DARK PASSAGE

By Andrew York

DARK PASSAGE

ANDREW YORK

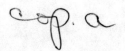

PUBLISHED FOR THE CRIME CLUB BY

DOUBLEDAY & COMPANY, INC.

GARDEN CITY, NEW YORK

1975

All of the characters in this book
are fictitious, and any resemblance
to actual persons, living or dead,
is purely coincidental.

ISBN 0-385-11240-8
Library of Congress Catalog Card Number 75-14848
Copyright © 1975 by Christopher Nicole
All Rights Reserved
Printed in the United States of America
First Edition

CHAPTER 1

A mistral had come sweeping down the Rhone Valley, churning the Gulf of Lyons into whitecaps, sending the boats in the old harbour at Marseilles surging against each other, scattering its chill over the sun worshippers in Poquerolles and Levant. The Gulf of St. Tropez seethed, and in sheltered Antibes the yachts bobbed gracefully on their moorings in the Vauban Marina.

Antibes was crowded with boats, although it was early June. No doubt many of the splendid vessels were permanent residents, but there were sufficient already at the visitors' quay, under the watchful eyes of the berthing masters in the huge, circular harbour office. Harrington spared them only a glance. He did not like boats. He did not even care for the South of France. The twentieth-century obsession with self-cooking had never attracted him, and he liked his women to have white skin. He liked to be able to count the blue veins. He enjoyed historical novels.

So the mistral suited him. He was able to draw his raincoat tighter and think to himself, Bloody fools. Tomorrow he would be back in England, where the skies were properly grey and one took off one's clothes only to have a bath or go to bed.

By profession, Harrington was an accountant, and he looked the part; he was not quite six feet tall and topped a somewhat narrow body with a sharp-featured, narrow face. He wore rimless glasses, on to which he had clipped shades. His hair was also thin, still entirely brown, and today a little windswept. But even the mistral could do little about the essential air of tidiness.

And no one could doubt that he was a successful accountant. His suit had been hand made in Rome, the narrow trousers accentuating the flatness of his belly, as they were intended to do, the two-button jacket increasing the neatness of his blue silk shirt, his narrow tie, and his spotless collar. He wore black leather shoes. In Antibes he was an outsider.

He left the dockside and climbed the shallow hill through the old town, found the Place Général de Gaulle and sat at a table with a cold beer in front of him. In the shelter of the houses the mistral dwindled to a fresh breeze, and the sun began to burn. Harrington lit a cigarette and watched the passers-by. Antibes contained as many foreigners as French; it was interesting deciding which was which. But he watched with a purpose, too. He did not intend to be discovered by the wrong person, and had bought himself a copy of *Le Monde* behind which he could hide, if necessary. He also intended to be noticed by the right person, and there she was.

As Riviera women went, whatever their original nationality, she was amongst the worst, from Harrington's point of view. Her skin was burned a uniform deep mahogany, and she wore only a sheer white mutton-cloth blouse over the skimpiest of bikini bottoms; the red and blue flowered design on the front of the blouse did nothing to disguise the nipples beneath. Her hair was concealed by a red silk scarf which isolated her face and made her seem even more of an Amazon than she was. He thought of her as the Great Bitch. He liked giving his women nicknames.

She crossed the square, slowly, throwing one leg in front of the other, muscles rippling in her thighs, buttocks rolling beneath the eye-catching briefs, belly pouting as she breathed.

Harrington snapped his fingers and ordered a Ricard and another beer. He did not get up, and she sat down beside him with a faint sigh.

"You are an amazing man," she said, her voice hardly more than a whisper. "You said nine-thirty on the morning of June the fifth, and here you are, at nine-thirty on the morning of June the fifth."

Harrington watched the waiter set their drinks in front of them and wedge the chit beneath the ashtray. "I would hope that gives you confidence."

"Oh, it does," she said. "What news of our friend?"

"Angel comes out of prison the day after tomorrow." Harrington peered into his beer.

"Oh, my God."

"Too soon for you?"

She drank some Ricard. "No . . . No, I want it to happen. We have waited too long."

"Well, it can't happen for another couple of days, at least," Harrington said. "Is Jarne impatient?"

"Very. He keeps grumbling about your disinterest in his hobbies." She shrugged. "I tell him there can't be any replies to the advertisements. And of course, I remind him how necessary it is to get the right sort of man. He trusts me, you know. But my God, if he were to find out . . ."

"You arouse the most delightful fantasies," Harrington said. "But he cannot find out unless you tell him. As you say, he trusts you. If he didn't, none of this would work. You must see to it that Angel also learns to trust you."

"If only I knew a little about him. I mean, personally."

Harrington smiled. "Stick to the externals. He is a mountain of a man, who would squash you flat. If he wanted to. Like so many very big men, he is curiously gentle in his habits. Or he used to be. I do not know what three years in Parkhurst will have done to him. In fact, I am told that he has spent a lot of time saying just what he proposes to do to various people when he is released. But as he won't be able to get at any of them, he will merely become frustrated. Again, like a great many big men, he is a trifle slow to react. I do not anticipate any trouble in persuading him to fall in with our plans."

"And this irritated giant must learn to trust me, overnight?"

Harrington closed one eye. "He will also be sex starved, my darling."

"What will happen to him, afterwards?"

"That depends on what he does, afterwards. On whether or not he panics. On which port he puts into. If he comes back to France, he may well be guillotined. That would be rather amusing. I'm not sure what the Spaniards do to you. But I'd rather be dead than spend ten years in a Spanish gaol."

The woman shivered, or appeared to do so. "I wonder . . . he has suffered so much already, for nothing. Now . . ."

"He'll be used to it. He's one of life's born losers, my darling. You just don't want to start going soft on me. You'll be feeling sorry for Jarne, next."

"No," she said. "I hate *him*. I don't care what happens to him."

"So put Angel in the same class. You don't want to forget that it is possible he might react badly towards you."

"I have thought of that. I can take care of myself. But what about the Doll?"

This time Harrington's smile showed genuine amusement. "Now that is the most interesting aspect of the whole situation. I think *her* reactions to what will happen, and Angel's reactions to her are going to be quite fascinating. But no doubt the Doll can also take care of herself. Or she will learn to very quickly."

The woman finished her drink, stood up. "I came into town to buy bread. So I'd better be getting back. When do you figure?"

"Two days, if all goes according to plan. Say Friday morning. I shall not see you again until it is finished. You're sure you remember everything of what you have to do?"

"I remember. I think of nothing else."

"Then I'll say goodbye. Don't I get a kiss?"

She regarded him for a moment, and for the first time he realised that her eyes were even colder than her face. "No," she said. "There'll be time enough for that, afterwards. And right now I don't feel much like kissing."

"But you won't go soft on me, my darling," Harrington said, still smiling. "Because if you do, by Christ, I'll skin you alive."

"And smile while you do it," she said. "I won't go soft on you, Martin. Send me Angel, and I'll do the rest."

*

Angel filled his lungs. He was six feet five inches tall and had shoulders to match; when he inhaled, he seemed to swell until he blocked the small doorway. The ill-cut suit and the shabby raincoat only accentuated the tremendous strength which was trying to get out; it was blowing half a gale and the wind sweeping off the Solent and across the Isle of Wight cannoned into him as it might into a lighthouse, before howling on its way across the prison yard.

As Angel grew, the warder seemed to diminish. "You've a nice day for it," he remarked. "What did the boss say?"

Angel smiled. He had features which once had been craggy without hardness, as his eyes had been a cool blue which lacked hostility. Now the hardness, the smouldering anger, showed in the flat mouth and the jutting chin, even in the faint hook to the big nose. And now the eyes were cold, rather than cool. Angel, with his size and his gaze, had always suggested an eagle confined amongst sparrows, during exercise time. And yet, when he smiled, for a moment he looked almost friendly. "He said to forget it." His voice was soft.

"Good advice," the warder suggested. Here was genuine concern. He liked the big man. Most people did. And those who didn't preferred not to show it.

Angel picked up his suitcase; it was not very large, and hung by his side like a handbag.

"And you want to stay away from people like Dave Bracken," the warder added. "You don't want to mix with the pros. I mean, we wouldn't like to have you back."

"You won't," Angel promised.

"We will, if you look too hard. Brood on it, Tommy."

Angel walked down the road to the bus. He knew the Isle of Wight well. Not only from having lived here, compulsorily, for three years. He could remember it from the old days, the pubs in Wootton and Bembridge, the turbulence off St. Catherine's Point, the long, lazy days spent drifting with the tide from Beaulieu down to Lymington.

It had not changed. The bus took him to the ferry, and the ferry took him across to Southampton. The water was the same pale green, the buoys lay scattered across it in the same profusion. Angel stayed on deck, despite the wind. The other passengers went below. No doubt they could tell, from his clothes and his pallor, that he was an ex-convict. But the wind was strong.

He stayed on deck to look at the sea, and remember. Remembering increased the anger in his system, the hate which had taken control of his mind. Remembering prevented any risk that he might take the governor's advice.

But there were few yachts on the Solent, this morning. It was a stormy weekday, in early June, and they were all still in harbour or ashore, being painted and antifouled and varnished, having their engines and their rigging overhauled, preparing for the season. Perhaps *Marianne* was amongst them. She knew these waters as well as he; they had learned them together.

He had never liked Southampton Water, from a sailing point of view. Too much traffic, too little water. Too many houses and chimneys to interfere with the wind. It hadn't changed, either. He waited for the other passengers to disembark before moving for the gangway himself. And suddenly realised that he was, at last, free. Because his prison sentence, at least in his mind, had started when he had boarded this ferry, going the other way. So when he set foot on that dock he was actually saying goodbye to Parkhurst and everything that was associated with it. He felt strangely reluctant to move.

Because freedom was a vacuum. Freedom supposed that this was Tommy Angel returning from a Sandown weekend; that he would run down to the Hamble and enjoy two pints of bitter before rowing himself out to *Marianne*. Freedom supposed that he would call at Smiths and restock his charts for the trip down to Sète, and that, being lazy, he would apply to the French Government Tourist Office in Piccadilly for a *permis de circulation* to enable him to pass through the Canal Lateral à la Garonne and the Canal du Midi, instead of beating all the way around Spain and Portugal, and freedom also supposed that he would start looking for a strong young dolly bird to help him work the locks, and do various other things, as well as the cooking.

And while he waited for his charts and his permit and his bird, freedom supposed that he would read a good book, and get a little drunk, and watch some end of season rugger and maybe even a little early season cricket, and that he would work on his boat. And be happy. Freedom supposed that above all. Freedom and happiness were synonymous.

So Tommy Angel was not free. He was going to do some of those things, save search for a certain dolly bird. And not with locks in mind.

He wondered why. It would be so simple, to forget, as the governor had advised. But with the freedom the dolly bird had managed to remove his self-respect, his reputation, and his boat. And thus his way of life.

He took a very long breath, walked down the gangway, presented his ticket, and did not look at the little man. To Angel all men were little, and for three years he had been taking orders from too many of them.

"Mr. Angel?"

Another little man, but one who existed in the big time. A blue pinstripe suit beneath the burberry, a little black moustache, youngish, thin faced and pale faced. But his paleness was from a choice of afternoon-to-dawn living.

"What's it to you?" Angel asked.

The young man smiled. "I'm on your side, Mr. Angel. Really. I represent Rehabilitations Incorporated. Perhaps you have heard of us?"

"No," Angel said. "And I'm not in the mood for charity."

The young man continued to smile. "We do not offer charity. We are, I suppose, technically a prisoners' aid society, but we are international in our scope and very selective in our clients."

"And you have selected me?"

"You claimed at your trial to be innocent. We believe that you are."

"I wish I had your patience," Angel said.

"Well, of course, there was nothing we could do with the evidence," the young man said. "It was all against you, after all. Nor do we make a habit of approaching people with promises which we might not be able to fulfil. But we were very relieved to observe you settling in as a model prisoner, and thus becoming certain to obtain full remission. We have kept an eye on you."

"Thanks," Angel said. "And now you are going to rehabilitate me."

"We are going to offer you our assistance in rehabilitating yourself," the young man said. "And in your case I think it is going to be very easy. My name is Smith, by the way."

"They call me Brown."

"And easier yet if you really have retained your sense of humour. My car is outside. If you like we can talk while we drive to London."

"Are we driving to London?"

"Is there somewhere else you'd rather go?"

"London will suit me fine," Angel said. The address was burned into his brain. So she would certainly have moved. But it was somewhere to start looking.

The car turned out to be a three-litre Rover. It was a long time since Angel had sat in anything quite so comfortable. And Smith handled her well. "Smoke?"

"I don't," Angel said.

"But I imagine you could do with a drink, eh? It's a bit early for the pubs, but there's a bottle in the glove compartment."

Angel opened the box, looked at the bottle of scotch, and put it back again. "I'll wait until I have something to celebrate."

"And you were talking about patience? You're a good bet, Angel, for our organisation. Would you like to look at these?"

He took a cardboard folder from the parcels shelf, laid it on Angel's lap. It contained a mass of testimonials, letters, some replies on good notepaper, headed by the name Rehabilitations Incorporated with an address in Great Portland Street, and a list of officers, including two titles and the name of the secretary, Peter Smith. There was even a balance sheet, revealing prosperity.

"So I'm impressed," Angel confessed.

"Then we can co-operate. What do you want to do first?"

"I'm easy."

Smith glanced at him. "What about the girl?"

"What girl?"

Smith took a cigarette from the packet on the logia, lit it with the dashboard lighter. "One thing we appreciate from our customers is honesty, Mr. Angel."

"I was convicted for *dis*honesty, Mr. Smith."

"So let's start again." Smith flicked ash. "As I understand the case, Mr. Angel, you were returning from the South of France in your yacht *Marianne*. She represented your entire worldly wealth, and you had been chartering her in the Mediterranean during the previous four years. Correct?"

"You seem to know it all," Angel agreed.

"Unfortunately for you," Smith said. "You had collected a young woman in Sète, and she helped you up the canals."

"One needs help," Angel murmured.

"Even more unfortunately, for you, she also had along half a million pounds' worth of uncut diamonds in her washbag, and someone had tipped off the British customs that she was worth looking at. Which made you rather angry."

"I broke a policeman's jaw," Angel agreed. "Easy to do in the heat of the moment."

"I couldn't agree more," Smith said. "But you were innocent. I mean, you had no idea that Francine Dow was carrying anything like that."

"I said so at the time."

"So you were entitled to be angry. And even angrier when you were sentenced to five years in prison, and had your yacht confiscated into the bargain. I'd be surprised if you weren't looking for Miss Dow at this moment."

"She was sent to gaol as well."

"Oh, indeed. Three years, wasn't it? With remission, she'd have been out over a year ago. Wouldn't you *like* to see her again?"

Angel shrugged. "I think we've said it all, Francine and me."

Smith opened the ashtray, stubbed out his cigarette. "Well, if I may say so, Mr. Angel, I find that a very mature and reasonable point of view. Very encouraging for our organisation. Very. I am so very pleased. Yes, indeed. Now, let me tell you what we have done for you. First of all, we have rented you a flat in London. Only Earl's Court, I'm afraid, and when I say flat I am stretching it a bit; two rooms, really. But it'll be a base, to work from for a day or two. The rent is paid for a week, and then you'll need money. In the glove compartment, behind the whisky, you'll find a hundred pounds in English notes. Enough to go on with, would you agree?"

"It sounds unbelievable. Who pays for all this?"

"Oh, you do, Mr. Angel. You may regard it as a loan, until you are on your feet again. But as you may imagine, this makes us all the more anxious to get you settled into a job as quickly as possible."

"I'm sure."

"So we have found you a position which seems to be just up your street. What do you say to skippering a yacht in the Med? Next best thing to being the owner, wouldn't you say?"

"That depends on who the owner is."

"You'll appreciate this one. Have you ever heard of a man called Justin Jarne?"

"I read the papers. He's some sort of a property speculator."

"I imagine he would prefer the word magnate, to speculator. Justin Jarne is probably the biggest property magnate in the world. Or perhaps I should say was. He's just about retired, now. And he is passionately fond of sailing. Unfortunately for him, his wife isn't. So Jarne sails during the summer, out of one of those delightful places like St. Tropez or Antibes, with a professional crew. Wait for it. The other half of the crew is a girl. She cooks and does the deck work. But he needs a skipper to look after his engine and check up on his navigating and that sort of thing, and he's just lost his regular man. The poor fellow was knocked over by a truck, and I'm afraid won't be available again this summer."

"And the wife raises no objection to her husband gallivanting around the Med with a dolly bird?"

Smith grinned. "The wife, Mr. Angel, is fully capable of taking care of herself. Believe me. Think you can handle it?"

"You said something about sailing."

"A ketch. Forty foot over-all. But all possible aids, electric winches, and that sort of thing. And the last word in equipment; radar, and auto pilot and everything you can think of."

"Engine?"

"A big Perkins diesel. Suit you?"

"I wouldn't complain if she was mine."

"Then I take it you'll accept the job?"

Angel watched the hedgerows whizzing past. So this whole situation was too unreal even to be considered. Or was it? Hadn't he been so damned unlucky that he deserved a little turn in the wheel of fortune? Weren't there such things as prisoners' aid societies, even if he had never heard of this one? He couldn't really argue with the literature. Wasn't this real money he was holding in his hand? And, supposing he managed to catch up with Francine, might it not be a good idea for him to get out of England as quickly as possible, as soon as possible?

Supposing he managed to catch up with Francine. What *did* he mean by that? What had he always meant by that? Or had it only been a method of keeping himself from going mad throughout those long thirty-six months?

"Of course we realise that it's a big decision," Smith said. "Leaving England the moment you get out. But you don't want to think about it too long; it's a plumb job. With the money is your ticket to Nice, economy class, one way, for tomorrow morning. Don't worry about repayment. Our man in Nice will take care of it; your salary will be paid to him until your debt is clear, but that shouldn't take more than a couple of weeks with the kind of money you'll be making. It's four thousand a year, by the way. Pounds, not francs. I've managed to get Jarne to hold the job until tonight, so I'd like you to confirm your acceptance by eight o'clock at the outside."

"And this man Jarne will take on an ex-con? Or doesn't he know about that?"

"He knows about that, Angel. And he doesn't give a damn. He's that kind of a man. If anything, I think it's a point in your favour. Especially as you've been recommended by us."

Angel nodded. "And supposing I just take this money and the ticket, fly to Nice, and don't bother to look up your friend?"

Smith smiled again, and this time it was not quite so pleasant. "As you have just reminded me, you're an ex-convict, Mr. Angel. You don't want to forget that too quickly. And before you leave the car, if you take any of that stuff, you'll sign the receipt. But I'm sure you've seen enough of the inside of prison not to want to go back."

Angel looked at the road for a while longer, then he pulled out the packet of money and counted it, checked the ticket, put them and the key into his jacket pocket.

There was a pen attached to the receipt.

*

He stood on the pavement where Smith had dropped him, and looked across the street at the dingy building. All his, for a week, if he wished; for one night, if he was wise. But if the inside needed paint as badly as the outside, then one night would be more than sufficient.

And at this moment he had no wish to stay at all. He had waited for too long, to be free, in London, unknown and unexpected. Save to a man named Smith.

He climbed the steps, and a woman appeared from a doorway on the right. "Yes?"

The first woman to speak with him for three years. This one was past middle-age and plump; her hair was dyed red and her artificial pearls were stained yellow. So were her teeth. She smoked a cigarette.

"My name is Angel. I'm the new tenant for . . ." He peered at the key. "Four B."

"No noise," she said.

"I'm the proverbial mouse."

She looked him up and down. It took a long time.

"The fact is," Angel said diffidently, "I'm on my way to an appointment, so I won't be going up right now. I wonder if I might leave my bag here for an hour or so?"

She shrugged, and returned to her sitting room.

*

Angel caught a tube to Hyde Park Corner, and walked, past the Hilton and down Curzon Street, before turning off into the maze of little lanes and alleys which surround Shepherd Market. It was years since he had walked down here. Or driven down here. Because once he had even owned a car. How long ago *that* seemed.

It was a cool afternoon, in June, and people wore coats and huddled against the breeze which swept up Piccadilly and out of Green Park. Short skirts flew and boot heels thudded. He had suddenly entered a forest of female legs, long legs and short legs, fat legs and thin legs, good legs and bad legs, legs concealed to the ankle and legs revealed to the crotch—they all looked good to him. So what would they say when they found Francine? Sex attack on London model? She would certainly be described as a model. Would it be a sex attack? Would he be able to keep his hands off her? And having laid his hands on her, would he be able to do anything else? He'd never actually killed anyone in his life. For all his size he had never actually set out to harm anyone in his life, except in self-defence—even the policeman came into that category. He had had it very easy, he supposed, until Francine.

But wouldn't the lads have a laugh if Angel, the man with the anger burning holes in his soul, got out, found his bird, and was returned on a charge of rape.

He was there before he knew it, staring at the little row of numbers and their accompanying bells. He half expected to see her name. Half hoped, perhaps. But of course even if she were still here she would hardly work under her own name. And Francine was her real name. That had come out in court. But the number was there, all right. Seven C. The name was Doreen. He rang the bell, and started up. He climbed slowly. He did not want to arrive out of breath. He was not sure that he wanted to arrive at all.

The door was in front of him, and another bell. This he also rang, to be admitted by a middle-aged Negress.

"Madam don't work before two," she said.

"I can't wait that long," Angel said, and entered a small lobby. This was shabby, but the living room beyond contained a new carpet and clean paint, three comfortable armchairs and a settee, a colour television set, and a table on which were scattered a selection of Scandinavian sex magazines.

"I will tell her," the Negress said. "You sit down. You wish to watch the telly?"

"No." Angel sat down, flicked a magazine. But suddenly he was completely disinterested in sex. He wanted to see her again. Just see her. There was a joke. But it was more than a little true. Whatever she had done to him, the fortnight before they had landed in England had been a dream. What would he do when she came through that door?

The door opened, and he rose as if pulled on a string. The young woman smiled at him, with a surprising amount of real warmth. "A gentleman on a Thursday morning?" She held out her hand. "Welcome. Rose says you have a problem."

Angel gaped at her. She was slender, and wore a short red dress. Her hair was black, and thin, and long; it nearly reached her thighs. Her complexion was sallow, and her features pointed. But she had breasts and hips, and her legs, matchingly thin to the rest of her, were well enough shaped. Besides, she exuded invitation.

And sympathy. "You look as if you *do* have a problem." Gently she extricated her hand from his, and turned away. "Would you like me to wash you?"

The door to the bedroom was open, and this was furnished even more opulently than the sitting room. Doreen walked to the dressing table, stepped out of her sandals, lifted her dress over her head. She wore nothing underneath, had small, tight buttocks, and, when she turned, equally small, slightly drooping breasts. There were stretch marks on her belly, but it remained flat except for a slight pout. She smiled at him, and moved one hand to indicate the bathroom.

"I was looking for a Miss Francine Dow," he said, trying to be distinct.

And suddenly the invitation had disappeared, although she had not moved. Only her face seemed to tighten, but even this was more a change in atmosphere rather than a visible muscular reaction.

"You *are* out of touch," she said.

"She no longer lives here," Angel agreed. "But I'm sure you can give me her present address."

"Angel," she whispered. "By Christ, you're Tommy Angel. I should have known." Her eyes were flickering, past his left shoulder, and he turned, slotting himself against the wall as he did so.

Two men stood behind him, one was white and the other black. Both were large and unprepossessing, but neither was so large as Angel, nor, seen from a potentially opposing point of view, so unprepossessing.

"You leaving quiet, Angel, man?" asked the black man.

"Tell me where I can find Francine and I might."

They exchanged glances, almost in desperation, and moved forward together, bending low, looking for his thighs and his groin. Angel also moved forward, met them halfway, collecting their heads, one in each mammoth hand, and tossing them away. He did not want to hurt them, and they looked ridiculous as they tumbled backwards.

A vase shattered on the back of his head. The girl stood on the bed, rising and falling on the mattress, mouth sagging as she realised she had miscued. Angel caught her round the thighs, switched her away from him, and slapped her across the buttocks. His fingers left marks. She gave a yelp of mingled pain and anger and kept on going, landing on her hands and knees on the floor beyond the bed.

By now the two men were getting up again, and the white one had produced a flick knife. The afternoon had ceased to be even faintly funny. But Angel had spent three years in prison; he reached behind him, grabbed the pillow from the bed with his left hand, advanced once more, swung his right hand in a scything blow which caught the Negro on the shoulder and threw him against the wall, and came back in time to meet the first thrust of the knife. This went deep into the pillow, and foam rubber bubbled from beneath the slip. Angel closed his right fist and drove it forward with fifteen stone in hard-muscled weight behind it. The white man's face dissolved into a mass of blood and he hit the wall, and then the floor, and lay still.

The Negro was turning again, panting, and saw the destruction of his mate. He decided that things had gone far enough, rose to his knees and crawled for the door. "Help me, nuh?" he bawled, apparently at the maid.

But she was on the telephone. "Help," she shouted. "Help. You send somebody quick, eh? Two or three."

Angel closed the door. Doreen was slowly getting to her feet. Her backside glowed.

"I want to have a chat with you," Angel said.

She backed against the dressing table. And now he heard the wail of a siren. One of the neighbours must have complained to the police. He wondered what would happen when the maid's help arrived to meet the riot squad.

"Would you like to get dressed?" he asked.

Doreen remained still, her back against the table, every muscle in her naked body tensed and awaiting its opportunity to help in her escape.

The white man sat up, holding his jaw. "Oh, Christ," he mumbled.

"Lie down," Angel suggested, and he did so.

The girl continued to watch him.

"If you don't get dressed," Angel said, "and show me a quick way out of here, I am going to break every rib in your body."

He stepped towards her, and she congealed. "Please," Angel said.

She ran across the room to the wardrobe, took out a dark fur coat and a pair of boots.

"Speed is of the essence," Angel reminded her.

She sat on the bed, pulled on the boots, stood up, and wrapped herself in the fur.

"Now what about a back stairs," Angel said.

She stepped over her ponce, opened the bathroom door, and then what had seemed to be a linen cupboard. The jangling of the bell was very close. Angel followed her into a narrow stairway.

"Now remember," he said as they reached the bottom. "I can be a gentleman, when encouraged."

She opened the door, led him on to a narrow alley, littered with dustbins and even a cat. This promptly ran away.

The jangle was on the street behind them. The girl led him down the alley away from it. She stood on the corner, the breeze playing with the fringe of her fur, and pointed at the stream of traffic slowly making its way up Curzon Street. "You can always get a taxi here."

Angel extended an arm, and a car halted. He gave the address, ushered the girl in, and sat beside her. "It has always been one of my ambitions," he said, "to sit next to a naked girl in a taxi."

She drew the fur coat closer about her.

"Why don't you tell me about Francine?" he asked. "That way we might even part friends."

She looked at him, sucking breath into her lungs. "She's dead," she said. "Don't you understand? She's dead. She was murdered."

CHAPTER 2

The woman lay on her belly on the foredeck of the big ketch; here she was sheltered from the gaze of the curious passers-by behind the canvas dodgers which lined the rail of the moored yacht. She was naked, and as she breathed her body glued itself with its own sweat to the hot teak, nipples, shoulders, belly, hips, knees, and toes. She would never lie on a towel; she enjoyed the physical discomfort, was fascinated by the mottled dark brown and pale brown when she arose, which so quickly turned back into the uniform mahogany.

She felt, rather than heard, Jarne come on board. The ship rocked beneath his weight, although for a man of his age he moved lightly. In many ways this was the most detestable thing about him. She often thought, were he really old, hideously old, with wrinkled skin and empty balls, then what she and Harrington planned would be entirely reasonable. Almost an act of mercy. But although he was past sixty his figure remained as slender as a boy's. Even his hair was still streaked with black, and his face was lean and aquiline, almost handsome. As a young man he must have been quite irresistible. Even now he was irresistible. She felt the boat move again as he entered the wheelhouse, and waited. A moment later he re-emerged, and she heard the pop. She began to tense, and another moment later the drops of champagne fell on her back. There was a soft thump beside her as he dropped to his knees, again with the careless energy of a boy, and then his tongue flicked her flesh, sucking the champagne and suntan lotion away from it as a frog might demolish a family of flies.

Now she moved, because she had to. "I didn't hear you come on board," she said. "I suppose I was dozing."

He sat beside her and extended the bottle. He delighted in doing inelegant things, such as drinking champagne from the bottle, enjoyed the knowledge that it would give her wind where it would have no effect on him.

She raised herself on her elbow, sipped, and he lowered his tongue to hers. He was always anxious, always willing, and he was old enough to be her father, comfortable. But he was also Justin Jarne. This she found exciting, because as much as she enjoyed physical discomfort, if controlled by herself, she also enjoyed the feeling of living dangerously. He made love to her as no other man had ever done, or, she supposed, would ever do. And suppose he discovered but a tenth of the thoughts that lay in her mind, what would he do to her then? She had no idea. Yet that possibility made the juices flow more than anything.

"Telegram from Harrington," he said. "He's managed to find a suitable crew."

"About time."

"Apparently most of the good people are already taken," Jarne said. "I suppose June is a bit late to start looking for a qualified skipper." He smiled. "This man has just finished three years in prison. I find that rather amusing."

"I find it frightening. Harrington must need his head examined."

"Harrington assures me he was innocent of the charge." Jarne drank some more champagne and gave her the bottle.

He stood up. "I think this man, his name is Angel, will help to make the summer more interesting. He will be here tomorrow. You can flirt with him, if you like. A little."

He upended the bottle, and the champagne splashed on her belly. He smiled at her, and went aft. She lay on her back, gazed up at the sun, and felt the sticky liquid drying on her flesh. Flirt with Angel? That would not be difficult. She'd enjoy that, in fact. Because when Angel got here, Jarne would be about to die.

*

The taxi had stopped. "This the corner, guv?" asked the driver.

Angel came to. "It looks like it. Come on, Doreen."

"Me?" Doreen asked. "I shouldn't even be speaking with you, Mr. Angel. Why, they'd . . ."

"Whatever they are going to do, they are going to do it now, Doreen," Angel pointed out. "You had better look on me as the only friend you have in the world. And you wouldn't really want me as an enemy, would you?"

He held her arm and got her out of the taxi before she could argue. The driver winked as he engaged gear.

"Won't your landlady object?" Doreen whispered.

"Not if we're quiet."

The red head popped out of the sitting room, glared at Doreen, and withdrew. Angel collected his suitcase, and showed the girl the stairs.

"Look, Mr. Angel," she said. "I'd really take it as a favour if you'd let me walk away from here. I can talk my way out of any trouble I'm in."

He grinned at her. "You can practice on me. You can even cook me a meal. Oops. I forgot to buy anything."

She pulled a face, and climbed to the third floor. Angel unlocked the door, showed her in. The sitting room, which doubled as a bedroom, judging by the let-down settee, contained little else; a straight chair, an ancient carpet, and a couple of hunting prints on the wall.

"I'm not in the game for love, you know," Doreen said.

"Convince me," he suggested, and closed the door behind them. At the back a curtain led to the bathroom, and there was a kitchenette with a gas ring, and a gas fridge. There was also a gas heater, and this Angel lit; the place was distinctly damp. "Now you can make yourself comfortable."

She took off her coat, which she carefully folded across the chair. Angel preferred not to look at her this moment; she was too much of what he wanted too badly. He investigated the kitchen instead. There was a bottle of scotch on the table. "Thoughtful fellow, Smith." He opened the fridge and received another surprise. "Well, what do you know," he said. "Beer, cold meat, even some lettuce. They *were* thinking of us. Hungry?"

She was already preparing the bed.

Doreen was a professional, used to handling men in some need, or some anxiety. He was in great need, and even greater anxiety, after three years. But it was unnecessary.

*

"You are worth every penny of your three pound fifty," Angel said, putting his hands beneath his head.

"I charge five pounds."

"Which gives us ample room to negotiate."

She went to get two bottles of beer. She gave him one, and took the other herself, sitting at the end of the bed, facing him. She looked as cool and as fresh as when she had first entered the room.

"You were going to tell me about Francine."

"Was I?" She had regained her confidence. "It'll have to be made worth my while."

Angel sighed. But there was only one way to handle this situation, or he'd be looking up from here on. He went to the bathroom himself, returned and finished his beer, then sat beside her. She gazed at him with complete composure, which only began to fade when he wrapped the fingers of his left hand around her neck.

"Holding you like this," he explained, "I can break every rib on the right side of your body with my right hand, and you wouldn't make a sound, except, of course, for the click of fracturing bones. Alternately, were I to hit you, I could make such a mess that you'd be out of business permanently. Would my reluctance to do either of those things constitute making it worth your while?"

He allowed his fingers to relax, and she gasped a little.

"I thought you were all right," she whispered.

"I am, at the moment, and my aim is to remain that way. You thought I was a sucker. I can't quarrel with that. Francine took me for a sucker, and she was right. But three years is a long time to stay a sucker. And before I let anyone mess me about again I'm perfectly prepared to commit murder myself. Now tell me. When?"

Doreen was slowly regaining control of her breathing. "Three days ago."

"Three *days?*"

Doreen's head bobbed up and down. "That's right, Mr. Angel. Funny thing, I had a drink with her only the week before."

"Did you see her often?"

"She came by now and then."

"But you had known her before she went to prison?"

"Oh yes. When she was put away I took over her lease for her."

"Tell me how she died."

"She was hit by a truck in the Fulham Road. She was knocked thirty feet. Hit and run, the police said."

"Only you know it wasn't a hit and run."

"Could I have a cigarette?"

"I don't smoke." But he moved back up the bed.

Doreen searched her handbag. Her fingers trembled as she flicked the lighter three times, before being able to inhale with great satisfaction.

"You were saying," Angel reminded her.

"It was . . . well, the Big People. You know?"

"No."

She shrugged. "Everybody belongs. You know that, Mr. Angel. Nobody owns himself. So I'm looked after by Alf and Billy. They see nobody messes me about. At least, they did before you came along. In return, they take seventy per cent of what I make. But they don't own themselves, either, and they don't keep all that seventy per cent. They work for one of the Big People. And even the Big People all belong to one of the Giants. So Francine figured she'd do better by taking on a little courier work. I was approached about that, once. I had more sense. Stay in the small time and nobody cares. Start peddling snow or rocks and you get the minks and the rides in the Bagliettos, but you also get the eye from the Big People, and it don't pay to let them down. As Francine found out."

"Because she was caught?"

"I figure."

"And for that she was murdered?"

Doreen shuddered. "She was knocked thirty feet, Mr. Angel, and then driven over. At night it was. When they found her she just didn't have a face left. So the papers said."

"Seems a little hard."

"I think she must have talked. Only a little, while in gaol," Doreen said. "But then there was you. The Big People know everything that goes on inside. So you were muttering about what you'd do when you came out. And it figured you'd go looking for Francine."

"Darling Doreen," Angel remarked. "Very little of what you are saying is making sense. Supposing we accept that my threats mattered a damn to anyone except perhaps Francine herself, then instead of rushing around killing her wouldn't it have been much easier to kill me?"

She shrugged again. "I don't know anything about their plans. I told you, I don't know anything about them. I just know they're there. I don't *want* to know anything more than that."

"I'm almost prepared to believe you. If it wasn't for the way you reacted in your place when you worked out who I was."

"So the word was out. Yesterday."

"You mean I'm blacklisted in the underworld? I think you are trying to make me believe I'm important. Just how did this dire warning come?"

"A telephone call," she said. "A man's voice. 'There's an ex-con
called Angel,' he said. 'Big chap. He may come to the flat and start
asking questions about Francine. He's poison.' That's what he said."

"And *you* asked no questions? I'm sure you can do better than that,
Doreen. Why don't you brood on it while you fix us something to
eat?"

She uncoiled herself and walked across the room. By now he
wanted her again. Three years was too long. And returning to normal
life was too confusing. So he needed his head not only examined but
dissected. In the first place for stopping by that table in the cafe in Sète
at all, and buying that long-legged ash blonde a drink. For that he had
paid, and paid and paid. But now, to feel angry because that same
long-legged ash blonde had been murdered was just bloody stupid.
Yet he was, suddenly, very angry.

Doreen returned with a plate of cold meat and salad. She had not
bothered to fix any food for herself, but had poured herself half a glass
of neat scotch, and drunk half of it. "That's what he said, Mr. Angel.
In my business it don't pay to ask questions. I don't know how important you are. I don't know anything about you at all, except that you
are not good to know. Do you think I could go home now?"

She saw his gaze, the way it kept dropping to her breasts and her
belly. "Or would you like another one first?" she asked, her confidence
returning once again.

He wanted to tell her no. He wanted to kick her out. He hated her
and all her kind, as much for what they had done to Francine, who
had been one of them, as for what they were. And there was nothing
more to be got out of her. But she was woman. Willing woman, and
three years had been too long.

She smiled, finished the whisky, and came towards him, hips swinging, face arranging itself into the necessary words and smiles, to pause,
with an almost ludicrous suggestion of a collapsing house of cards, as
there came a knock on the door.

*

For a moment Angel was too taken aback by the dissolution taking
place in front of him to worry about the identity of the visitor. The

smile slowly disappeared from Doreen's face, her mouth started to droop at the corners, her shoulders followed suit, and her very breasts, a moment ago riding high with confidence, seemed to slide downwards.

He reached out of the bed, collected her fur coat and her boots and dumped them in her arms, and pushed her towards the bathroom.

"You won't . . ." she whispered.

"We'll play this one by ear," he promised.

The knock came again, more forcefully.

Angel pulled on his underpants, made sure the curtain was in place, and listened to another ratatat. No one in all London knew he was here, save the girl in the bathroom and the man Smith. And supposing anyone else did know he was here, would they be interested enough to call?

He opened the door, stepping to one side as he did so. The man outside was about average height. He was also slender, middle-aged, with sharp features and grey hair. He wore a topcoat and heavy shoes, a striped tie and a striped shirt. He looked entirely ordinary, and yet entirely confident. There was only one profession in the world to which he could possibly belong.

"Welcome," Angel said. "I don't think we have met. Inspector?"

"Detective Inspector," the man corrected him, with half a smile. "My name is Hibbert. May I come in?"

"I'm sure you have a warrant." Angel stepped back.

"This is a courtesy visit." Hibbert entered the room, removed his hat, looked around him, and inhaled. "Where's Doreen?"

"In the head," Angel said. "She seems to have a very nervous disposition."

"With reason, in view of the company she keeps. I'd let her go, if I were you, Angel. That way she might keep her skin, and you and I won't be interrupted."

"What do you think, Doreen?" Angel asked the curtain.

There was a short hesitation, and then she came out. She wore her coat and boots and had brushed her hair. "You owe me."

Angel took out his wallet and gave her ten pounds.

"Ta. I suppose there's no use asking you not to let me down this time?"

The door closed behind her.

"Do you mind if I smoke?" Hibbert asked.

"Not if you'll let me get on with a late lunch. And you can tell me how you found me."

"We knew you'd home on Francine's old address, Angel. When news came in of a fight there, we didn't have any doubt who had started it. You've been under surveillance since leaving Doreen's apartment. You actually were under surveillance since leaving Parkhurst, but we lost you in Southampton. Our man said you were met. We didn't know you had so many friends."

"I wonder why so many people are interested in me. Especially with Francine dead."

"Sad case," Hibbert agreed. "Mind you, like Doreen, she didn't pick her friends very carefully. I wonder if you're any better at that, Angel?"

"I'm hoping you'll tell me."

Hibbert sighed. "I don't blame you for being suspicious. Three years is a long time."

"I also lost my boat."

"And that rankles more?" Hibbert really did smile this time. "Now, what about all this wild talk of getting hold of Francine when you came out?"

"Francine is the only person I know who could prove my innocence."

"And you seriously supposed that she would, having refused to do so in court? Or maybe you meant to beat it out of her. Maybe you sent someone out to do it for you. Dave Bracken, perhaps."

"You mean you haven't made an arrest?"

"We're working on it."

"Dave Bracken is a friend of mine," Angel said. "Right this minute I'd say he was probably the only friend I possess."

Hibbert sighed some more. "As I said, you people can pick them. What about the friend who collected you at the ferry?"

"He's just an acquaintance."

"Let's try another one, then. What do you figure on doing now that Francine is unobtainable? Seems to me you're stuck with the situation."

"Looks that way," Angel agreed.

"So?"

"I'll cut my losses and get myself a job. As a matter of fact, I've already been offered one."

"By the man who picked you up?"

Angel masticated his last mouthful. "Could be." He went to the fridge and poured himself a beer. "Join me?"

Hibbert shook his head, stubbed out his cigarette, got up, and walked about the room, slowly. "He get you this dump as well?"

"You can always leave."

"Angel, you have developed an unfortunate habit of antagonising policemen. I seem to remember you broke the jaw of one, when you were arrested."

"You may not believe this," Angel said, "but that was the first time I had ever hit someone that hard."

"And now you've got the habit?"

"Meaning?"

"Your friend's boy friend also has a broken jaw. You're just too big to go around hitting people, Angel."

"And you mean to do me for that?"

"I imagine Alf deserved it. I'd like you to consider, though, what he's likely to do to Doreen when he gets out of hospital."

"I'll send her flowers," Angel said.

"You don't want to lose your sense of perspective. Would it interest you to know that I believe maybe you *were* a patsy?"

"Shame you weren't at my trial."

"It wouldn't have made much difference. Even you must know that the skipper of a yacht, or any other kind of vessel, is responsible for whatever happens on board, unless he can prove he was being had. All you could produce was a flat denial, which is what the most guilty person would have done."

"And you have waited three long years to come along and greet me on my release and tell me all this? It would have been simpler to send me a postcard, Hibbert. But as you've done the decent thing, I'll do the decent thing as well and again offer you a drink."

"I'm on duty." Hibbert lit another cigarette. "I came along, Angel, because whatever started in Sète three years ago isn't over yet, by a hell of a long shot. It never is, for us. But surely it must have occurred to you that it isn't over for you either? Partly your own fault, of course. Breathing threats is standard procedure, but we can forget that, from our point of view. You were steamed up. Trouble is, you're the sort of chap that certain people feel they just have to take seriously. And that meant curtains for little Francine Dow. So she shopped you. But she didn't deserve to be squashed flat."

He's trying to be friends, Angel thought, incredulously. Or is he? "I figure she knew the risks she was taking."

Hibbert sighed yet again. "I wonder if she did. She was at least on the inside; you claim to be on the outside. So, supposing in some way the Angel/Francine setup has become poison to someone, don't you think it would have been simpler for someone in prison to slip a knife between your ribs on a dark night? Or certainly for someone to sidle up to you when you came out and started looking." The cigarette came up, pointing. "And I can tell from your face that the thought had crossed your mind. So here are a few more thoughts you might like to start moving around that brain of yours, Angel. Francine died three days ago. So she was a tart and she hardly made a paragraph in the centre page. But her death must have been news to someone. Yet not a word got to you in prison."

"Maybe nobody wanted to upset my last week."

"All those friends you were telling me about. But you don't believe that either. Angel, whether you like it or not, you're still alive and kicking, and Francine is dead, just because someone wants it that way. Shall I tell you why?"

"It looks as if you are going to whether I like it or not."

"Francine didn't pick up those stones in a poker game. She was a pro in every possible sense, on the game in a big way here in Mayfair, and when she travelled, part of an organised route. The route consisted of a boy friend with a small motor cruiser. Every summer, they'd nip across the Channel and go down the canals, do the Riviera, and come back up in the autumn. Everyone knew them, customs officers, lockkeepers, the whole crowd. And not a soul suspected that they were ever carrying anything more illegal than a spare bottle of gin. Whoever employed them was too smart to have them take more than one holiday a year, but try figuring the amount of diamonds they must have brought in over five years, even at that rate. Then three years ago they had bad luck. Francine's friend must have eaten a rotten oyster, and was taken ill with food poisoning just after they reached Sète on the way home. He passed out and had to be rushed to hospital, and was unconcious in the intensive care unit for several days. Francine panicked. She couldn't get to him. Worse, from her point of view, all their money was in his name. She was stranded with nothing but her clothes, her passport, and half a million pounds in diamonds. But she had to get the stuff into England by a certain date; the people she worked for didn't accept excuses. So she took a chance and picked you up."

"That didn't come out at the trial."

"Why should it? She wasn't going to implicate her friend, and we weren't going to let on that we had been tipped."

"To search my boat?"

"To find Francine Dow. The young man had talked in hospital, while delirious, and the French police passed the information on to us. Just the name. But as they had come to Sète by boat, we figured that she might just be continuing the same way. So Customs and Immigration at the seaports were especially alerted. But we never doubted you were a regular as well. You fit the bill, you know. You're a fairly well-known commuter from the Riviera. And it made sense to suppose that when her companion had dropped out, Francine had switched to a reserve. And as it happened, when that young Customs lad saw Francine's passport and got excited, there the stuff was."

"And now you have come along to tell me how I can get hold of the boy friend."

"You'll need a medium. Food poisoning can be deadly. And it was, accidental food poisoning, Angel. So maybe you're one of the world's unlucky characters. I've come along because, as I said just now, I think you *are* unlucky, and were innocent. Which means that, innocently, you are still involved. Which means you might like to clear your name. Properly."

Angel gazed at him.

"We can't give you back your three years. We *can* give you back your boat, or the equivalent."

"And what do you think I might have to offer, at this late date?"

"I wish I knew. Maybe you have something without knowing it. Maybe that girl slipped something amongst your clothes, or maybe she gave you some information, about something, information which led to her death, but which so far has led to your life. At least until they can get it off you. Because whatever it is, they'll come looking, some time soon. So keep in touch. Nothing more than that."

"And one night find myself alone on a street with a runaway truck," Angel said. "I was doing some thinking, before you came, Mr.

Hibbert, and I have been doing a lot more since you started talking. So I wanted to get hold of Francine. I figured that she was operating on her own, and that she hadn't wanted to take the full rap. I could understand that. But as we had both served our sentences, I also figured that she wouldn't too much mind putting me in the clear. And if she was still reluctant, I was prepared, maybe, to be aggressive. So I breathed a lot of threats. There's nothing else to do, in a cell. But I always figured she'd be reasonable. Nothing more than that. Since coming out, not yet twelve hours, I've had a fight and become, maybe, involved in something really nasty. In any event, the only person who can clear my name is dead, and I'm not really cut out to be a police spy. So I'm a coward. I'm going to cut my losses, and take the governor's advice—forget it. I have been offered a job. I wasn't too keen, on it or the man who offered me it, down to half an hour ago. But I think I am going to take it. It means I shall be leaving England for a while, and to tell you the truth, I won't be at all sorry to go. Or do you mean to impound my passport all over again? It's nice and dusty from its three years in the Parkhurst safe."

Hibbert picked up his hat and stood up. "And you think these people won't be able to reach you outside England?"

"Supposing they really think I'm worth worrying about, I'm sure they can. But my reasoning is that I'm just not worth worrying about. That's why I'm still alive, Mr. Hibbert. And I aim to stay just that unimportant."

Hibbert went to the door. "You're a fool, Angel. I'm the only hope you have. The next time I see you, I figure it'll be on a slab."

CHAPTER 3

Harrington sat at his desk, leaned back, unbuttoned his waistcoat, and lit a cigar. He had lunched well.

His desk was four feet across and six feet wide. There were trays, and a blotter, and a small file, within reach. The rest was empty, highly polished oak. Beyond his desk there were twelve feet of deep pile carpet, maroon in colour, leading to a glass wall which looked out over London. This floor of the J and J building he had designed himself. He liked space, the right to look for miles, to know that there was no more solvent firm of merchant bankers in England, which in this context still meant the world. Thus there was nothing to interrupt his vision. Three comfortable leather armchairs waited on either side of his desk, but he looked down the tunnel in the middle. So far as he knew there was only one more splendid office than this in the whole city, and that was at the other end of the floor, presently and usually empty, while the Chairman soaked up the Mediterranean sunshine.

But soon to be filled, once again. He watched the smoke rising from his cigar. He searched for the top, for the true ceiling, and was only academically interested in the outward show. So, the directors of the J and J, as honest and straightforward a group of tycoons as it was possible to imagine, would undoubtedly elect a new chairman from amongst their own kind, rather than even consider elevating the company secretary, however efficient he might be.

And yet, it could be swung. Perhaps. Something to think about. Having accomplished everything else, to become chairman of the J and J would surely be simple.

The door opened and Shelley entered, checked on seeing him, her eyes widening in surprise. "I'm sorry," she said. "I should have knocked." But there was no apology in her tone. She was not the sort of girl who apologised easily. She was small and solid, and white skinned, and had wavy yellow hair; her brown eyes suggested that this might be dyed, but there was no other flaw in her appearance. Her pale grey suit came from Harrods, her yellow blouse from Fortnums, and her accent, as well as her parents—according to her file—from Wiltshire. Her hobby was horses. She was everything Harrington found desirable in a woman, and she knew it. If she was ever disconcerted it was that she remained, after more than a year, nothing more than his secretary. "I didn't realise you were already back."

Harrington gazed at her through a cloud of cigar smoke. This was one of the most satisfying moments of the day, just gazing at Shelley on top of a good lunch, mentally removing her smart suit and imagining what would lie underneath. If anything. Except, of course, white skin. He fully intended to do something about her, one day. But not until this business was completed. Harrington prided himself upon his self-discipline, his knowledge of when he could afford to relax and when he couldn't. "I left early," he reminded her. "Any messages?"

She opened her notebook. "Nothing important. Someone called Peter Smith telephoned, just after you left. He was rather anxious to speak with you personally. We have five Peter Smiths on file. I really can't say which one it is."

"None of them," Harrington said. "This is a personal matter. Anything from Antibes?"

She shook her head. "When Mr. Jarne goes on holiday, he really goes on holiday, doesn't he, Mr. Harrington? Has he found a crew yet?"

"I sent him down some names and particulars. If he can't find someone from amongst that lot, then he never will. There won't be any dictation this afternoon, Shelley. It's been one of those days."

"Very good, Mr. Harrington. And the man Smith? He left a number."

"So dial it for me, will you?" Harrington waited, fingers drumming, until his phone buzzed. "This had better be good, Peter, my lad."

"I thought you'd like to know that despite all, Tommy went looking."

"I never supposed he was putting up anything more than a smoke screen," Harrington agreed. "Any trouble?"

"Alf is seeing a doctor, and Billy's hair has turned white. If you follow me."

"But Tommy is all right?"

"So far as I know. Trouble is, he took the girl with him."

"So?"

"I just thought you'd like to know."

Harrington considered the end of his cigar. "He is probably employing her in a professional capacity. Three years is a long time."

"I haven't finished. While she was still there, they had a visitor. Name of Hibbert. Detective Inspector Hibbert."

"I know the name." Harrington frowned. "Go on."

"So after a minute or two, Doreen left. A little flustered. Hibbert stayed an hour."

"I wonder what he wanted. Unless he supposes our boy knows something about that Francine business."

"You don't suppose *this* business might have got out of control?"

"This business will not get out of control," Harrington said. "Just as long as everyone does what they're told. That includes you, Peter. Bags packed?"

"All ready to go."

"Well, I'm sure you are going to have a marvellous holiday. Is your crew looking forward to it?"

"He says it'll be just like old times."

"Keep an eye on him. But neither of you is to stir a muscle until Tommy has left the country."

"I've got that. And Doreen?"

"What about her?"

"Our boy may have told her something. Or she may have told him something."

"I never realised how nervous you were, Peter," Harrington said. "Neither of those two *has* anything to tell each other, about you and me. They don't know we exist, except as other human beings."

"It's just that I thought it might be simpler . . ."

"It wouldn't. It would be an unnecessary risk. I still think you were lucky last time. From here on in, keep your nose clean." Harrington smiled. "We'll just let our Tommy get himself knotted, shall we?"

*

Angel locked the door, sat on the bed, and decided against any more beer. Instead he poured himself half a glass of scotch. He had promised himself this for three years, amongst so many other things. And it was as disappointing as all the others. Maybe because he was still worked up about Doreen, a sexual urge compounded by the hideous fate of Francine.

Or maybe because he was just realising how frightened he was. Maybe he hadn't been lying to Hibbert, after all.

He had not really been frightened before, ever. Not even at the prospect of going to prison. Angry, yes. Bitter, yes. But not frightened. And how secure life had been, in prison. One did what one was told, and one lived according to a set of rigid rules. And one dreamed only of getting out into the world of vice and viciousness.

And if one was lucky, one made friends. He had been very lucky. But then no doubt he had been born lucky by being born large. The block at Parkhurst in which he had found himself had been dominated by David Bracken, and Dave, having looked Angel over, had decided the big man would be more useful as a friend than as an enemy. And Angel, in turn, had liked the ex-boxer with the broken nose. Dave Bracken was an unusual character. His boxing career had been totally unsuccessful, and he had graduated, apparently without regret, into the dreg society of the sporting world. Yet he was an intelligent man. According to those who claimed to have known him on the outside, his muscles and his violence were for hire, and Dave himself had never denied that he was in prison for strong-arming a raid on a security van. But he had been the only one arrested, and he had kept his mouth shut. That was sufficient to earn the respect of the regulars, and yet his privileged position had to have had more behind it. Inmates and warders alike had feared Dave Bracken, and that he had formed a liking for Angel had been sufficient to make the three years much easier than they might have been. Dave had been let out over a year ago, but by then Angel had himself been established. Thus he had avoided all of the misery which can so easily be inflicted upon a loner.

So Hibbert was also aware of Dave's standing, and Hibbert was looking for a lead, any sort of a lead. But Dave was certainly not mixed up in smuggling. So no doubt Hibbert's tail was still hanging close behind. He'd find nothing to interest him in Bracken's gynasium.

Whereas Angel had never felt so lonely in his life. Besides, he desperately needed information and advice.

Surprisingly, the gymnasium was exactly as Dave had described it and Angel had imagined it.

"I don't manage," Dave had said. "I have a good site and I rent the space. If anyone wants advice they're welcome to it. I've experience, man."

So there were half a dozen rings and a variety of earnest, sweating young men, clad in trunks and vests and head guards, pounding at each other; around them a crowd of older men in cloth caps and checked vests and other equally out-of-date gear smoked incessantly and muttered or shouted at each other and at their protégés. The huge room stank of resin and sweat and nicotine and sheer effort, and wore an air of hopelessness; even Angel could see at a glance that there was no talent on view.

But with his entry there was an audible sigh. Heads turned and guards dropped. He was certainly past the age at which anyone could consider taking up boxing as a career, but his size and his obvious fitness and the slightly aggressive air given him by the whisky combined to raise a murmur of what might have been, which was shattered by a great shout. "Tommy Angel, well glory be."

Dave Bracken was small only alongside Angel, and he had the shouldered slouch and the broken nose which made him seem bigger than he was. Sometimes he could add a glare of real menace, which, it had occurred to Angel, should have won a great many of his fights before he had even landed a blow.

This afternoon it was absent, and his ruddy cheeks and thick lips glowed as he hurried forward, right hand outstretched, left hand brushing the short, crisp black hair backwards on his forehead in a gesture which denoted at once embarrassment and shyness.

"When did they let you out?"

"This morning." Angel shook hands.

"And you're only now coming to see me?" Bracken frowned. "Or maybe you had other things on your mind."

"Maybe," Angel agreed. "I'd like a word."

"Man, you have the floor. Not here. These bums don't know when to keep their mouths shut. Out of the way, stupid." He thrust one man aside and the others hastily moved to the walls. Still grasping Angel's hand, Bracken led the way up a flight of scuffed steps into a surprisingly cosy living room. "Lu," he bellowed. "Lu. Come out here and meet Tommy Angel. What do you think of the place, Tommy?"

"Something out of Runyon," Angel said. "If Runyon had ever known London."

Bracken glanced at him, frowned again, and then grinned and
threw his arms wide. "Meet the wife."

Lucy Bracken was short and plump and dark. She wore an apron
over a beige sweater and beige slacks; her breasts drooped and her
thighs trembled. She smelt of cooking oil. But she had one of the
widest smiles Angel could recall, splitting her rather rugged face into
two and stretching all the way up to her hard brown eyes. "Tommy,"
she said, and took his hand between both of hers. "Dave has told me
so much about you. I have to thank you for looking after my man inside."

"The boot was on the other foot, Mrs. Bracken. Believe me."

"Lu," she said. "To my friends. You'll want a drink. Scotch? Or
will it be rum, like Dave?"

"I didn't know you were a rum drinker, Dave," Angel remarked.

"He got the habit in the Navy," Lucy Bracken said.

"For crying out loud," Angel said. "He never let on about that, either. And here I was supposing that when I talked about *Marianne* I
was boring the pants off you."

Bracken was frowning yet again, and Angel, turning back to face
the woman, was surprised by the sudden tightness at the mouth
which he had last seen smiling so generously. "The tub I was on was
no yacht. Sit down, Tommy, sit down, man."

"Rum will suit me fine, Lu," Angel said, and sat down. "When you
come out," Bracken had always said. "Come and see me, Tommy,
man, and we'll have a jar and talk about what comes next." But maybe
he hadn't expected the invitation to be taken up. Apparently he had
thought more into their friendship than had actually existed, Angel
decided, regretfully.

But Bracken was grinning as he raised his glass. "How was it?"

Angel glanced at Lucy, standing beside him. She had regained her
composure, but remained somewhat resigned. She anticipated words
with her husband, afterwards.

Or, with David Bracken, would more than words be involved? Yet
Lucy Bracken looked well able to take care of herself.

"It was lonely," he said. "And long."

"The bastards," Dave said. "So what do you figure?"

"Ever heard of Rehabilitation Incorporated?"

Bracken finished his drink, handed the glass to his wife. "From
time to time. But they don't deal with people like me."

Angel sighed. "You have just taken a load off my mind. This character met me in Southampton. Called himself Smith. Offered me a job, skippering a yacht for some rich raver down in the Med."

"Sounds like that outfit," Dave agreed. "Anyone who can't earn a couple of thousand doesn't interest them. The Med? Isn't that your line of country?"

"That is what was bothering me. It all seemed just a little too pat."

Bracken took the full glass from his wife. "Tell me about the man. Smith."

Angel shrugged. "Thirty-fiveish, slim, small build, little black moustache, very well dressed, driving a Rover thirty-five hundred."

"Was there more than talk?"

"A hundred pounds, a flat for a week, and a plane ticket to Nice."

Bracken's frown was back. "You want to watch it. They'll be around for their pound of flesh, man."

"So I'm looking for advice."

"Nor for Francine, any more?"

"Francine is dead. Or didn't you know?"

Bracken sighed. "I know, Tommy. But I figured, what the hell, if Tommy happens to have forgotten about her, why drag it up?"

"You haven't asked me how I found out."

"Maybe you read a newspaper."

"I chatted up a girl called Doreen," Angel said, speaking very slowly. "A tart working from the same address Francine used to have. Oh, what the hell, you may as well have the whole story."

Bracken listened, as did his wife, while she refilled their glasses for a third time.

"I've heard of that bastard Hibbert," Bracken said, when Angel had finished.

"So why should he have mentioned your name?"

Bracken grinned. "They've all got my name on their minds, Tommy. I never split in that heist I was done for. And nobody else was ever nailed. As far as they're concerned, I'm still worth having."

"And are you?" Angel asked.

"Once is enough for Dave Bracken." But the frown had returned. "You're not still bearing a grudge? The girl is dead. So maybe whoever did her in is the chap responsible for your going up in the first place. Take a tip from an old hand, Tommy. Stay out of that game. You'll wind up with a knife in your back down some dark alley."

"That also worries me," Angel said. "How come I haven't already?"

Bracken sighed. "You used to be happy taking my advice in Parkhurst."

"You usually managed to convince me, then."

"Okay. So I knew where I was. Now I don't, as regards you. Maybe Hibbert had something. Maybe these people have got something on you, something they figure might do for them. Whatever happens, you don't want to play. So the word is that these Rehabilitation Incorporated people are a lot of usurers. It'd still be worth your while to get out of this country for the next couple of years. Pay them their thirty per cent or whatever it is they want. You'll be in the clear. Get on with your new employer and you can give them the stiff middle finger. Believe me, Tommy, I'm only thinking of you."

"I suppose you're right."

"When do you have to let this Smith know?"

"Presumably I've already accepted the job by taking his money and his ticket. But I'm to confirm by eight o'clock tonight; he gave me a number to call."

"So you've time for a meal. Lu cooks like nobody else in this whole town."

"We'd like you to stay, Tommy," Lucy Bracken said.

But she wasn't convincing. Neither was Bracken. Maybe they hadn't expected him; maybe the death of Francine had convinced them that they didn't want to mix with him. What had Doreen said? The word was out, stay away from Tommy Angel. Tommy Angel is poison. It would have reached Dave as well.

"Thanks all the same," Angel said, and stood up. "I'd better get to bed early. Seems to me tomorrow may be a long day."

*

The mistral had died away, for the time being, and Nice was hot. Angel had forgotten what it was like, to be in the South of France, to inhale the sea-laden air, to feel a breeze in June without the slightest temptation to button up his jacket—rather a strong desire to take it off. For a moment he could almost forget what he was, now, and remember what he had been, pretend all over again that he was only a train ride away from *Marianne,* and total freedom.

For a moment. Even had he been able to forget the smug satisfaction in Smith's voice on the telephone, the new suit, a shade tight at the shoulders, would have reminded him. And even had he been able to forget the suit as well, his own self-loathing would have kept him fully aware of just what he was, now.

Which was so damned ridiculous it was almost funny. To get caught up in a smuggling ring in the first place was sheer stupidity, a judgement if ever there was one on his four years of total indulgence, of picking up birds whenever he felt like one, of taking a drink whenever he felt like one. To spend three years breathing vengeance had been childish, even if no doubt the anger had kept him from going mad. Actually to attempt to do something about Francine had been crazy, only calculated to land him back behind those ugly walls. And now that he had been saved by circumstances, to feel sorry for the girl, to feel that maybe in some way he had caused her death, to feel like looking for whoever had been responsible, to feel guilty, because he was running away from England and the nameless them, the Big People, was utterly absurd. He had allowed himself to be sucked into something beyond his understanding, and in the course of time the whirlpool had thrown him back out. He should at last count himself truly lucky.

And, he reflected as he went through the glass doors, even had he been able to forget all that, there would still be constant reminders. A man waited for him. A thin man with a hooked nose and a pointed chin, sunburned face arranged into a friendly smile, sports shirt freshly laundered and flapping at the collar, feet protruding from white duck trousers to allow his bare toes into flipflops.

"Angel? My word, but you *are* a big fellow. I'm Colne."

He did not offer to shake hands, and Angel hastily checked the instinctive forward movement of his right arm.

"My pleasure."

"Makes a change, what? But you know the Riviera, of course." He did not offer to take Angel's bag, either, and was already turning and leading the way across the arrival lounge, but not, Angel realised with surprise, in the direction of the exit.

"I've been here," he said.

"Of course you have, my dear chap. I suppose you know Antibes as well. You're booked for *Twin Tempest*, you know, but there has been a slight complication."

"Not really," Angel said, his heart sinking.

Colne gave a short laugh, and halted at the door to the bar. "We had hoped to get you straight on board. But I'm afraid Mrs. Jarne has found out about your arrival. I suppose old Jarne must have told her something. So I'm afraid you'll have to go with her."

"That's bad, is it?"

Colne scratched his nose, carefully. "You'll want to watch it, old man. But then, as you say, you know the Riviera. I'll just introduce you, shall I?"

"Do that," Angel agreed. "But there is one small matter I'd like to mention. I still have seventeen pounds out of the hundred Smith gave me in Southampton. Actually, I changed them into francs before I left London. Do I give the money back to you, now?"

Colne raised his eyebrows. "My dear fellow, I have no idea *what* you are talking about. My motto has always been to hang on to whatever money one can. You never can tell when it'll come in handy." He smirked. "Buy the lady a drink. Over here now, and I must say again, old chap, do please be careful."

"I've had some," Angel said. He followed the direction of Colne's gaze, and felt his blood begin to tingle. He had indeed had some; it was inseparable from the chartering business. Elderly gentlemen who had at last made their fortunes and decided that a Mediterranean retirement was the life for them, and who came equipped either with aggressive, bad-tempered, and utterly repulsive wives or with equally aggressive, good-looking but utterly dumb dolly birds. He had not anticipated that the Jarne setup would be the least different, and felt suitably humbled.

The woman in the upholstered chair was of an indecipherable age, but he would have settled for thirty. She was tall; her legs were long enough to guarantee that. They were presently encased in yellow bell bottoms, but the ankles were exposed before the matching flipflops were reached, and the bare flesh, slender and firm and brown, promised there would be little change on the long, slow climb up to the slender hips and the flat belly lying behind the huge buckled leather belt.

Her blouse was a deep green, and loosely buttoned; only two were fastened. The flesh that showed was a uniform brown. There were no wrinkles on the slightly long neck, and the hair, which, judging by the dark eyebrows and her general complexion, would be black, unless she cheated, was concealed beneath a yellow head scarf which matched her pants and shoes.

Her face suffered from a certain remoteness; she looked at him, established that he was looking at her, and appeared to lose interest. She did not doubt that if he *was* looking at her, he would not readily stop. Angel was not prepared to argue with that point of view. The only word for her features was chiselled, the forehead high, the chin a sliver of bone contained within a frame of not less firm brown flesh, the mouth wide and lacking lipstick, the nose a perfect retroussé, so perfect he was inclined to suspect that in this respect she *might* have taken some trouble with a good surgeon. Her eyes were a deep brown and inexpressibly arrogant. Again with reason. She was perhaps the most beautiful woman Angel had ever seen, off a screen, and she needed none of it, now. The pearl earrings would have established that, even had she removed the five rings. The one on the third finger of her left hand was pure gold and simple enough, the rest reflected lights of various colours, one green, one red, one blue, and the biggest facets of shimmering white. Her wrist watch was a thin gold Omega.

"Mrs. Jarne?" Colne asked, nervously. "This is Tom Angel, Mr. Jarne's new skipper."

She nodded. "Would you like a drink, Angel?" Her voice was low, and had the assurance of her eyes. Her accent was international. She was the sort of woman one either fell in love with at first sight, supposing it was remotely possible that she could be afforded, or, lacking that sort of bank account, hated at first sight. In any event, Angel was in a hating mood, this morning.

"I'd love a drink."

"We will have it in the car." She stood up, and a man in a green uniform, with a green peaked cap and black boots, emerged out of the shadows at the side of the room to hold her chair. "Thank you, Mr. Colne," she said, and left the room.

Angel gazed at her back. So did every other man present.

"You'd better go, old man," Colne muttered. "She really doesn't like to be kept waiting."

"Does she come with the boat?" Angel asked.

"Mrs. Jarne uses the boat for sun bathing," Colne explained. "When it happens to be here. She does not like sailing of any description. And believe it or not, Jarne seems to like to get away from her for months on end. I suppose he needs the rest."

"I'm glad of that," Angel said. "Or you could just book me a passage home. See you."

He went outside, blinked in the brilliant sunshine. But he didn't have far to look. The giant Mercedes was waiting on the No Parking sign, and the chauffeur was still holding the door wide.

Angel sat beside the woman, behind the tinted glass, and for the first time inhaled her perfume. He supposed it must be Adoration or something equally expensive. Certainly he had never smelt anything like it before.

"I will have a vodka and tonic," she said.

The car was already gliding on to the street. Angel opened the bar, poured two. "Cheers. You'll forgive my surprise. I had not expected to run into a bird the slightest bit like you. And I'm just out of prison. Or didn't they tell you about that?"

He was being deliberately rude, a measure of his own uncertainty. Yet she almost smiled, allowed her fingers to brush his as she took her glass.

"I knew about that, Angel. And so I wished to look you over before allowing my husband to go away with you. And I, also, am surprised. When they said a big man, I had no idea they were being so literal. Now tell me, are you equally pleased?"

"I read somewhere that beauty is only skin deep."

Now she did smile. She looked quite delighted. "And you even have a gift of repartee. Small, but promising. I assume that you were paying me a compliment. I am pleased, Angel. Tell me what they sent you to prison for."

"Smuggling."

She frowned. "That is not an interesting sort of crime."

"You'd have preferred rape?"

She inclined her head. "I could forgive a man anything, Angel, were I sure it was done with passion. But smuggling is a petty way of trying to get rich."

"If it will make you feel any better, I didn't do it," he said, and could have kicked himself. Apart from the stupidity of the protest, why should he defend himself to this bitch?

She laughed, and he had seldom heard a more delightful ripple of sound. "You were framed, Angel? That rather disappoints me as regards your intelligence."

"We all have our faults."

Once again she laughed, and this time said something in Spanish to the driver. He nodded.

"I do not think there is any necessity for you to go straight down to the boat," she said. "As I know my husband has no intention of leaving before this evening. I think you should come to the house and lunch with me."

"If you're sure Mr. Jarne won't mind."

She shrugged, very slightly. "My husband lacks passion. At least as regards me, Angel. Do you find that hard to believe?"

"Very."

Again the shrug. "Perhaps I lack passion as regards him. We obtain our pleasure in different ways. He is much older than I, and so perhaps our paths have drifted apart."

"I think you should know," Angel said, speaking very slowly and carefully, "that I am all through being a patsy, for anybody. Even for you, Mrs. Jarne."

She glanced at him without changing her expression, and then waved her hand. "That is our house."

The Mercedes was descending a gentle slope, and in the far distance, beyond some more villas and spreading gardens, was the sea. Closer at hand, on the right there was a thick little wood, beyond which white walls enclosed a large landscaped park, scattered with trees and ornamental ponds. The house was almost invisible, and now disappeared altogether as they approached two square white-washed gateposts, each some four feet thick. He had even lost track of where they were, although he figured they had to be somewhere close to Antibes. But the Mercedes was turning into the concrete drive, and he saw the swimming pool, and then the terrace. The house now came into view, brilliant white and vaguely Moorish in design. There seemed endless galleries and few doors, and these stood open.

As did the door of the car, held by the chauffeur. Mrs. Jarne got out and Angel followed her, to check as a black Doberman trotted across the patio, hair bristling.

"Jupiter," Mrs. Jarne said. "Jupiter looks after me when my husband is away. Do not bite Angel, Jupiter. He is going to be a friend, I am sure."

The dog reached Angel, and stopped, head thrust forward to sniff.

"He always does what I tell him," Mrs. Jarne remarked. "Come along, Angel."

Angel stepped round the dog. The next obstacle was a white-coated butler, who waited at the entrance to the house.

"Two for lunch, Henri," Mrs. Jarne said in French. "Calamar, is it? We will eat now. And a bottle of Clicquot." She stepped out of her shoes and on to the soft carpet, walked down a side hall, and opened a door to a deep pink tiled bathroom. "I imagine you would like to wash your hands."

He did, in fact, only want to do that, which he realised was probably fortunate, because to his surprise she remained in the room, leaning against the door. "My name is Lampagie."

"That's reaching back a bit." Angel dried his fingers on a soft pink towel. The entire room carried her scent.

She led him back into the hall. "Tell me."

Angel tried to remember. "The Princess Lampagie was the most beautiful woman of her time. She was the daughter of Eudo, Count of Toulouse, and lived at the beginning of the eighth century. To cement an alliance intended to save Eudo's lands from invasion, she was given in marriage to one of the Moorish emirs in Spain."

She led him across the entry hall, and down three steps to a dining room which looked through french windows at the lawn. Here was a huge mahogany table, at which two places were laid, leaving an enormous expanse of highly polished wood to gleam in the noon sunlight. And here too was a chandelier and a great sideboard on which waited a fascinating accumulation of crystal decanters. Lampagie Jarne sat at the head of the table, and motioned him to the chair beside her. "Go on."

Angel sat down. "The story has an unhappy ending. The emir was in revolt against the Caliph, and the next year he was defeated and executed. And Lampagie went to the Caliph's harem. After that she disappears from history and legend."

Lampagie clapped her hands with pleasure. "A sailor, from prison, with a classical education. But there is a measure of her beauty, and her talents. She was not a virgin when the Caliph took her. I think that must have been unique. As to her ultimate fate, no doubt she took her turn in the holy bed, developed unusual relationships with some of her companions in misfortune, and with some of her eunuchs, like everyone else in her position. But I would like to think she also became a mother, and that her blood still flows, somewhere."

"In your veins, perhaps?"

"Who knows. I am proud to bear the name."

"I'm afraid I can do no better than Tom."

"I prefer Angel." She waited as the butler entered with a tray on which there were an ice bucket containing an opened bottle of champagne and two glasses. He placed this next to his mistress, and left again. "Will you pour?"

Angel obliged, and she took her glass, sipped, and gazed at him over the rim. Just for that moment her eyes held his, and he felt a whole lot better. The eyes were deep, haunting, and haunted. Her arrogance was in her consciousness of wealth and beauty and power. Not in her soul.

"Would you like to make love to me?" she asked.

CHAPTER 4

It occurred to Harrington that it was going to be impossible to do any work this afternoon. Presumably by now Angel had arrived in Antibes. He might be on board the yacht this very moment, and no doubt Jarne would be anxious to get to sea.

Smith would also be in the South of France by now. With his crew. Waiting.

And Colne would be wondering what was happening.

What of the Great Bitch? Harrington rather thought she would like Angel. She would think that a man who was so big in general must also be bigger than average in particular. She might even be right. The best of luck to her.

And the Doll? Oh, the Doll would also like Angel, he had no doubt at all. They were two of a kind, the Great Bitch and the Doll, and Angel had the physique, and sufficient intelligence—going on the reports he had received from Parkhurst—to appeal to each of them. It occurred to Harrington that they might even fly to Angel's defence, afterwards. That would be amusing. He might have to do something about that. And that also would be amusing.

But work today was out of the question.

The door opened. "Good afternoon, Mr. Harrington." Shelley wore a pale green miniskirt and seemed all leg. Another reason for finding it difficult to work, if one was in the mood to be distracted. "Had a good lunch?"

"Very," Harrington said. "Anything come in while I was out?"

She shook her head. Her wavy blond hair moved to and fro. "June is a quiet month." She leaned over the desk to place the evening paper in front of him, and Harrington's mind was suddenly made up; her white nylon blouse was high necked but quite sheer. There was no point in thinking of anything else, really. Except what might be happening in Antibes. And he did not want to do that.

"Miss Beattie," he said. "I propose to take this afternoon off. Would you care to accompany me?"

She straightened, regarded him with a faint frown.

"I thought we might drive into the country," Harrington explained, feeling unaccountably nervous. "It really is too nice an afternoon to spend sitting in an office in London."

Shelley nodded, slowly and thoughtfully. "Suppose Mr. Jarne telephones? Do you remember . . ."

"He won't," Harrington said. "Not this afternoon. His new crew was due to arrive today, and he will be too happy showing off his boat and making plans for his departure."

"Shelley continued to look sceptical. "Liz Hartnell got the sack," she pointed out. "Because she wasn't there when Mr. Jarne telephoned."

"Should that occur," Harrington promised, "I will employ you on a personal basis, Shelley. Will that do?"

"That would do very nicely, Mr. Harrington."

"Then grab your handbag and meet me outside, and telephone the garage and have them send the car round."

He watched her walk to the door. She had been to a finishing school in Switzerland, and placed her feet carefully, one in front of the other, as if she were balancing books on top of her head. Perhaps mentally she was. He had never been to bed with a real lady before. He had never had the guts. It occurred to him that he was taking his first step into freedom. After thirty-seven years of imprisonment, first of all by his background and then by Jarne, he was going to be free. In a day or two he was going to be the freest man in the world.

And then Lampagie would be nothing. He remembered the contempt with which she had glanced at him, the one time Jarne had ever invited him home. He wondered what she would be like, the next time they met.

*

"Tell me about Mr. Jarne." Shelley leaned back against the leather cushion, sighed, and closed her eyes.

"I didn't bring you on an afternoon's outing to talk about Jarne." Harrington also relaxed; the Rover was through Guildford and at last out of the heavy traffic.

"Just for a moment," she said, without opening her eyes. "It is

rather odd, to work for a man you have only seen once, and never
even spoken to."

"I keep reminding you, my darling," Harrington said. "You work
for me."

"But you work for Mr. Jarne," she said with maddening logic. "So,
indirectly, I must also."

Harrington sighed. But presumably she would be worth it. And
besides, suddenly he wanted to talk about Jarne. For the very last
time.

"I suppose you could call him a self-made man," he said. "He
began after the war with nothing but his gratuity, slowly built it up
into a fortune."

"You mean he really did start from scratch?"

"Behind scratch, if anything."

"That sort of thing always fascinates me. I thought men who could
come from nothing to be millionaires went out at the end of the last
century."

"Not quite," Harrington said. "So maybe nowadays they have to be
more shady than once upon a time. And maybe Jarne was a shade
more shady than most. But he got there."

"What do you mean by shady?"

"Mind your own business," Harrington said, and pulled off the
road, directing his car across the bumpy grass to the place he sought.
From the brow of this hill they looked out over the Weald, in June an
endless green panorama, disturbed but not destroyed by the electricity
pylons and the ribbons of road.

"Anyway," she said, "he was never caught out."

"Not our Justin," Harrington agreed. "And then he diversified, got
his fingers into more and more pies. Even I only found out just how
many after I had been working for him a good five years."

"What exactly is your relationship with Mr. Jarne?" she asked, sitting up. "I mean, you're more than just secretary of the J and J company, aren't you?"

"That's a minor post." Harrington gazed at the view; he liked endless space almost as much as he liked white skin. "I work for Jarne,
and nobody else. So the J and J is his front company, and it is con-
venient for him to have me where I can keep an eye on everything
that's going on." He took off his glasses.

"I see," she said thoughtfully. "You still haven't told me what sort of a man he is. I mean, he must be a terrific businessman, mustn't he?"

Harrington picked up her right hand, turned it over, and kissed the palm, then allowed his mouth to follow the arm upwards. His right hand rested on her left knee, his fingers gently snaking beneath the short skirt.

"I really would like to know," she said. But she made no move to stop him.

Harrington raised his head. His right hand was buried beneath the skirt, its fingers just reaching the nylon clad warmth of their goal. And still she hadn't moved; he could afford to be generous. "Anyone would think you had your eye on him rather than on me."

"It's a good way to learn about a man, finding out about his employer," she said, still with total composure, and now he had reached hair as soft as the nylon. She was either totally lacking in passion, or she could control her feelings better than any woman he had ever met. Either way, her ultimate arousal promised a pleasure that he had never encountered before, either.

"Well, then," he whispered, his face inches from her neck. "Justin Jarne is the hardest man I have ever met. As you'd expect. He is also the toughest, most ruthless man I have ever met. You want to stay away from him, my darling. He'd roll you up and chew you into pieces and spit you out, fit only for the dustbin."

She smiled at him. "I think you admire Mr. Jarne, Martin."

That surprised him. He had never thought about it. "Why, yes," he agreed. "In many ways I suppose I do."

"And if you work for him, you must have those qualities too, or he wouldn't employ you, would he?"

"I never thought of that," Harrington said, smiling in turn, and she thrust out her tongue to touch his.

"I had," she whispered, and put her left hand on the nape of his neck to bring his face forward.

*

"*Would* you like to make love to me?" Lampagie asked again, still sipping champagne. "Believe me, it is not something I often permit. I find lovemaking incredibly boring, nine times out of ten. But you are at least physically different."

Angel stared at her. So many brilliant, witty, cutting replies crossed his mind. But he merely said, "No, I would not like to make love to you, Mrs. Jarne." And that was a lie. "I came down here to do a job of work, and I would like to get on with it. Where is your husband's yacht moored?"

"I will take you there. After lunch."

The butler entered with another laden tray, served them each a plate of squid, and refilled their glasses.

Lampagie smiled at Angel. "Please. It is very uncivil to refuse to lunch with your employer's wife."

Angel chewed, slowly.

"I have shocked you," she said sadly. "That is a shame. If I can shock a man I doubt whether I can ever be friends with him. And I had hoped you were different. I still think you are. You are a poor liar. It was no more than a rhetorical question, you know. But I am interested in why your refusal was so quick and so definite. Is it my husband?"

"Wouldn't that be natural?"

She shrugged delicately. "I really would not trouble yourself, Angel. Shall I tell you about Justin Jarne? He is a very rich man. I understand he is one of the richest men in the world. But it was not always so. He came out of the British Army in 1946 as a soldier with nothing but his discharge pay. Somehow he got into business, and found he was good at it. So far a great success story. And it went on and on and on. Money makes money, they say. I know very little of his business activities, but I believe he owns a lot of property and a lot of shares and has a lot of people working for him, now. He is a financial wizard, perhaps, as the newspapers would say. And he sees himself as an emperor. As an emperor, therefore, he has decided, over the past dozen years or so, to indulge his various vices. Justin has a sadistic streak which runs through him like a disease. Obviously I did not know this when I married him. Although I should have suspected something. I am his fourth wife. One died, one committed suicide, and the other was divorced. Four years ago he married me. I come from a very good family, you know. A better family than any of the others. And so I was a very good prize for him. He courted me like a prince, and as he is a very handsome and very courteous man, and a very generous one, when he wishes to be, I thought my every dream had come true. Of course I had made a serious mistake. Justin's sadism is physical, often, but he also likes to indulge in mental torture. He can tear a person's mind to shreds, and enjoy doing it, much as he can mark a body. Then he will restore the person, body and mind, to health again. So that he can destroy them, again, when he feels like it."

She sucked at the squid.

"You'll have me weeping in a moment," Angel said. "But you have survived him for four years. That must be better than any of the others managed."

Again the delicate shrug. "His first wife lasted longest. She even bore him a daughter, I believe. But she doesn't get on with her father. I suppose that is natural."

"Why *are* you telling me all this?" Angel asked.

"Who knows?" she said. "Perhaps I am lonely, and like to talk with strangers. Perhaps I do not wish you to be under any misapprehension as to the man you are going to work for. He has a young woman on board now, who I imagine is his current mistress. But she will not be the only one, and I suppose that he is tormenting her as much as he torments me. You will find that regularly in the course of this summer he will pick up one or two of those itinerant young women who are always to be found in Mediterranean seaports, and bring them on board for a day or two, without the slightest concern for her feelings, or for yours."

"You sound almost jealous."

She smiled. "Oh, I suppose in my own little way I try to copy Justin. It is my only means of survival."

"And he doesn't mind?"

Lampagie finished her fish, carefully sucked each finger, and then washed them in the little bowl of lemon water the butler had placed beside her. "Why should he? I am everything he really wishes in a wife, even after he has sucked me dry emotionally. I am very beautiful, and I am a very good and much respected hostess. I am very socially acceptable. I never make scenes about his girl friends, or about anything else. And I am always here, waiting for him when he decides to return home. This amuses him, to own, so absolutely, someone like me. But outside of that, he has the utmost contempt for me, and for you, and for everyone else. He has a theory, that the world is a pyramid of people. Those at the bottom are really nonexistent. They merely prop up the rest. Above them are the Little People, who dictate events to the nameless mass, but are really of no account in themselves. Then there are the Big People, who dominate the Little

People. But above all the Big People there are one or two Giants, and they run the world. Justin counts himself one of the Giants. And who knows, he may even be right." She struck the gong, and the butler appeared. "Cork this bottle, will you, Henri? And put it and another one in the boot of the car." She pushed back her chair and stood up. "Now I will drive you down to the boat."

*

"So what's in it for you?" Angel asked. He wondered why. He was not really interested. Apart from the fact that he had suddenly become obsessed by a nameless worry, which he could neither place nor understand, but which he was sure had been caused by something she had said, or done. Which covered a lot of territory. But even had he been able to remember what it was, he would still have been preoccupied. She had decided to drive herself, had exchanged the big Mercedes for a little Alfa Romeo, and seemed determined to reach Antibes without ever using all four wheels at the same time.

She laughed. Her head went back and the slither of sound drifted behind the car as it swayed across the road. "For what reason should I change things, Angel? Occasionally I am made to suffer. The rest of the time I am allowed to live as very few people do."

"There's a thought." People. Big People and Little People. Doreen had used that expression. She had delivered the formula as her own. An uneducated tart and a business tycoon. But it really wasn't a particularly original or startling point of view. In fact, although perhaps not all would have put it so succinctly, it was a point of view shared by most of those at the top, and by not a few of those at the bottom. Only the ones in the middle were ever reluctant to admit just how small they really were.

Like Angel.

The car debouched from the sloping streets on to the esplanade—the house had, after all, been only a few miles from Antibes—searing past the moored yachts in their endless rows, and came to a screaming halt at the end of the main jetty, not quite demolishing a telephone booth.

"So here we are." Lampagie Jarne led Angel round the harbour office, and pointed. "The big ketch. My husband's true other woman. And the only good thing in his life. Do you like her?"

"It would be difficult not to."

"And you do not find it strange that a man who could afford the *Queen Elizabeth the Second,* if he really wanted to, should spend so much of his time on that overgrown lifeboat, where he has to work as hard as any sailor?"

"I find it reassuring," Angel said. "And I wouldn't exactly describe that as an overgrown lifeboat."

He could not keep the envy from his voice. *Twin Tempest,* as Smith had promised, was a forty-foot-long ketch. As her description had implied, both of her masts were forward of the enclosed wheelhouse, which meant that each of her three working sails, mizzen, main, and foresail, would be small enough easily to be handled by one man. She was built of wood, probably iroko on oak frames, he figured, with obviously teak laid decks and superstructure; her hull was painted black and her deckhouse white. Ketches, being as a general rule designed to go as well under engine as under sail, are not often very fast boats, but *Twin Tempest* did not look particularly slow. More important, she looked a good sea boat, and Angel could tell without going a step nearer that she was fitted out for real open sea work; the mizzen was topped by an enormous loop aerial for radio direction finding, and halfway down the mast a bracket supported a big radar scanner.

"You will find," Lampagie remarked, "that everything Justin possesses is in very good working order."

For the first time he felt embarrassed. "I'm sorry, Mrs. Jarne, about lunch. Maybe, as I just got out of prison yesterday morning, I'm still a little confused."

"Maybe," she agreed, and smiled. "I was not offended, Angel. I'll see you again. If I choose to. Come along."

She walked across the concrete dock, seized the bell at the end of the gangplank and gave it a resounding ring, and then stepped out of her flipflops and went on board. Angel carried his bag behind her, checked as he reached the deck; a young woman had emerged from the wheelhouse doorway.

As Lampagie had remarked, everything Jarne owned looked in good shape. But it occurred to Angel that his new employer also liked them large. This girl was blond, and no doubt genuinely so; her pale yellow hair complemented the blue of her eyes, and it was long, straight hair which wisped on her shoulders. So, in colouring, she contrasted with Lampagie, and also in her features, which could hardly be described as beautiful. Rather were they clipped, short nose and chin and small mouth all inclining together to give an impresson of strength rather than hardness. But like Lampagie's, her eyes were remote. No doubt Justin Jarne had this effect upon all his women.

On the other hand, who would waste even five minutes worrying about her face? She wore a black bikini, and a great deal of lotion had no doubt gone into helping the sun to overcome the natural fairness of her skin; it was a uniform golden brown from forehead to toes. And there was a lot of it. Long, powerful legs eased into wide thighs, separated by a rounded belly which stretched the bikini briefs. The bra top was distended by the swelling breasts. Even her shoulders were suitably broad. Angel had no doubt at all that as a deck hand she was going to be the very best.

"This is Alison," Lampagie said with utter contempt. "Mr. Angel is your new skipper."

"I'd figured that." Alison was very obviously English. "Hi." She held out her hand. "You'd be a hard man to miss, Mr. Angel."

"I'd have to be pretty careless myself." Her fingers were dry and firm.

"My God," Lampagie said. "A mutual admiration society. I'm sure you'll be glad you waited, Angel. Where is my husband?"

"Still in siesta," Alison said. "But he'll be up in a few minutes. Come aboard, Mr. Angel."

"The name is Tom."

She waggled her eyebrows at him, led them into a large and very well appointed wheelhouse. Companionways led both forward and aft.

"Aft is Mr. Jarne's sleeping cabin and bathroom," Alison explained, and went forward, down the steps into the saloon, the port side of which was a U-shaped dinette, while the starboard contained the galley and the fridge. "Tea, beer, or something stronger?"

"Beer will suit me fine," Angel said.

"I will have tea," Lampagie said. "Just to be a nuisance." She took off her head scarf, and thereby accentuated the difference between herself and the girl; her hair was raven, and cropped before being swept forward in a bouffant style. Angel wondered if the careless gesture was really a very deliberate piece of upstaging. Certainly the isolated face only gained in beauty. "Come along, Angel," she said. "I will show you your cabin."

She opened the jalousied door in the forward end of the saloon. Angel glanced at Alison, who shrugged. He picked up his bag and followed Lampagie into a small lobby.

"Loo on the right, bathroom on the left. I'm sorry, I don't suppose that is very nautical. Then here is a double cabin, presently occupied by Alison, and forward," she opened another door, "is the forecastle, with a berth to port and stowage to starboard. That's better, isn't it? It also has its own washbasin and another loo. Up there in the bow. I don't know what arrangements you will come to about quarters. As you are the skipper I would put my foot down."

"You can sleep in here with pleasure, Tom," Alison said, from the double cabin. "Or if you prefer it, I will move into the forepeak."

"I'm sure that won't be necessary," Lampagie said. "She very seldom sleeps down here, in any event, Angel. The kettle is boiling."

Alison made tea, opened Angel a beer. Remarkably, she did not seem embarrassed by Lampagie's sallies.

Lampagie sat at the table with her tea in front of her, one knee draped across the other. "You may sit beside me, Angel," she suggested, and then glanced at the steps to the wheelhouse. "Or perhaps you would rather meet my husband first."

CHAPTER 5

"Do you realise," Shelley asked, "that it is not yet six o'clock?"

It was still difficult to believe it had really happened.

"I should be going," she said. "Unless you'd like me to spend the night."

Let her go, now? Let her go, to be left with nothing to do but wonder what was happening in Antibes, whether everything was all right with Smith, whether the two bitches would not get into each other's way and foul everything up, whether Jarne might not change his mind at the last moment and remain in port?

But Justin Jarne never changed his mind, or his method. There was the secret of his success.

"If I'm going to stay the night," Shelley said, "I'd like to eat. Will you take me out, or shall I cook you something?"

Harrington released her and lay back. "You don't mean you can do that, too?"

"I haven't shown you a fraction of the things I can do," she said, and slipped her legs out of bed.

"There's champagne in the fridge." Harrington put on his glasses to watch her walk across the room. She looked almost as good from the back as from the front. It occurred to him that he could easily marry this girl, because she was the sort of young woman of whom he had always dreamed. Others might be more beautiful, and possibly even more sexy, although that was doubtful. But no one had ever matched her combination of sexuality and breeding. Possibly Lampagie Jarne might be able to do so. But he had never got Lampagie Jarne into bed, and he was not sure it would be a good idea, even were it possible. Lampagie was the only woman in the world of whom he was frightened.

*

Angel put down his beer and stood up, grazing his head on the deck beams. He was surprised, and was apparently intended to be surprised. Justin Jarne looked delighted.

"You'll be Tom Angel," he said, coming forward with outstretched hand. "Welcome aboard."

His fingers were dry and strong. He wore only a pair of red bathing trunks, and his flesh was as brown as either of the women's, and far more remarkable, appeared to be as firm textured. Only the grey hair, still streaked with black, and the lines on the face, suggested that he was at retirement age. For the face itself was as lean as a boy's.

"It's good to be here, Mr. Jarne," Angel said. And for the first time was unconditionally glad he had not touched Lampagie. He was going to like this man. There were calluses on the hand which was now releasing his. Justin Jarne was no bridge-deck sailor.

"I'll bet." Jarne glanced at his wife. "I see you've met Lampagie. Do you like her?"

"I . . ."

"What he means is," Lampagie said, "do you find me beautiful? The correct answer, of course, is yes."

Jarne smiled. "Aren't women fascinating, Tom? Women, the sea, and ships, are the only interesting things left in this overcivilised world. Shall I tell you why? Because they are the only *un*civilised things left. No law or government will ever civilise woman. No government can ever own all the sea. And every time we poor men put out beyond the twelve-mile limit we are our own masters, and may throw civilisation to the wind." He sat beside his wife, took her left hand in his, and gave it a gentle squeeze. "Sure you won't come for the ride, dearest? We are going to cast off at eighteen hundred, and sail direct for Ibiza. It will take us two days and three nights. Doesn't that sound entrancing?"

"I should need my head examined," Lampagie remarked.

"There's a wife for you, Tom. Before we were married, I couldn't keep her off the boat. What are you drinking?"

"Beer."

"Leave it. We shall drink champagne."

"Oh, bother," Lampagie said. "I even brought some down, to cele-brate, and left it in the car. Angel . . ."

"I'll get it, Mrs. Jarne." Alison stepped past her employer.

"In which case it will be too hot to drink at this moment," Jarne said. "It will also be Clicquot, which I abhor. You'll find a bottle of Krug in the fridge, Tom."

Angel opened the fridge, took out the bottle of champagne, and released the cork with a gentle pop. Lampagie had already placed four glasses on the table. Now she raised the first full one. "I will drink to a happy summer, Justin."

Jarne smiled at her, rather as a father might smile at a young and wayward daughter. "What she means, Tom, is that she is glad to see the back of me, so that she can return to her more normal life of dusk-to-dawn parties, and dawn to dusk in bed. Seldom alone, I might add. But then, it keeps her looking young, wouldn't you say?"

Angel put down his glass. "I think I should change my clothes, and start getting the ship ready for sea."

"Don't be absurd," Lampagie said. "He is only saying things like that because you are here to embarrass."

"And in any event," Jarne said, "my ship is always ready for sea. You can change your clothes in a moment. Tell me, Tom, do you like women?"

"I've rather gone off them," Angel confessed. "At the moment."

"I suspect a story. I know," Jarne said. "A woman was responsible for your being sent to gaol."

"But it wasn't rape," Lampagie said. "I asked."

"I never doubted that you would," Jarne said. "And do you mean that he wouldn't rape you either? You have had a boring day, dearest. But I take your point, Tom. There comes a time when one runs out of things to do to women."

"There, in that little word 'to,'" Lampagie said. "You have an entire masculine philosophy. I wouldn't dream of asking for a 'for,' but you could perhaps have tried 'with.'"

"I have tried 'with,'" Jarne pointed out. "And when I was very young, and equally innocent, rather like Tom here, a few years ago, I imagine, I went in for the 'for.' But now that I am older and have seen a great many women doing their worst for me, I come to rest on 'to.' I envy the old sultans and gothic kings, who could snap their fingers and do what they liked. There was once a sultan of Turkey called Mohamed the Second, you know, Tom, who was my ideal man."

"Tom has a surprisingly thorough knowledge of history," Lampagie said.

"Have you?" Jarne sounded genuinely surprised. "Then you are even more of a treasure than I supposed when I first saw you. What story would you say I have in mind, Tom?"

Angel poured himself some champagne. In a most remarkable fashion he seemed to have known these people all his life. In a dream, perhaps. Mainly because it was impossible to judge whether or not the Jarnes really did loathe each other, or were not actually extremely fond of each other. Either way he was feeling more relieved every moment. To become involved emotionally with this pair would be like placing one's head in a noose.

"I would go for the tale of how he asked a visiting artist to paint one of his more beautiful concubines, and the artist protested that he never painted human beings because he did not know enough about the muscles and sinews of the human body, and so Mohamed had the girl's head struck off so that his protégé could see how everything worked."

"What a splendid conception," Jarne said, and placed the forefinger of his left hand on Lampagie's chin, slowly and gently stroking it over the throat and down to the shoulder. "What a delightful picture that conjures up."

"Except that surely you would not allow anything so brutally unaesthetic as striking off the girl's head, Justin," Lampagie said. "Wouldn't it be far better and more interesting slowly to cut it off, slicing through layer after layer and vein after vein, and artery after artery, and finally, sawing away at the vertebrae? Why, she might not die for a couple of seconds."

"Isn't she delightful?" Jarne asked. "Have you had a successful scavenge, Alison?"

She was slightly out of breath, but carried two bottles of Clicquot; one of them was only half full, left over from lunch, and recorked by Henri the butler. "They are a bit warm."

"Then put them in the freezer," Jarne said.

"But be sure you drink them tonight," Lampagie said. "If they've been chilled, and then warmed, and then chilled again, they'll go flat. Certainly the open one."

"And that would be a disaster," Jarne said. "Two whole bottles of champagne gone flat. Besides which, if we forget them, they might explode, which would be rather amusing. Do you know, dearest, I

think you're right. Beheading is always too quick. Mohamed also went
in for impalement. It was the favourite form of execution in the East
in those days. Can you imagine, Tom, an impalement?"

"I'd rather not," Angel confessed.

"Do you know, it actually does chill the blood," Jarne said. "Even
my blood. Can you possibly imagine the feelings of someone con-
demned to impalement, told perhaps a night or two before, and left
to brood on it? No bracing yourself for a short, sharp shock, as with
hanging or beheading. No grim determination to die with dignity,
because of all deaths it is the most degrading. No certainty the agony
will not last for hours. And of course, while it will not last for hours, it
will certainly last for several minutes, and every second of each
minute will seem an eternity. Imagine the courage needed to face
such a fate. Or did anyone possess such courage? Were they not all
dragged, screaming, to the dreadful stake?"

"I think it is time I was getting back to the house," Lampagie said.
"I have some people coming in to dinner."

"To celebrate my departure?"

"Of course." She went to the companionway, stopped, and glanced
over her shoulder. "Have a pleasant voyage, Angel. Bring him back in
one piece. I want to be standing by his bedside when the rot finally
breaks through the surface." She looked at the champagne glass she
still held, then shrugged and threw it on to the deck, where it
smashed. "Clean that up, will you, Alison," she said, and left.

*

Justin Jarne stretched. "She really has no sense of humour. Do you
know, Tom, that is the most difficult thing to find in all the world? A
woman with a sense of humour. And to find a beautiful, or even a
pretty woman with a sense of humour is absolutely impossible. If I
ever make such a discovery, I am going to take her with me to the
most deserted island I can find, and just hibernate. From time to
time. Alison has no sense of humour." He stood up. "But I suppose
you will have to clean up that glass, dearest. Whenever you've
changed, Tom."

He climbed the ladder to the wheelhouse. Angel looked at Alison.

"I imagine they are, really, very fond of each other," she said.
"Relationships like that are generally harder on the help than on the
principals. Thank God she doesn't like sailing." She dropped to her

hands and knees, pulled a dustpan and brush from one of the lockers, started hunting for glass splinters.

"Amen to that," Angel agreed, and went forward to change his shore clothes for blue denims and canvas deck shoes. Then he joined Jarne in the wheelhouse.

"Do you know the Perkins?" Jarne asked.

"I had one of the fours in my boat."

"This is a six." Jarne rolled back the carpet to lift the floor boards.

"Oh, very nice," Angel said, and the admiration was genuine. The green painted engine might just have come from the makers. There was not a spot of rust, not a drop of grease, to be seen.

Jarne sat on the floor, legs dangling, and then dropped down on to the engine-room sole. "Engines," he said, "are the only reliable things left in this imperfect world of ours, Tom. Treat them right, and they'll treat you right. Treat people right, and they will kick you in the teeth. Engines only let you down when you neglect them. So we treat this engine right. That means every morning, and I mean *every*, you'll check the oil levels in the sump and in the gearbox, and the water level in the exchanger, you'll take out the intake filter and make sure it is clean, you'll check the grease in the gland and turn it tight, and you'll wipe the lot over with a clean rag. Understood?"

"Understood," Angel said. "Does she make any water?"

"There's a drip from the gland when we're under power," Jarne said. "Nothing in harbour or under sail. Here's the electric pump, with a hand beside it. I have another pump operated from the wheelhouse. And here is the automatic fire extinguisher. There are two others."

"Insta alarm?"

"In the wheelhouse by the controls. Fire, bilge, oil pressure, and engine heat. We cook off electricity, so the generator gets a lot of work, but at least we have no gas problems. Happy?"

"Ecstatic," Angel said.

"So close it up." Jarne climbed back out, leaned on the wheel, and watched Angel putting the boards back into place before straightening the carpet. "You and me ever met, Tom?"

"Not to my knowledge, Mr. Jarne. I've heard of you, of course."

"You've used all these instruments?"

"I think so." Angel gazed at the big Sailor radio telephone. "I like that."

"There's the loop for direction finding. We get about sixteen good miles on the radar. So there we are. Glad you like her." He glanced at his watch. "Lay me a course for Ibiza, round the north coast of Majorca."

Angel leaned over the chart table, picked up the parallel rule, and drew two pencilled lines on the small-scale chart. He then walked the rule from the first line to the compass rose. "Two two three true . . ." he scribbled on the pad of notepaper beside the chart. "Deviation?"

"Two west on anything south westerly," Jarne said.

"Magnetic variation just over three . . ." Angel muttered, still scribbling. "No tides . . . I make it two two eight magnetic to clear Dragonera Island of the north west corner of Majorca, and then two two three for Ibiza Harbour." He laid down the rule, picked up the dividers, and walked them down the lines. "Distance four hundred and twenty nautical miles. What do you reckon to make in this wind? There's not much of it."

"I regard navigation as an exact science, Tom," Jarne said. "And it is the most interesting part of cruising, so everything about cruising should be subordinated to accurate navigation. Thus we cruise at seven knots, no more and no less. If there is enough wind to make that under sail, then we do so. If there is too much wind, then we shorten sail to maintain that speed. And if there is insufficient wind, we use the engine at whatever revolutions are required to make up the difference. Under engine alone, she also cruises at seven knots."

"What happens if you run into bad weather?"

"This ship will maintain seven knots in up to Force Nine," Jarne said. "I had her built for that purpose. I've never been caught out in anything more than that, and I don't intend to let that ever happen. You'll see today's forecast from Grasse Radio entered on that pad. Keep it up to date. As from tomorrow, you'll use Barcelona. Do you speak Spanish?"

"Enough for a forecast," Angel said.

"Then you won't have any problems. Should you need any assistance, though, Alison speaks excellent Spanish. So, we shall leave here in twenty-nine minutes, at exactly eighteen hundred, and we will arrive in Ibiza at zero six hundred on Monday morning. Understood?"

"Understood," Angel said.

"So now you can help me bend sail on. I've already signed us out and settled the harbour dues. Do you know, I feel like a schoolboy going home for the holidays. I always do, when I am about to put to sea."

Disappeared as if he had never existed was the verbal sadist of a few minutes before. Disappeared even was the champagne-drinking millionaire. Justin Jarne went to work with the energy and strength and certainty of a man half his age, and it was all that Angel could do to keep up with him as they hanked on mizzen, main, and foresail, stowed the spare deck gear which always seems to accumulate on a boat when it has been in harbour for a few weeks, and generally prepared the yacht for sea. Like a schoolboy, Angel thought, and realised that he felt like that, too. After three years, to be on a ship again, and what a ship. As Jarne had claimed, properly handled *Twin Tempest* would drive on quite happily through even a severe gale, and he hadn't the slightest doubt that she would be well handled.

"I never had the opportunity to thank you, Mr. Jarne," he said, when the owner seemed at last satisfied and stood on the foredeck, surveying his ship with a smile, "for giving me this chance."

"You were lucky," Jarne told him. "Colin Blaine was hit by a truck. Both his legs were broken, and an arm. Bloody hit-and-run driver. They haven't got him yet."

Angel frowned. "Now, that's odd."

But Jarne was staring at him again. "Angel," he said. "By Christ, Tom Angel. I must be getting old. You did three years for diamond smuggling."

"I was told you knew."

"I knew you'd done time. By God. I wonder . . ."

"If you don't like the idea of putting to sea with an ex-convict, Mr. Jarne, I'll leave now. If you want my opinion, I don't think you need a skipper."

"Don't be a damned fool. I wasn't thinking of you, Tom. I was thinking that perhaps my secretary should have been more explicit. But of course he wouldn't have known either."

Angel scratched his head. "I'm not with you, Mr. Jarne."

Jarne smiled, and slapped him on the shoulder. "So forget it. You've been inside. That doesn't bother me, Tom, so long as you're a seaman. And I can see that you are. Just remember that what I say goes, and on every subject you can think of, and we'll have a happy ship." He pointed at the wheelhouse, where Alison had just appeared.

"I'm not a jealous man, Tom. But it's up to her, as regards you. If she complains, you're out. Keep that in mind. It's time we left."

He went aft and started the engine; the magnificent throb of the diesel filled the boat. He looked out of the wheelhouse door. "Let go aft, Alison. You'll start taking up the anchor, Tom."

Angel pressed the switch, and the electric winch whirred. Slowly the chain came in, and *Twin Tempest*, even more slowly, moved out from the dock, engine still in neutral, all the weight being taken on the winch. But the anchor came up steadily and straight, broke the surface a few seconds later. Angel gave the thumbs-up sign, and the beat of the engine changed as Jarne put her into gear. Angel went aft, into the wheelhouse. Alison had again disappeared below, and the most tantalising smells were starting to rise from the galley.

"We'll have sail up as soon as we're outside," Jarne said. "There may be a bit more wind away from the coast. The forecast is for three later on, anyway, and from the east, so it'll be a nice reach for us."

Angel nodded, and returned on deck. The pier heads and Fort Carre slipped astern, and to their right the overcrowded promontory of Cap d'Antibes itself blocked out the drooping sun. Jarne brought the ship round into the faint breeze blowing off the shore, and Angel set the mainsail. The yacht paid off, and up went the jib, followed by the mizzen.

"Sheet them in for the time being." Jarne reduced the engine revolutions just enough to bring the speed back to seven knots, and engaged the automatic pilot. "Two two eight it is. I'm going to eat now, Tom. Alison will bring yours up here. We do four hours on and eight off."

"Alison too?"

"On night passages, yes. During the day she is just cook and deck hand, when required. She's as strong as a man, and as good. She'll relieve you at twenty-two hundred, and I'll take her from zero two hundred to zero six hundred. Understood?"

"Understood." As Lampagie had said, her husband went to sea, apparently, to work as hard as any sailor. Angel was just content to be left in command of such a ship at last. He left the wheelhouse doors open, stood on deck leaning against the coach roof, watching ahead for the crab pots that were always a problem close to shore, the remote control in his left hand ready to override the pilot should it become necessary to alter course. Behind them Antibes dropped astern, and now, beyond the cape, the skyscraping flats and even more myriad yachts of Cannes slowly began to unfold from behind the Îsles de Lérins. It wouldn't be dark for a couple of hours, but tomorrow morning there would be nothing but sea. Freedom, at last. Humour Jarne, and he had all the freedom he could manage. Even the freedom to flirt a little with the girl Alison. Supposing she wanted to.

She was there now, at the top of the steps from the saloon, with a plate of stuffed peppers and a fork. "Shall I keep watch, or feed you?"

"Neither," he said, and took the plate.

"Here's some more champagne." She handed him the glass. "Or don't you drink on watch?"

"I imagine I can absorb one more glass of champagne," he said. "I'm in the mood to celebrate as much as anyone else."

"There's lots more where that came from." She hesitated. "I have to go down and sit with Mr. Jarne. I hope you don't mind."

"Not in the slightest. I'm just enjoying being on a boat again."

Again the hesitation. Then she said, "He really is a very charming man, you know. So he's wealthy enough to behave a little oddly from time to time. I think he does it mainly to annoy his wife."

Angel grinned at her. "Relax, Alison. I'm the sort of crew who doesn't criticise his employer."

She gave a quick smile in her turn, and went below. Angel took out the binoculars and scanned the sea horizon. Nothing out there. Most of the fishing boats would be in, unloading their catches, and they wouldn't be putting to sea again much before three in the morning. He looked aloft, at the canvas only half filling as the light easterly breeze puffed and died. Below his feet the diesel throbbed with a steady, reassuring persistence. But the wind was proving fitful. He moved the throttle a fraction forward, and the needle on the electric log settled at just over seven.

The only other sounds were the swish of water past the hull, and the whine of the autopilot as it corrected the helm. By God, he felt good. He left the binoculars round his neck, walked forward, and then went aft again. Beneath him the lights came on in the saloon, but he resisted the temptation to look in through the skylight. So she was Jarne's mistress. He couldn't really understand any man turning his back on Lampagie, but if one did, then presumably Alison was as good a substitute as one would find anywhere. Alison who? He must find that out. Why, he wondered? Jarne had told him to do what he could, there. Had the invitation been genuine? A threesome, on board a small yacht?

It occurred to him that he was becoming a little heady with the champagne, and the boat, and the sea. Even Parkhurst was beginning to fade, just a little.

Anyway, he thought, as he returned to the wheelhouse, hadn't he also walked away from Lampagie? Maybe she was just a shade too beautiful, too assured, too amoral.

Even for Justin Jarne?

The sun disappeared, and within a few minutes it was dark. The clock on the console showed nine-fifteen. Three hours. Three of the most blissful hours of his life. But there would be so many more.

Alison came up the steps from the saloon. She smiled at him, a trifle nervously, he thought, and went down the after companion to the master stateroom. A moment later Jarne also came up. He swayed just a little and carried a half empty bottle of champagne.

"Everything all right, Tom?"

"Everything is just fine, Mr. Jarne. If you'd like to take the night off . . ."

"Because of a little champagne?" Jarne laughed, a dry sound. "You have a lot to learn about me, Tom. I'll turn in now, and set my alarm for zero two hundred. Alison will relieve you in an hour." He stood before the console, checking the pressure gauges, peered into the radar-screen for a few seconds, turning it up to maximum range. "A nice empty ocean, save for that fellow. Have fun, Tom."

He followed the girl down the after companion, and Angel moved to the set. There was a fairly large blip, which must only just have left the land, now some twenty miles astern of them and just out of radar range. The blip showed on the extreme edge of the screen, on the starboard quarter. A big yacht, or fishing boat, out of St. Tropez or Port Grimaud.

The stateroom door was shut, and Alison had not returned. So she was not due on watch for half an hour. And in that time she would amuse Jarne until he went to sleep. God damn and blast. He had known all about the situation, so why was he feeling angry? It was rather illogical.

The door closed softly at the bottom of the companion, and a moment later she passed him, without a word. But she smelt of woman. So then, was he a dog?

He stared at the darkness of the night, listened to the clink of dishes from the saloon. Then she was back again, carrying a bottle of champagne and two glasses. "Isn't it a glorious night?"

"No moon," he said.

"That's even better. It's so clear. Drink?"

Angel shook his head.

She smiled, and sat on the settee berth which filled the starboard side of the wheelhouse. "You'll be off watch in a minute or two. This is Mrs. Jarne's effort, and as she said, it's been opened and recorked. If we don't drink it, I think it *will* go flat. Mr. Jarne doesn't like Clicquot."

She was already pouring.

"You have four hours up here," Angel said. "I don't want you to think I'm a square . . ."

"But you don't think I should have any more. Okay, Skipper, you're the boss. But you can."

"One more," Angel said. But the situation was getting to him. He wanted to be angry. No, he wanted to be contemptuous of her. She was, after all, just a little tart. Correction, a fairly large tart. But she was smiling at him, and he thought he could see the invitation in her eyes and her mouth, even in the darkened wheelhouse with only the glow from the binnacle, which just reached her chin. So maybe there was invitation in her chin. "Although if you'd like me to stand your watch for you, I wouldn't mind. I'm not in the least sleepy, and to be honest, I'm so tickled at being at sea again I just don't want tonight ever to stop."

"Whereas you figure I might just have that languorous feeling creeping over me," she said.

She wanted to make an issue of it, right now. Perhaps that was the best way, if they were going to spend the summer together.

"I didn't say that."

"You thought it. But you can forget it. My job is to keep Mr. Jarne happy. He doesn't figure there is any need for reciprocation."

"So you're still on heat."

She stared at him for a moment. "No, Tom," she said. "He doesn't even turn me on that much. So stay, if you really want to. But don't feel obliged because of me. I've crewed Mr. Jarne for over a year now. I'm not exactly a stranger to night passages."

"I didn't suppose you were," Angel said, and checked the radar again. The blip had closed to fifteen miles.

"Something there?"

"Something. About our size or a little bigger, on a converging course. But she's only making about ten knots, I figure, so it won't be much before the small hours when she catches up."

"I'll keep an eye on her," Alison promised, and stood up. "Twenty-two hundred. I'm in charge."

She handed him his glass, refilled, and Angel made way for her at the screen. She still wore only her bikini, and he looked down at the curving line of vertebrae, which disappeared just above the cleft of her buttocks. God, how he wanted to touch.

She straightened without warning, and he had to step back in a hurry. A wave of perfume shrouded his nostrils. "I've got him," she said. "As you say, he'll be a few hours yet. Isn't it fantastic? This whole empty sea, and a yacht going our way."

"But not necessarily to Ibiza," he said. "Could be Palma or Mahón. If you're lucky, she'll pass under our stern in an hour or so. But don't forget she's there."

She nodded, and sat in the helmsman's seat. Now the binnacle light managed to settle directly on the droop of her bra, seeming to double the swell of her breasts. Angel finished his second glass and put it down on the chart table. He discovered he was sweating. But then, it was a warm night.

And suddenly he was feeling distinctly odd.

Alison yawned. "I suppose it's because this is our first night at sea, after so long," she said. "But I feel quite sleepy."

"I don't think the champagne has helped much," Angel said, and was distressed to find himself slurring.

Alison laughed quietly. "Oh, I won't have another. At least, not until I come off watch. I imagine you don't think much of our seamanship, Tom."

"I can't really criticise, as I'm feeling as odd as anyone. Which is damned silly in my case; I should have had more sense after three years. But if you don't mind, we won't make this a nightly occurrence."

"You're the skipper. Listen, I really am quite all right. Why don't you turn in? I'll call you if I need you. Take the starboard bunk."

Angel considered. But a blanket seemed to have descended over his mind, and obviously the sensible thing to do was to have at least an hour's rest and wake up as good as new.

"If you're sure you're all right," he said.

"Of course I'm all right."

He heaved himself to his feet. "Seems a shame. I was going to spend the next hour or so chatting you up."

She smiled at him. He could hear her breathe in the darkness. "I rather hoped you would. But you have all summer to chat me up. And you can kiss me good night, if you wish. Mr. Jarne always does that."

For a moment he hesitated. She was too obviously trying to be nice, on this occasion. Trying to dissipate the anger she knew he felt. The anger of jealousy. But why look a gift horse in the mouth? He had already done that once before today.

He swayed across the wheelhouse, and his hands touched the bare flesh of her shoulders. There was nice and nice. Her mouth was open, and her tongue tasted of champagne. Before he could stop himself his hands had slid round the front of the bikini top.

Her mouth left his. "You are too sleepy, and I'm on watch," she said with the utmost gentleness. "I just told you, we have the whole summer. Let's take it slow."

"I'm sorry," he mumbled, wishing that his head would stop swinging. "I suppose it's . . ."

"Those goddamned three years," she said. "The only thing I want you to do is stop talking about them. Put them out of your mind. Listen, if you really feel that way, I'll give you a nudge when I come down at two o'clock. Just to see if you're awake. Now go get some sleep, or it won't be worth it."

Angel half fell down the companion ladder into the saloon, staggered forward, and reached the forecabin. Now the boat was rolling scuppers under, and dipping her bows into the waves as well. On a flat calm night with no wind? He shook his head violently, and the motion eased a little. What he really wanted to do was wash his face in cold water. Yes, he thought. In fact, the best thing to have would be a cold shower. He'd do that, he thought, in a couple of minutes. But for that couple of minutes he just wanted to lie down and let his head settle.

He rolled on to the starboard bunk, and allowed his breath to escape, slowly. He listened to the creaking of the rigging, the sluice of the water past the hull. Up here the diesel was muted into a low hum. Five minutes, he thought. He'd count up to three hundred, and then get up and have a shower.

Angel slept.

CHAPTER 6

Justin Jarne threw the bedroom door wide, and pointed. "You, Martin," he said. "You."

Harrington sat up, the sheet dragged to his throat, and tried to move up the bed. But his back was pressed against the headboard, stuck to it with his own sweat. "Justin?" he whispered. "What are you doing here? You're in the Med. You're at sea, Justin. You're . . ."

"Dead." Jarne smiled. "Oh yes, Martin. I'm dead. And Angel will hang for it. But I won't forget you, Martin. Oh, I won't do that. I'm coming for you now, Martin."

"He won't be hanged," Harrington gasped. "He'll be guillotined. Guillotined. Guillotined."

"But you won't see it," Jarne said, advancing slowly across the room. "You won't be alive. You'll be coming with me, to hell."

He was coming closer with every step, smiling. Harrington's back strained against the bed head. He gasped for breath, and tried to speak, to beg, but his tongue seemed cloven to the roof of his mouth. Slowly Jarne came closer and closer, his mouth spreading wider and wider into that terrible smile. Harrington managed to get his hands up, pushed at the body as it advanced. Surprisingly, Jarne's chest seemed soft. But the harder Harrington pushed, the closer it came, and now he could feel breath on his face.

Jarne slapped him, crisply, on the cheek. Harrington's head jerked, and his eyes opened. He gazed at Shelley, hair untidy, frowning.

"Thank God for that," she said. "Do you often have nightmares?"

Harrington continued to stare at her, looked down at his hands, one resting on each of her breasts.

"Are you all right?" she asked.

He nodded. But was he all right? "Was I shouting?"

"You were mumbling, something about being guillotined. Were you dreaming about the French Revolution?"

"Yes," he said. "A historical nightmare. Damned odd, what?"
Gently he moved her to one side, got out of bed, went through to the
kitchen and drank some water.

"*Are* you all right?" She leaned in the doorway, naked, and smiled
at his reaction. "I guess you are, at that."

"Just a nightmare." Harrington looked at his watch. It was half-
past four. It must be done by now. If it was going to be done at all.
But by now it would be over. As he had subconsciously known. Now
the real work would begin.

But not until someone telephoned the news. He must wait for that,
remain absolutely normal until that happened. He crossed the room,
put his arm round her shoulders. "Just a nightmare. But I don't feel
much like sleeping again, right this minute."

She smiled at him, as only Shelley could smile. "Neither do I," she
said.

*

The deck beams above Angel's head slowly came into focus. They
were painted white, and were two feet away. For a moment he
thought he was back on board *Marianne*; she also had had teak laid
decks. But this wasn't *Marianne*; the motion was different. This was
Twin Tempest, on which he was the new skipper, and on which he
had made a prize fool of himself last night, first of all by getting jealous of the crew, and secondly by getting drunk. Of all the bloody
stupid things to do. Although, thank God, only the girl Alison had
been aware of it. But then, she had been responsible for the whole
thing in the first place.

He could see the deck beams. Therefore it was dawn. He looked at
his watch. Three minutes to six. Thank God for that; he wouldn't be
late for his watch. He rolled out of the bunk, landed on the deck, and
stopped to wipe his brow. His head seemed to be opening and shutting like a swinging door, and each bang went through to his heels.
Well, that figured. But he decided to get on deck right away, relieve
Jarne, and when the owner had gone to bed and he had made sure the
horizon was clear, he could have a wash and brush his teeth.

He pulled the towel off the rack and wiped his face, gazed at
Alison. She lay on the port bunk, on her face, a pillow clutched in her
arms. She was naked, a magnificent expanse of muscular, sun-
browned, and entirely female back. And last night she had become

quite pally. Or had she also had too much champagne? Or, even more likely, had she known what was going on in his mind, and so had determined to keep the peace? But, *if* she wanted to keep the peace, there was a hopeful sign.

She had been going to wake him up when she came down. Maybe she had changed her mind. Maybe he hadn't been that easy to wake.

He hoped it hadn't been the champagne. Not with a back like that. The only thing he remembered accurately about her front was her smile. He had liked that, too.

He went back through the empty saloon, listened to the whine of the autopilot, gently keeping *Twin Tempest* on course. He crossed the saloon, checked at the foot of the companion ladder, gazed at Justin Jarne's feet. He scratched his head. So he had a distinctly odd employer. But would Jarne really go to sleep on the wheelhouse floor, immediately above the engines, when there was a settee berth available? Even if he had got hold of another bottle of champagne?

Angel climbed the steps, gazed down at Jarne, the suffused face, the staring eyes.

For a moment he swayed in time to the boat, unable to move. Unable to think. Unable to function. Then he carefully stepped over the inert body, and dropped to his knees on the other side. Still his brain was numb, unable to grasp the enormity of what had happened. There was a dead body cluttering up his wheelhouse, and it belonged to the owner. That was not good seamanship.

Then he wondered if he was still asleep and having a nightmare.

But Justin Jarne was definitely dead. He had been strangled, with great efficiency, so far as Angel could tell.

He rocked back on his heels, looked around the wheelhouse. There was nothing disturbed, no sign of a struggle, no evidence even of Jarne having fallen. Having killed him, his assassin had gently laid him on the floor. Angel wiped the back of his hand across his brow. Now thoughts, emotions, fears, alarms, were rushing across his mind. For a moment he felt almost hysterical. He wanted to shout, "No, no, no." He wanted to shake Jarne into life. He couldn't, he didn't, have the right to have this happen, just when, after so long, everything had been going so well.

Then, slowly, the seaman began to take over. Jarne had been dead for several hours; the body was quite cold. And presumably, throughout that time, the ship had been making her way steadily south out of the Gulf of Lyons; the autopilot continued to whirr reassuringly.

Angel scrambled to his feet, grabbed the binoculars, swept the dawn horizon. It was hazy, promising another fine day, and he doubted that visibility was much over three miles. But those three miles, on every side, were empty. He put down the glasses and buried his eyes in the radar screen. Slowly the sweep went round, emptily. He left the set and looked at the electric log. It recorded just over eighty-three miles, which made them at the very least seventy miles from Cap d'Antibes, and about thirty miles from the nearest part of the French coast, which, on the course they had been steering, would be the Isles d'Hyères.

He checked the compass, found it still pointing to two two eight, and beneath his feet the engine purred steadily. Hastily he shut it down, and then went on deck and hove the ship to. And then wondered why. Somehow things seemed less out of control with the ship not actually moving through the water, only rolling lazily in the Mediterranean swell.

But the silence was terrifying.

And at his feet, Justin Jarne lay dead. Someone had gripped his throat with tremendous force, and squeezed the life out of him. Someone.

But there was no one else on board.

Angel sucked air into his lungs, half fell down the companion ladder, stumbled across the saloon, and dragged open the door to the forecabin. Alison had not moved, sighed faintly in her sleep. Angel seized her shoulder and shook it. She sighed some more, half turned, and flapped her hand at him. She was certainly in a deep, apparently conscienceless sleep. Angel held on to her shoulder and her thigh and tumbled her out of the bunk. She came down feet first and her knees buckled. He grasped her under the armpits, straightened her again, and slapped her on the face.

Her head jerked, and her eyes flopped open, before flopping shut again.

"Wake up," Angel said. "Come on. Wake up."

But her knees were buckling again. No one could be that asleep, unless she were drugged. Still holding her under the arms, he backed across the swaying cabin, into the head. Here he propped her against the bulkhead and let her go. She gradually slumped down the tiles and then sank into a squatting position, head against the locker under the basin. Angel seized the shower head, pulled it from its bracket, switched the cold water up to maximum, and directed the stream at her face, slowly bringing it closer. For a few seconds she didn't move, and he had to take the jet away to allow her to breathe. Then her eyes started to flicker, and her mouth to move, and he brought the cold water back. Now she reacted violently, jerking her head and slapping at the water with her hands, pushing herself up the bulkhead, gasping and spluttering. "You . . . you bastard," she shouted. "You . . . do you think that's funny?"

Angel switched off the water. "Outside," he said.

Something in his tone made her check the shaking of her head. She frowned at him, while dragging her fingers through her hair to get rid of the worst of the water.

"Come on," Angel said.

"I don't think that was the least amusing," she said, more quietly. "I was in a deep sleep." She stepped out of the head, leaving damp footprints on the carpet. "Do you mind?" she asked. "I'll put on my robe."

"I mind," Angel said. "Get in there."

Once again the long stare, accompanied by a faint frown. "Have you gone round the bend?" she asked.

She was either a brilliant actress, or she *was* quite unaware that anything had happened. Angel grabbed her arms and propelled her through the saloon. He didn't want to think about it for the moment. Thinking involved too many unanswerable questions.

Alison started to climb the steps to the wheelhouse, still being pushed by Angel, and checked. "Oh, my God," she said. "Mr. Jarne?"

The only sound was the creaking of the rigging.

"You'd better take a closer look," Angel suggested.

She hesitated, and her head half turned as she felt his fingers release her. Then she moved forward again, very slowly, holding the grabrail. Water trickled out of her hair and down her back, rolled over her buttocks, and dripped past her legs to dampen the carpet. She reached the wheelhouse floor and sidled round the dead man. "Did . . . did he fall?"

"He has been strangled."

Alison's head came up slowly. For a moment she gazed at him. Then she leapt over her dead employer, reached the back of the wheelhouse and the steps to the after cabin, and skidded down them, all in one long breath.

"That isn't going to do any good," Angel told her, entering the wheelhouse.

But she had already disappeared into the stateroom, although without shutting the door. Angel stepped across Jarne's body, stood at the top of the companion. "Come on back up, Alison. You and I have got to talk about this."

"We'll talk," Alison agreed. She had got her breath back, and with reason. She carried a small automatic pistol in her right hand.

"What do you propose to do with that?" Angel asked. Remarkably, he did not feel in the least frightened of her, or even alarmed. "Shoot me into the bargain?"

"Back up," Alison said. "Or I *shall* shoot you. I'm awake now, Mr. Angel. Don't make a mistake about that."

"I'm glad to hear it." But he retreated across the wheelhouse, reached the radar screen, peered into the display unit for some seconds. The ocean remained empty. "I didn't kill him, you know," he said. "I was also asleep, until half an hour ago. I wish I still was."

"I was, Mr. Angel," she pointed out. "Until you woke me up. Do you mean to call Grasse Radio?"

"To call . . ." Angel straightened. "I suppose that will have to be done. But I rather thought you might like to discuss the situation first."

She stayed on the far side of the cabin. "I don't see what there is to discuss, at this moment." After her initial shock, she had become remarkably composed.

"Happens every time you put to sea, does it?" Angel asked.

"Nor do I think this is the time to be funny. Will you call Grasse Radio, please?"

"You think I killed him?"

She stared at him, her mouth making a slight O. "He didn't strangle himself, Mr. Angel."

"And I think you must have done it, because I didn't."

Once again the O. "I suppose you think that makes it perfect," she said. "You accuse me, I accuse you. So where's the answer. Is that it?"

"I should think the French police will come up with a very simple answer, that we did it in cahoots, darling," Angel said. "I would brood on that one, if I were you."

"Mr. Angel," she said, "I have sailed, quite happily, with Mr. Jarne for over a year. In all that time we have never even exchanged a cross word. On the other hand, I never saw you before in my life, until yesterday afternoon. And . . ."

"I am just out of gaol. I haven't forgotten that. And suppose I told you that Justin Jarne was just a name in a newspaper to me before two days ago, when I was offered a berth on his yacht?"

"As you say, Mr. Angel, we'll let the police sort it out."

"But the prospect doesn't bother you?"

She almost smiled. "Mr. Angel, you may not believe this, but I liked Mr. Jarne. I won't pitch it stronger than that. He paid me well, and he wanted me in return. Fair enough. I could quit whenever I got fed up. But I never did quit, did I? And I wasn't planning to. I'm not going to break down and weep now he's dead. Not right this minute. But by God I'm going to see that they hang you for his murder."

"They don't hang you in France," Angel said thoughtfully.

"I forgot, they guillotine you. It's probably less painful. But I'm sure a good lawyer will get you a life sentence."

"*Crime passionnel*," Angel said, even more thoughtfully, switching on the radio. "We had a fight over the beautiful Alison . . . Do you know, I never did catch your last name."

"It's Somers," she said.

"I must remember. For the police, you know." He turned the receiver to the Antibes radio beacon, listened to the Morse signal, and slowly rotated the loop aerial until the whine faded. He made a note of the compass bearing, and tuned to the Sète beacon.

"What are you doing?" Alison demanded.

"I'm sure Grasse will want to know our exact position." The two lines crossed within half a mile of his dead reckoning fix, and he made a pencil cross on the chart. Then he switched the transmitter to two one eight two kilocycles—the distress frequency—and waited for it to warm up.

And all the while his instincts were shouting, Think, think, think, God damn you. But his instincts were also shouting at him to do all manner of ridiculous things. In the first place, to attack the girl, get the gun away from her—he did not doubt that he could, if he really wanted to—then throw Jarne's body over the side, and just sail, and sail, and sail. Where? Every boat must come to harbour eventually. But if he had the time he might persuade Alison to see things from his point of view. And if she didn't, well then, he could always kill her as well and throw her overboard after Jarne, and return to port with the story that they had both been lost in a storm. No one could disprove that.

And having killed Jarne, to kill Alison could not possibly cause him any problem.

But he hadn't killed Jarne, for Christ's sake. He was innocent. And therefore, she *had* to have done it. She had to have a motive, and it would probably be quite easy for the police to discover it. Perhaps Jarne had come on deck early, and had wanted her to do something quite unnatural. There might even have been a fight, and Alison had seized him by the throat . . .

Except that there was no evidence or even suggestion of a fight. Not even a cushion out of place.

So, then, perhaps Jarne had made a will and left her a large sum of money. And she had the perfect patsy along in Angel. So she'd never have a better opportunity to get rich quick than right now. She had just admitted she was along for the cash. But she had admitted it only to him, and that wouldn't wash in court.

On the other hand, everything that had happened on board was just between the pair of them. The police would have to sort the whole thing out. And if they could not prove that he had strangled Jarne, well then, what *could* they prove?

Only that Angel had just been released from prison, with a growing suggestion that he was becoming mentally conditioned towards violence. And that perhaps he did not know his own strength.

Would they need anything more?

Because the person who had strangled Jarne had very definitely known his own strength, and had used every last ounce of it.

"I'm sure the set has warmed up by now," Alison said from behind him.

But I'm innocent, he wanted to shout. And to run will solve nothing. In the end. God, how tired he suddenly was.

He pressed the handset button before he was quite ready. "Grasse Radio, Grasse Radio, Grasse Radio." How calm and quiet was his voice. "*Twin Tempest, Twin Tempest, Twin Tempest*, calling Grasse Radio. Do you read me. Over."

The set crackled faintly.

"Try them again," Alison commanded.

"Grasse Radio, Grasse Radio, Grasse Radio; *Twin Tempest, Twin Tempest, Twin Tempest* calling Grasse Radio. Do you read me? Over."

"*Twin Tempest, Twin Tempest, Twin Tempest*," came the faintly foreign voice. "Grasse Radio, Grasse Radio, Grasse Radio calling *Twin Tempest.* Over."

Angel took a long breath. "I wish to report an accident on board." He stared at Alison over the microphone. "A man has been killed. Over."

There was a moment's silence. "Would you repeat your message, please, *Twin Tempest.* Over."

"I say again, there has been an accident," Angel said. "A man has been killed. The owner, Mr. Justin Jarne. Over."

Another brief hesitation. "What working frequencies do you have, please? Over."

"For God's sake," Angel grumbled. "Doesn't he think this is a distress call?" But he pressed the handset button. "I have Channels One, Two, Five, and Six. Over."

"Very good, *Twin Tempest.* Will you speak on Channel One, please, and listen for me on one nine zero seven kilocycles. Would you spell the name of your ship, please. Over."

Angel made the necessary adjustments to free the distress channel. "My ship's name is Tango—Whiskey—India—November—Tango—Echo—Mike—Papa—Echo—Sierra—Tango," he said. "Do you read that? *Twin Tempest* listening on one nine zero seven kilocycles. Over."

"*Twin Tempest*," the voice said. "And what is your position, please? Over."

Angel studied the chart. "My position is forty-two degrees, twenty-eight and a half seconds north latitude," he said, "and five degrees fifty and a half seconds east longitude. I am thirty-four miles due south of Cap Sicié. Over."

"And do you require any immediate assistance? Over."

"Not to work the ship," Angel said. "I think I require some policemen."

Another brief hesitation. "I will inform the police department, *Twin Tempest.* I think the best thing is for you to make for Toulon. Your speed, please? Over."

"Seven knots," Angel said. "I should make Toulon by eleven hundred hours. Over."

"Keep your radio on this frequency, *Twin Tempest*," the voice said. "We will send a boat out to meet you. Would you spell the name of the dead man, please?"

"The dead man is the owner of the vessel, Mr. Justin Jarne. Juliet—Uniform—Sierra—Tango—India—November—Juliet—Alfa—Romeo—November—Echo. Over."

"Justin Jarne," the voice said, thoughtfully. But it remained disinterested. "Would you tell me who else is on board, please? Over?"

"I am the captain," Angel said. "And there is one crew member. My name is Angel: Alfa—November—Golf—Echo—Lima. Thomas Angel. The crew is a woman, Miss Alison Somers. Sierra—Oscar—Mike—Echo—Romeo—Sierra. Over."

"Thank you, *Twin Tempest*. Is there anyone we should notify apart from the police? Over."

My God, Angel thought: Lampagie. He had completely forgotten about her. But she had to be told. He wondered what her reaction would be. "Mrs. Jarne lives at a villa outside Antibes," he said. "Over."

"We will notify Mrs. Jarne," the voice said. "Is there anyone else? Over."

Angel looked at Alison.

"I don't know," she said. "There is Mr. Jarne's secretary. A man called Harrington. But I don't know . . . this will have a big effect on the value of Mr. Jarne's companies and investments, and things like that."

"I think we'll leave that decision with Lampagie," Angel said. He pressed the switch. "I do not know of anyone else to inform at this moment," he said. "Over."

"Very good, *Twin Tempest*. We shall be waiting for you south of Cap Sicié. Please keep your radio standing by on this frequency, in case I wish to contact you again. Do you understand? Over."

"*Twin Tempest*, making for Toulon, and standing by on one nine zero seven kilocycles," Angel said. "Over and out."

He closed down the transmitter, replaced the microphone on its hook, gazed at Alison.

"You'd better get us back under way," she said.

"And Jarne?"

"Just leave him be," she said. "You can put a sheet over him, but you mustn't touch anything."

What she said made sense. Angel did as he was commanded, then put the engine into gear once more and turned the ship north. He engaged the autopilot, and once again glanced at the girl. Alison sat on the settee berth, the pistol pointed at him. "Do you mean to keep aiming that thing at me for two hours?" he asked. "I've told Grasse that I'm bringing the ship and the corpse in. And they know where we are. I can't change, now. And to tell you the truth, I'm starving."

"I am quite comfortable," she said. "But I would like you to fetch me some clothes. You'll find them hanging in my locker. Then you may get yourself something to eat, if you wish. I will eat when we get to Toulon."

*

The day stayed hazy. The sun rose and hovered immediately above them, and it grew steadily warmer. It was impossible to think about what might be happening under the sheet. It was almost a relief to hear the calm voice on the radio, calling them every half an hour for a position check as they approached the coast.

If only his mind could be similarly controlled, similarly unemotional, similarly logical, Angel thought. Because there had to be an explanation for what had happened. Alison had been on watch from about ten o'clock, when he had gone to his bunk. He had been feeling under the weather. Right. So he had fallen into a very deep sleep. And then, no doubt, Jarne had come back on deck to be with Alison, and they had quarrelled, and she had throttled him . . . and then gone to her bunk and fallen into a sleep quite as deep as his own.

It was all too illogical. Because if she had had the strength to strangle Jarne, then she also had the strength to drag him on deck and throw him over the side. And then she could have called Angel in a state of hysteria and told him that Jarne had fallen overboard—he might have gone on deck for a leak or to check the set of the sails and missed his footing. The night had been moonless, and Angel could never have been sure whether they had just been unable to find him or whether he had in fact sunk like a stone because he had been already dead. But the second alternative would never have entered Angel's head, in the circumstances.

Except that all of that would suppose that Alison Somers was an utterly cold-blooded murderess. She did not look particularly cold blooded.

Which meant nothing.

And how much cold blooded could anyone get than calmly to go to bed and fall into a deep sleep after committing murder. Although clearly she had taken a couple of pills to assist her.

And just as clearly, he suddenly realised, she had slipped him a couple of pills as well. Probably dissolved them in the champagne. That was it. It had tasted a little odd, and she had said it was going flat. And it just hadn't crossed his mind before. But he had never felt woozy on four glasses of champagne before, either.

"My God," he said.

Alison Somers gazed at him from behind the pistol; she had put on denim pants and a light jumper, and looked at once composed and attractive.

But then, that figured. The composure, certainly.

"You drugged me," Angel said.

She frowned. "I have no idea what you are talking about."

"You put something in the champagne to make sure that I would sleep through any noise. And here I was thinking that maybe you and Jarne had a fight. But this murder was premeditated."

"I have no idea what you are talking about," she said again.

"You drugged me," Angel repeated. "And then you killed Jarne, and went to bed yourself, knowing that I would be the obvious suspect, being an ex-con. It won't work, Alison. We live in the age of women's lib, remember? You'll have to take your chances like anyone else. You forgot one thing. I may be an ex-con, but I didn't have any motive for killing Jarne. No matter how hard the police look, they won't be able to link me to him in any shape or form. While, if they look hard enough, and they are going to have to do that, I have no doubt at all that they are going to uncover your motive."

Her eyes remained coldly unimpressed. "I'm glad you've managed to work out some form of salvation for yourself, Mr. Angel," she said. "I suggest you try it on the police."

She pointed at the coast-guard cutter coming out of the haze on their starboard bow. Hastily Angel put the engine into neutral, went on deck, and hove to. To his surprise, Alison helped him. No doubt she felt safe enough now the police were actually in sight. But she kept the pistol tucked into the waistband of her pants.

The cutter came gently alongside. She seemed crowded. Apart from her crew there were also several uniformed gendarmes, as well as a couple of obvious plain-clothes men, and two equally obvious doctors. They boarded *Twin Tempest*, saw the body at a glance. Alison stood by the wheelhouse door, Angel remained on deck. The two ships nodded gently on the calm sea, their fenders softly rubbing. The crew of the cutter gazed at Angel, and Angel gazed back at the crew of the cutter.

One of the plain-clothes men returned on deck. He was a tall, thin man, with pointed features and nervous fingers; they constantly flicked or rubbed forefinger and thumb, although always without noise. "You are the man who telephoned Grasse?" His English was very good.

"That's right," Angel said.

"Thomas Percival Angel. My name is Levasseur. Inspector of detectives, you understand."

Angel nodded.

"Mr. Jarne has been murdered."

"I know that, Inspector. But I did not kill him."

Levasseur nodded, and sucked his lower lip under his teeth in a faintly comical gesture. "You and Mademoiselle Somers are the only people on board, yes?"

"Yes."

"And Mr. Jarne is dead, yes?"

"Yes."

Levasseur nodded again. "So there will have to be an investigation, you understand."

"I understand," Angel said. "As you have pointed out, I am the man who telephoned Grasse."

"I know you telephoned," Levasseur said. "But I should inform you that Miss Somers says she made you do this."

"Has she accused me?"

"I am afraid so, Mr. Angel. Is it true that you have just been released from prison?"

"Quite true. It is also true that I never met Mr. Jarne before yesterday, whereas Miss Somers has sailed with him for over a year."

"Of course," Levasseur said. "Believe me, monsieur, I have not yet formed an opinion on the matter. That is for the magistrate. I must only be sure of the facts. So I am taking you and the yacht into custody. On the way back to Toulon I will be pleased to have a full statement from you."

"And Miss Somers?"

"Oh, I am taking her into custody as well, Mr. Angel. It is for the magistrate, as I said, to decide which of you will be charged with causing the death of Mr. Jarne. If either. Or both." He turned away, and then checked, and looked over his shoulder. "But I should advise you that the doctor who has examined the dead man has already given it as his opinion that whoever gripped his throat possessed unusual strength. Strength certainly far beyond the capability of any normal woman to produce." Again the peculiar sucking in of the lower lip. "You would describe Miss Somers as an entirely normal young woman, would you not, Mr. Angel?"

CHAPTER 7

The telephone rang. Harrington, sitting before his boiled egg, spoon in hand, hesitated, gazing from the smoothly ovalled shell up to Shelley's face. She had already started her meal, and was following her first mouthful with a piece of toast. She had showered, and brushed her teeth with his toothbrush, as she had brushed her hair with his hairbrush. She looked cool and relaxed. She had not yet bothered to dress.

Neither had he. He had wanted to extract every last ounce of intimacy from last night and this morning, to watch her cooking his breakfast, naked, to watch her moving around the flat, naked, to know that she was his.

To know that this was a beginning, and not just an episode.

And to prevent himself thinking about anything else. Because everything else, everything that mattered, was coming closer and closer. He was, in fact, just beginning to feel agitated because it had not yet arrived.

And there it was. That jangling sound could be nothing else, at eight-thirty in the morning.

"Don't tell me it's another woman," Shelley remarked.

"Eh?"

"You are suddenly looking very odd," she said.

"Sorry." He got up. "I was suddenly reminded that our night has come to an end."

"As finally as that?"

"Of course not. I hope." He stood by her chair, looking down at her.

She smiled at him. "Then what's a telephone call? But you'd better answer it."

Harrington had never properly noticed the telephone before. It was red, and suddenly he felt that was a rather silly colour for a telephone. Or was it merely symbolic?

But he didn't really want to touch it.

He reached out, convulsively, picked up the receiver. "Yes?"

"Mr. Harrington?"

"Yes."

"Mr. Martin Harrington?"

"Yes." His heart was starting to pound. Yet the voice was English.

"Will you hold the line, please. I have an overseas telephone call for you."

Now the pounding was threatening to block his ears. He held the receiver a little distance away from his head, discovered that Shelley was watching him.

"An overseas call," he explained, surprised at the evenness of his voice. "Old Jarne, I'll bet. I thought he was safely tucked away at sea, by now."

A good line, that. "Perhaps he's calling from his yacht," she suggested. "He never really cuts himself off, does he?"

"Mr. Harrington?"

Another English voice. But another strange one, as well. He had forbidden Smith to call, of course, and he had not really expected *her* to call; it would not have fitted her circumstances and her emotions of the moment. But at least it could have been Colne.

"Yes," Harrington said.

"Would I be right in assuming that you are the Martin Harrington who is private secretary to Mr. Justin Jarne, of the J and J Corporation?"

"Who is this?" Harrington asked.

"You don't know me, Mr. Harrington. But I have some rather bad news for you."

"What?" Harrington asked. "What did you say? Where are you calling from?"

"I am calling from Toulon, Mr. Harrington. There is a rumour here that Mr. Jarne has been killed in an accident at sea."

"An accident?"

"I'm afraid I don't have any details. It happened on board his yacht, *Twin Tempest*. But it appears as if there may have been suspicious circumstances. A coast-guard cutter has gone out to escort her in."

"Good God." Harrington searched his brain for the right questions. "But . . . how did they know? You say it happened at sea?"

"The crew telephoned in, apparently. I wonder if you could give me your reaction to this news, Mr. Harrington?"

"What paper do you work for?" Harrington demanded.

"Free lance, Mr. Harrington. But I thought you would like to know."

"Yes," Harrington said. "But you say it is only a rumour."

"Something has happened out there, Mr. Harrington," the voice said. "The cutter left Toulon just after dawn, and I believe it is expected back about lunchtime. Have you any comment on this news, Mr. Harrington?"

"I'll comment when I find out the truth," Harrington said, and hung up.

"Bad news?" Shelley asked. "Was it Mr. Jarne?"

Harrington frowned. "Something about an accident on board *Twin Tempest*. But it's only a rumour."

"An accident?" Shelley's turn to frown. "To Mr. Jarne?"

"That's what he said. I'd better get down there, I suppose. Come to think of it, if I'm not here the press boys won't be able to get on my back. Ring British Airways, and get me a flight to Nice. First available seat."

He hurried to the bathroom, checked in the doorway. Shelley still sat at the table, staring at the telephone.

"Shelley," he said. "My darling, I just have to get down to Antibes. This may be more than a rumour."

"Yes," she said. "I'm sorry, Martin. It's just . . . you don't think it's anything serious, do you?"

"I don't know," Harrington said patiently. "That's what I mean to find out. Why don't you come with me? There's an idea. You'll like the Riviera."

"Me?" she asked. "Oh . . . I'd . . . No, I think I had better stay here." She stood above the telephone. "You will be coming back. Soon?"

"Of course, my darling. I'll be back tomorrow, I should think. But make the return half of the ticket open, will you? Just in case." He pulled on his clothes, watched her dialling through the opened doorway. Her back was turned to him. But he could swear her fingers trembled.

*

Toulon nestled securely behind its surrounding hills and islands, already scorching in the noonday sun. The military port was filled with warships, the commercial port with merchant vessels. And the Quai la Sinse with people, as Angel brought *Twin Tempest* alongside, watched in the wheelhouse by Inspector Levasseur and two of his gendarmes, while the coast-guard cutter hovered on his port quarter like a sheep dog.

By now Justin Jarne's body had been wrapped in a sheet and removed to the saloon table. Alison had returned to the after cabin, and two of the crew of the cutter had come on board to handle the sails on the return journey; now they took care of the mooring warps. No doubt Alison had said all that she had to say, for the moment; Levasseur had spent over an hour in the cabin with her before coming up to take Angel's statement in turn. So he also had said all that he had to say. And felt no better for it. Last night the pair of them had been working themselves up towards something which had promised a great deal. This morning they were accusing each other of murder.

But Justin Jarne was dead, and he hadn't done it. He had no reason to have done it. But if he went on thinking in circles like that he'd go mad. Besides, there were more pressing problems immediately at hand. In addition to the swarms of reporters and cameramen and sightseers being restrained by the police, there was also Lampagie Jarne, wearing a brown pants suit beneath a broad-brimmed toreador hat, her faithful chauffeur at her side. Her face was in shadow, but it was composed.

And now the yacht was alongside, she was being helped on board. A policeman held her arm as she swung her legs over the rail. This time she did not bother to remove her shoes, and they clumped dully on the teak of the deck. For a moment she was framed in the doorway, then she came into the wheelhouse.

"Where is my husband?" she asked, her voice low.

"In the saloon, madame," Levasseur said. "I did not mean to expose you to this."

"It was my decision to come here." Lampagie went to the companion ladder. "Did you kill my husband, Angel?"

He opened his mouth to let go all the protests which came crowding up, and managed to choke them back. "No, Mrs. Jarne."

"Then it was the girl?"

"We do not know, as yet, madame," Levasseur said. "Mademoiselle Somers also denies committing the crime."

Lampagie continued to gaze at Angel. Her eyes were the coldest he had ever seen, and her mouth was a rigid line. "But you will find out the truth, Inspector?"

"Of course, madame. Shortly."

Lampagie went down the steps. Levasseur gave some instructions in French to his assistant, and followed her. The detective sergeant touched Angel on the arm.

"You will come with me, monsieur."

"Am I under arrest?"

The sergeant almost smiled. "You are going to help us with our inquiries, monsieur." Perhaps he had studied in England.

"What about my gear?"

"We shall take care of it. It would be best if you came now, monsieur."

Angel nodded. Everything the man was saying, everything that Levasseur had said, had made sense from the beginning. The pair of them could not have been more helpful or more noncommittal. But the fact remained that he was their number one suspect. Because Alison could not have committed the crime. There was the rock on which all his denials must founder.

The detective sergeant stepped on to the deck. He wore a small black pencil moustache, and this he stroked from time to time. It was his only sign of concern for the situation, or even of humanity. The gendarmes pushed the onlookers back, but still there were cameras snapping. Then there was a car, and Angel sank into the back seat. Three years, and it was all happening again. And again he wanted to shout, No, no, no, this can't be real. It's not me sitting here. It's a dream. A nightmare. I didn't do it.

But then, who did?

The police driver engaged gear and his siren at the same moment. An armed gendarme sat in the front seat beside him, turned round to stare at Angel. The detective sergeant sat in the back beside Angel and drew the blinds. He felt in his breast pocket and produced a packet of Disc Bleu.

"I don't," Angel said.

The sergeant shrugged, as if to indicate that in his opinion Angel soon would, and lit one for himself.

"I didn't do it, you know," Angel said. He wondered why.

"It might be better to confess," the sergeant said, half to himself. "The girl . . . she is very good looking, eh? Sexy. One sexy girl, two men on a small boat . . . there is a bad combination. In France, we are sympathetic towards that situation."

"*Crime passionnel*," Angel said. "I wondered when you'd settle on that."

The sergeant stroked his moustache. "There would be a prison sentence, of course. But it will be better than life, or the guillotine."

"Not for me," Angel pointed out. "I've just spent three years in prison, remember?"

The sergeant nodded.

"But you'd still be sympathetic," Angel said.

The sergeant resumed work on his moustache. "We are a sympathetic people, monsieur. I can say no more than that. We have arrived."

The car stopped in the courtyard of a police station, and a policeman was opening the door.

"What happens now?" Angel asked.

"You wait, monsieur. The magistrate will see you as soon as he has studied the facts."

Angel got out. "Am I not allowed a lawyer?"

The sergeant shrugged, this time as if to suggest that would be a total waste of money, in these circumstances. "If you will give me the name of your lawyer, I will see that he is informed of the situation."

My lawyer, Angel thought. I haven't got a lawyer. I haven't got a single solitary friend in the world, save for Dave Bracken. And Dave would be as much use here as a mouthful of sand to a man dying of thirst in a desert. Smith? His business was rehabilitation, not defence. Besides, he had not liked Smith.

"Well, monsieur?" the sergeant asked.

Angel looked up at the sun, burning down on the courtyard. The Riviera sun. He had looked forward to that.

"Forget it," he said, and followed the gendarme inside. The room was bare. There were a table and two chairs. The policeman closed the door and leaned against it. He also lit a cigarette, but unlike his sergeant he did not offer the pack.

Angel sat down at the table, took off his cap, and placed it in front of him, ran his hands through his hair. There was salt on his fingers. By God, how long was it since he had had salt on his fingers?

And how long would it be again before he had salt on his fingers?

He was tired. Strain, he supposed; he had certainly had a good night's sleep. But his brain kept going round and round in circles. Justin Jarne. Justin Jarne. Justin Jarne.

The last time he had seen Jarne, alive, had been about nine o'clock last night. He had gone to his cabin, behind Alison, carrying a bottle of champagne. He had been in a high good humour. Well, who wouldn't be, in that situation? But Jarne had been in a high good humour all afternoon. He had been looking forward to reaching Ibiza. And he had been going to come on watch at two in the morning. To relieve Alison.

And when he had done that, he had been killed. Someone had been waiting for him, and had seized him by the throat, and had crushed the life out of him. Someone.

The door opened, and another policeman brought in a tray of food. Remarkably attractive food; a small dish of *moules*, then a pork chop, with fried potatoes. And a carafe of *vin ordinaire*.

Angel discovered how hungry he was.

Could he have done it? Had he undergone some sort of a personality change in prison? He had felt a remarkable thrill of excitement when the girl Doreen's boy friend had tried to scar him . . . when was that? Two days ago. He had not meant to break Alf's jaw. But he had meant to hit him as hard as he could. And that had been enough. He had not meant to break that policeman's jaw, three years ago, either. But again it had taken only one punch.

But he had not broken Justin Jarne's jaw, because he had not used his fist. He had used his fingers, of both hands together.

Christ almighty, what was he thinking? He had never been tempted to strangle anyone in his life.

So, there had been something in the champagne to turn him into a homicidal maniac. Certainly he had felt very odd after drinking it.

But hadn't Alison drunk from the same bottle? He couldn't be sure about that. She had not had a drink in his company, because he had asked her not to. But she might have had a nightcap when she had come off watch. Certainly she had been sleeping the sleep of the dead when he had tried to wake her up. But she hadn't been dead. Then she had been drugged. By God, he had thought about that earlier, and then forgotten it. They had both been drugged, and by the champagne. Lampagie Jarne's bottles. But they had been left in the car, so that they would become warm, and thus not immediately drinkable. But Lampagie had insisted that they remember to drink it. She had made a point of that. And one bottle had already been opened, left over from their lunch.

Lampagie Jarne.

"Lampagie Jarne," he said, and drank the rest of the wine. "I must see Inspector Levasseur. Quickly."

The policeman gazed at him.

"Don't you understand your own language?" Angel demanded. "Inspector Levasseur. I have information. I . . ." He listened to the knock on the door, bounded to his feet. It was the detective sergeant.

"I never really thought I'd be glad to see you," Angel said. "Listen. I have thought of something."

The sergeant nodded. "You will tell it to the magistrate. He is waiting for you now."

"But listen," Angel said. "This is important."

The sergeant gave another of his half smiles. "It is murder, monsieur. I agree, that is important, if this is the word you would choose to use. You'll come with me, please?"

Probably the magistrate would be the best bet. Angel followed the sergeant outside, and once again into the car. Once again a gendarme sat in the front seat, staring at him. Once again they drove through the streets of Toulon, blinds drawn.

"How is Miss Somers?" Angel asked.

The sergeant shrugged.

"Is she also going to be interrogated by the magistrate?"

"But of course."

"And how is Mrs. Jarne?"

Once again the shrug.

Lampagie. Lampagie. Lampagie. He had decided, yesterday afternoon, that she either loved her husband or hated him. Then it had been none of his business. Now it was vitally his business. So she had hated him. She had drugged the champagne. But why? To turn them all into raving lunatics? That really was a bit too much like science fiction. Yet there had to be a reason. A motive. Surely all he had to do was give the police a motive, and a reasonable hypothesis, and they could take it from there.

But that required thought, analysis, detection, and all he wanted to say was, "I'm innocent, I'm innocent, I'm innocent."

Another courtyard, but this time there were fewer policemen about. Angel got out of the car, and followed the sergeant to a rather grand door. The policeman walked behind, staring at Angel's back. The door was opened by a concierge, and the sergeant showed Angel into a small lift. Their shoulders brushed as they went up together; the policeman ran up the stairs, keeping pace with them. He opened the door for them at the top and then another door on the other side of the lobby.

This was an office, furnished with three desks and two young women, one typing and the other on the telephone. This one now put down the receiver and smiled at the sergeant. "Maître Audier is waiting."

She did not look at Angel.

The sergeant nodded, opened the inner door. The policeman went back into the lobby, closing the door behind him. The sergeant gestured, and Angel stepped into a larger room; here the carpeting was new, in a patterned blue, and the walls were lined with books. There was a single large, old mahogany desk, and two comfortable chairs in front of it. Behind the desk sat a grey-haired man, slimly built, with pointed, shrewd features. He sat still, his hands resting on the blotting pad in front of him, one on each side of a sheaf of papers in a cardboard folder. Angel recognised the top sheet as his own statement.

"Good afternoon, Sergeant," the magistrate said in French.

"Good afternoon, Maître," the sergeant said. "This is the man, Angel."

"Sit down, Monsieur Angel," the magistrate said. "Would you rather speak in French, or English?"

Angel sat down. "I'd prefer English; it's three years since I spoke much in French. But I can manage."

"My name is Maître Audier," the magistrate said in English. "I have been appointed to inquire into the death of Mr. Jarne. Do you understand that?"

Angel nodded.

"Because you have been in France before, and you understand something of French procedure," Audier said. "But you have not been in trouble with the French police before?"

"No." Angel listened to movement behind him. But the sergeant was not leaving; he was sitting in the remaining chair, in front of the door.

"And now it is a case of murder," Audier said. Still he had not moved his hands, but his eyes dropped to look at the paper. "Would you like to add anything to this statement?"

"Yes," Angel said. "I have been thinking about the whole thing, naturally, and it occurs to me that I was drugged, last night." He paused, because it sounded rather silly, spoken aloud.

Audier did not look up. "I am going to help you, if that is possible, Mr. Angel," he said. "*If* that is possible. You understand that a man, your employer, has been killed on board a yacht, at a distance of . . ." His eyes searched the paper. "Thirty-four miles from the nearest land. He was certainly killed by a human agency. But there were only two human beings on board the boat. And it is the opinion of the doctor who examined the body that one of those human beings could not have committed the crime. You do understand all of that, Mr. Angel?" At last the eyes raised.

"Yes, of course I understand that," Angel said, trying to keep the panic from taking control of his mind. "But I did not kill Mr. Jarne. At . . ." He choked back the words. Even to suggest that he might have done so under the influence of some drug or other would be to concede their case.

"You were going to say?"

"I think I should discuss this with my lawyer. I don't think you are going to believe anything I say."

"I hope, Mr. Angel, to be able to believe *everything* you say, eventually," Audier remarked. "I have studied your statement for an hour, and I have also studied Mademoiselle Somers' statement, and I have been conducting certain inquiries since early this morning. Since, in fact, your call came through to Grasse Radio. But I would like to begin by going through your statement. Perhaps you would explain certain points for me." For a moment the lips twitched as if he had almost smiled. "I wish you to remember what I said just now. I am here to help you, as much as possible. But I am also here to find out the truth of the matter." His hand moved, to flick the paper. "Your name is Thomas Percival Angel, and three years ago you were arrested for smuggling diamonds into England."

"And that makes me a murderer?"

The eyes came up, and then dropped again. "Your defence on that occasion was a denial of any knowledge of how the jewels came to be on your boat." Once again the eyes rose. "And now you are denying any knowledge of how Mr. Jarne came to be killed."

"Now look here," Angel protested.

"You were released from prison on Thursday morning last," Audier continued, not appearing to notice the interruption. "And the same day were offered the job of captaining Mr. Jarne's yacht by an organisation known as Rehabilitation Incorporated." The eyes were back. "Would it interest you to know, Mr. Angel, that there is no organisation by that name known to anyone at New Scotland Yard?"

"So how do you think I got the job?" Angel demanded.

"I am hoping, Mr. Angel, that you are going to tell me that. But let me continue to the end. You arrived in Nice yesterday morning, and were met by Mrs. Jarne, and taken to her house outside Antibes for luncheon. Is that how wealthy English women generally treat ex-convicts they have never seen before in their lives, Mr. Angel?"

"Oh, for God's sake. Why don't you ask her? She is that sort of woman. And in any event, I think she is French, not English. And if you'll read that statement again, you'll see that I was met by a man called Colne, not by Mrs. Jarne. Colne works for Rehabilitation Incorporated."

"The organisation which does not exist."

"But Colne existed."

"Indeed, a Mr. Colne exists. He is a real estate agent, who, amongst others, looks after Mr. Jarne's various properties in the South of France. He was requested to meet you at the airport and hand you over to Mrs. Jarne."

"That is not how he put it to me. And who requested him?"

"Why, Mrs. Jarne did, Mr. Angel."

Angel gazed at him with his mouth open.

"That is according to Mr. Colne," Audier said. "We shall, of course, confirm that along with the other point, of Mrs. Jarne, at an appropriate moment."

"You wouldn't by any chance call right now appropriate?"

"Mrs. Jarne has just lost her husband, Mr. Angel. But perhaps you had forgotten that." The eyes returned to the paper. "So then you went down to the ship, and that evening Mr. Jarne put to sea. About one hour after you arrived, you have written here. Mr. Jarne put to sea with a man he had never met before in his life, for a two-day journey to Ibiza. Is that correct?"

"For God's sake," Angel shouted. "I am a professional yacht skipper. For four years I chartered my own boat out of Sète."

"That was before you were sent to prison for smuggling. Did you supply Mr. Jarne with references?"

"I was told it wasn't necessary. I was told Mr. Jarne knew all about my record."

"By these people from Rehabilitation Incorporated," Audier said, and sighed. He was beginning to remind Angel of Hibbert.

By God. Hibbert. "The next time I see you, I figure it'll be on a slab."

"Anyway," he said, "Mr. Jarne *did* know I had been to prison, and it really did not seem to bother him."

Once again Audier did not seem to notice the remark. "You left Antibes at eighteen hundred hours. That at least we know to be the truth. The harbour office confirms the time. You took the first watch. At ten o'clock you retired to bed. You had drunk too much champagne. About . . . four glasses, you say." Up came the eyes. "Champagne is a dangerous drink, eh?"

"No. I told you, I have a theory about that. It must have been drugged."

"So you said. But let me finish. You went to bed and think you passed out. When you awoke it was dawn, and the young lady, Miss Somers, was asleep in the bunk opposite you." Audier waggled his eyebrows, as if to suggest he had no idea where the French obtained *their* reputation. "So you hurried on deck, and there was Mr. Jarne, strangled. But you had not done it. So, you reason, Miss Somers must have done it. A lover's quarrel, you say. Unfortunately, medical opinion has it that Miss Somers could not have done it. But there is nobody else on board. That is quite a problem. One for a medium, in a séance, rather than a detective, don't you think?"

"Listen," Angel said. "I've been thinking since I made that statement. I was drugged. I realise that now. So, probably, was Miss Somers. And so, perhaps, was Mr. Jarne."

"Indeed? Who is responsible for this?"

"Mrs. Jarne. It's not as odd as it sounds. She loathes her husband. She virtually told me so."

The eyes flickered down to the statement. "Over this tête-à-tête lunch of yours."

"Yes," Angel shouted. "It happened. If she says it didn't, then she's a liar. And then she brought champagne down to the boat. But it was hot, and so we didn't drink it right away. But she reminded us that we had to drink it that evening, or it would go flat. And we did. I'll give you a sample, if you wish. Test that. Test Miss Somers. Have a post mortem performed on Mr. Jarne. You'll find traces of barbiturate drugs in all of us. I'll bet you what you like."

"I am not a betting man," Audier said sadly. "Which is unfortunate for me. We have already had a post mortem carried out on Mr. Jarne, and no trace of any drug was found in his stomach. Champagne, yes. A great deal. But no drug. However, if you will choose to give us a blood sample or a urine sample, I will have that arranged immediately we have finished our talk. But I should like you to tell me why Mrs. Jarne should wish to drug you all."

"Because . . ." Angel frowned.

"Because she wished her husband killed? Yes, indeed. I believe there could be some sense in that. Supposing she had a motive for wishing him killed, which is merely fantasy at this moment. But one of the people on board the yacht must have been left undrugged, or there would have been no one to commit the murder."

"And that means me? Even if I have traces of the drug still in my system?"

"It cannot mean anybody else, Mr. Angel. And you could easily have taken the drug yourself *after* committing the crime." Audier at last raised his hands, brought them together under his chin, and gazed at Angel. "Mr. Angel, so far there has been no official deposition. This has to be completed by me, and certified by me. I can tear up your statement and you can write another one, and no one in court will ever know about it."

"If that is a plea for a confession, Maître, you are wasting your time. You are going to come unstuck on the one vital fact in any murder case—motive. I had no motive for killing Justin Jarne. Before the morning I left prison I had never heard of the man in my life. Before yesterday afternoon I had never seen him."

Audier gazed at him for some seconds. Then his hands turned outwards. "Mr. Angel, you are a foolish young man. Now I am going to tell you your motive. What I am going to say has been the subject of a most secret police investigation, here and in your own country, over the past few weeks. But as you know it all, anyway, it can do no harm. And in any event, I presume the entire story will come out in court."

"I have absolutely no idea what you are talking about," Angel said. But his heart was beginning to pound most uncomfortably. There were too many factors about this business which everyone else seemed to know, and he didn't. And they all apparently pointed at him.

"You haven't," Audier remarked sceptically. "You were convicted of diamond smuggling, three years ago. You claimed to be innocent. Perhaps you were innocent. The facts we now possess seem to suggest that you were. In which case you have my utmost sympathy. Which is why I offered just now to help you. But there still remains the fact that your yacht was carrying a great many valuable stones. And those diamonds were part of a continuing traffic entering the United Kingdom from the Mediterranean. You will say, what is secret about that? The secret is in the organisation of this smuggling chain, which was unique, in its size and its scope, and in the fact that we have discovered that it was controlled by a single man.

"That man, Mr. Angel, was Justin Jarne."

CHAPTER 8

Shelley had not been very successful with the holiday bookings, and it was after four when Harrington's flight reached Nice. He had telephoned from Heathrow, and Colne was at the airport to meet him, wiping sweat from his brow as Harrington came through the doors.

"God, but I'm glad to see you, Martin. What a terrible thing."

"Let's get out of here. You've a car?"

"Waiting." Colne took the overnight bag.

"I'll have the details," Harrington said, getting into the front seat of the Peugeot.

"Very few, I'm afraid. It seems to have been that man Angel. I must say, I didn't care for him. You picked him, you know."

"I sent Jarne a list, and Jarne made the choice. You know Angel had done three years for some smuggling offence?"

"Yes."

"I think that amused Jarne. I tried to warn him, on the telephone. Angel also has a record of violence. But what exactly happened?"

"Well, of course, the whole thing is down in Toulon at the moment. I tried to get hold of what information I could, and was just getting set to drive over there when you called."

"What about Mrs. Jarne?"

"She went down to Toulon the moment she was notified."

"Did you see her?" Harrington asked.

"No. I telephoned the house, but was told that she had already left."

"And what about the other member of the crew? The girl, what was her name?"

"Alison Somers? So far as I know she's in custody as well."

"Good heavens," Harrington said. "Do you mean they were in it together?"

"Well, it seems likely," Colne suggested. "I wouldn't be at all surprised if Angel hadn't known her before, and if this thing wasn't planned between them. Something must have gone wrong, though. It seems they were on the radio telephone to Grasse first thing this morning, screaming for help."

Harrington allowed himself a smile. "Imagination boggles. I tell you what, Harry. I don't think there will be anything either you or I can do in Toulon, and we don't want to become involved in a police investigation, do we? I think our best course is to go to the Jarne villa."

"I told you, Mrs. Jarne isn't there."

"But I'm sure she'll be coming back," Harrington said. "And anyway, there'll be messages and God alone knows what else to be handled, and after all, I am supposed to be the old man's private secretary. I suppose I should say was."

Colne smirked. "But you'll be hoping that Lampagie will keep you on."

Harrington winked. "I think we should go to the house, Harry. Both to hold the fort and be there with sympathy when she gets back."

                                    *

"I'm beginning to get the message," Angel said slowly. "You figure I knew a lot more than the combined police of two countries."

"You were on the inside, Mr. Angel. The police are always on the outside. Believe me, I understand much of what must have gone on inside your brain during the past three years, and I can even sympathise with much of it. You had a reputation for brooding, in prison. Indeed, you did more than brood. You uttered many threats against the young woman who you claimed involved you in the smuggling. But she was also sent to prison. So perhaps, if you were innocent, she might have told the court. She preferred not to, and you were angry. That is very reasonable. But to stay angry for three years can be bad for a man. And while in prison, angry, perhaps you begin to hear a name, the name of the man who controlled the smuggling ring, who had employed Francine Dow, and who therefore, indirectly, had been responsible for your prison sentence. Perhaps before you were even aware of it your anger, now developing into hatred, had transferred itself to Justin Jarne. And then you began to plan. You wrote to Justin

Jarne, perhaps, and asked for a job. Or perhaps it was even more for-
tuitous than that. Perhaps you merely collected everything you could
on the man, meaning to settle accounts one day in the future. And
then, only a week or two before you were due to be let out, Mr. Jarne's
regular skipper met with an accident, and he advertised in one of the
yachting magazines for a replacement. You could hardly believe your
eyes. Immediately you applied. No doubt you told Jarne that you
were an ex-convict, soon to be released. You knew that would have no
ill effect on Justin Jarne. Perhaps you even reminded him that you
were the man his courier caused to be imprisoned. Who knows. In
any event, he took you on, and you travelled to Nice. I wonder, did
you then have any real plan in mind? I think, then, that you merely
wanted to be with the man, to study him, to plan for the future.
But . . ."

"But when I saw Jarne again, all my hatred and suppressed anger
bubbled over, and I waited until Alison Somers had gone to bed, and
strangled him."

Audier shrugged. "That is for you to say, Mr. Angel."

"After which I immediately called Grasse Radio and confessed."

"I do not remember your confessing. But I believe you may have
had that in mind. After all, Mr. Angel, you are not a bad man. You
are a most unfortunate man, made violent by endless misfortune. For
three years that violence, that hatred, that desire for revenge, has been
bubbling inside you. Until you actually committed the deed. Then, as
is so often the case, all passion left you as if you were a balloon which
has been punctured. And so, very properly, you called the authorities.
You could not then bring yourself to admit the crime of murder, but
that is not a point which will be held against you, I can assure you of
that. For just as the murder was premeditated, even if you did not
plan it to happen as it did, so I believe that your desire to confess and
give yourself up was instinctive, even if you did not express it in so
many words. I can assure you that the court will be sympathetic."

Angel stared at him. "You have it all tied up, haven't you? By God,
you'll walk with me to the guillotine with tears in your eyes, and
promise me that the blade will be so sharp I won't feel a thing. You'll
have seen to it, personally. Well, I'm not going to play, Maître. I am
innocent. I never saw or heard of Justin Jarne in my life, before I was
told by this organisation you claim does not exist that there was a job
waiting for me down here. And I figure that's a line of inquiry that's

well worth your while following up. Rehabilitation Incorporated might not be known to Scotland Yard, but it is known in the London underworld: I checked. So why should someone belonging to an underground group pick me up and send me off to Antibes to work for Europe's number one diamond smuggler? Just so I would be the obvious suspect for his murder? I'm just, I hate to be trite, a pawn in the game. Do you want to know something, Maître? A lot of what you suggested about me in prison was true. I worked myself up a hate against that girl Francine Dow. And I meant to have it out with her when I was released. But when I found out that she had been murdered I felt a little sick. I'll bet you don't even know yet that she *has* been murdered. She was knocked over by a truck. So was Jarne's regular skipper, just a few days earlier. Does that make you think at all? And I didn't do either of those two, Maître. I was still inside Parkhurst when they happened. If you want to get things straight, you should telephone Inspector Hibbert, at Scotland Yard. He knows all about me. He even suggested that something like this was being laid for me, and like a fool I laughed at him."

"And he was sorry about that," Audier said. "It may interest you to know, Mr. Angel, that Mr. Hibbert was one of the first people I spoke to this morning, when the news of Jarne's death reached me. And I asked him if he had ever heard of either of the members of Mr. Jarne's crew, and do you know what he said when I mentioned your name? He said, 'For Christ's sake, the stupid bastard. They've conned him into committing murder.' "

Angel continued to stare at him. His entire stomach seemed to have turned to lead.

Audier glanced down at the papers in front of him, and then closed the cardboard over the file. "I suppose I cannot blame you for refusing to admit your part in this, although it would be much better for you to co-operate. I do think that if you intended to deny the facts you should have prepared something better than this tissue of lies, as perhaps you should have planned the crime more carefully. As it is, Mr. Angel, I have no doubt at all that the police will be justified in preferring charges of murder against you, and I shall so inform them. You will, of course, remain in custody."

Angel slowly stood up. "And the fact that I am innocent?"

"You will have to prove that, Mr. Angel. You were found almost as red handed as it is possible to be."

Angel nodded. But the anger was coming back, now mixed with despair to make an incredibly explosive combination. "And Miss Somers?"

"I shall be interrogating her shortly. It is possible that she will also be charged as your accomplice, should we happen to uncover any links between you. But that remains to be seen."

"You will come with me, Monsieur Angel," said the detective sergeant, getting up.

Angel nodded again, turned, and hit the policeman on the chin. He deliberately pulled the punch, just a little, but it was sufficiently powerful still to drop the sergeant like a sandbag. Angel caught him under the armpits before he could fall to the floor and sat him in the chair; in the same movement he opened the policeman's jacket and removed his revolver.

Then he turned back to the desk. Audier gazed at him, still sitting, a slight frown between his eyes.

"That was an incredibly stupid thing to do, Mr. Angel," he said. "It provides the very last confirmation needed of your guilt."

"Then you want to remember," Angel said, "that I have nothing left to lose. So I would like you to tell me how I can get out of here without taking on the policeman in the lobby, which might involve your secretaries in a shooting."

Audier shrugged. "There is a private staircase from my office outside," he said. "I do not imagine either of my girls will attempt to stop you. But where will you go?" He carefully refrained from pointing out that he would be giving the alarm only seconds after Angel had left.

"If I told you that, Maître," Angel said, "you'd have a battalion of policemen waiting for me when I got there. But I didn't kill Mr. Jarne. On the other hand, I see your point, that I haven't done a very good job of proving it, and I don't really see how I am going to improve on this afternoon if I'm locked away in a cell."

The sergeant moaned, and moved in the chair. Hastily Angel knelt beside him, taking off his tie to gag him and using his braces to secure his wrists and ankles; leaving him trussed like a chicken on the floor.

Audier watched without changing expression. His hand rested next to the telephone, but he would not risk the two young women outside. His calmness was nonetheless disturbing. "If you feel there is some information you may be able to obtain, then it is your duty, and certainly your wisest course, to inform me, and I will have the police investigate."

"Do you wear braces, Maître?"

The advocate shrugged, stood up, and took off his gown.

"Would you lie on the floor, please?"

Audier lay down with a sigh. "Nothing I can say will change your mind? Things are going to go very badly with you, Mr. Angel. And if, mistakenly, you commit any more violent acts, it may even be impossible for the best lawyer in France to save you from the guillotine."

"My problem is that I won't be employing the best lawyer in France," Angel reminded him. "I don't have that kind of money. And the worst lawyer in France will probably find it quite easy to get me to the guillotine. Which also bothers me quite a lot." He pocketed the revolver, removed the advocate's shoes, used his socks tied together as a gag, stood up, and discovered he was sweating. "I apologise, Maître. This time I know I have committed a crime, in resisting arrest. But try looking at things from my point of view. Next time I see you, I'll have proof that I'm innocent."

*

Angel opened the door. He had placed the two men against the inside wall, and this was a solidly built old house, but of course it could only be a matter of seconds before they were discovered. Yet the two girls looked up with little interest.

"Free," Angel said in French. "No case. Isn't that splendid?"

They smiled at him.

"Maître Audier said I could use the private stairs," Angel explained. "There were reporters at the main door."

The older of the two girls pointed at the narrow staircase in the corner, sheltering behind an ornate bannister.

"Many thanks, mademoiselle. Oh, by the way, the maître asked if he could not be disturbed until he rings. I think he wants to have a word with the sergeant."

The girl nodded, still smiling. Angel smiled in turn, and ran down the steps, two at a time. At the bottom there was a small hallway, with three more doors opening off, and a fourth on to the street. Fortunately it *was* the street, and not the courtyard. He closed it behind him, stepped into sunlight. God, how good it felt. Sunlight, and freedom. For just a moment. Suddenly he realised that. There could

be no hiding in a crowd for Thomas Percival Angel. So it was necessary for him to think very quickly and very lucidly. And then to act,
very decisively. Before the police caught up with him.

He walked rapidly, found a small shop, bought himself a loaf of
bread, two bottles of beer, and a kilo of plain cheese, and a carrier bag
to put them in. Then he returned to the street and hailed a taxi.

"I wish to go to Hyères," he said.

The driver nodded, engaged gears, and braked as a wailing siren an-
nounced the arrival of two police cars, crowding down the street.
They had been even quicker than Angel had expected. He sat well
back, sliding down the seat. "There is something happening?" he
inquired.

The taxi driver shrugged. "There is always something happening,
monsieur," he remarked. He flicked the switch on his two-way radio,
reported that he had a fare, and was driving out to Hyères.

The car moved off again, and Angel sat up. In a car he looked like
any other tourist.

The buildings began to fade, but the taxi was sticking disturbingly
to Route 97, immediately beside the railway line.

"Where I actually want to go," Angel said, "is a little place called
Pierrefeu. It is quite close to Hyères. I don't suppose you know it?"

"But of course, monsieur," the driver said. "Why did you not say so
in the first place?"

"I thought I'd have to make inquiries in Hyères," Angel confessed.
"Can you take me to Pierrefeu?"

"If you wish, monsieur, naturally. It is a long drive."

"I'm in no hurry." Angel looked at his watch; it was half-past four.

They started to climb, but after a mile or two the taxi swung away
from the main road and on to hardly more than a lane, winding
through the valley between the Massif Maures and the foothills of the
Alpes de Provence. The taxi driver switched on the radio.

"Would you mind terribly if we didn't have that thing on?" Angel
asked. "I'm trying to think."

"I must report my whereabouts and my destination, monsieur," the
driver said. "It is company regulations."

"It is better for me if you do not," Angel said, and placed a fifty-
franc note on the front seat. "If my wife . . . you understand?"

The driver made a remark under his breath, but the radio was
switched off again and the money disappeared. Angel looked out of

the rear window, watched the houses dwindle. In another few minutes the car was completely alone, driving between hedgerows.

"Could you stop a moment?" Angel asked.

"But what is the matter with Monsieur now?" the driver demanded of the afternoon. He braked.

"I don't feel very well," Angel said.

The car had stopped. Angel opened his door and got out, listening. But there was no sound save for the hum of a distant aircraft. Angel stepped up to the front door, twisted the handle, pulled the door open and seized the driver by the throat, all in the same instant. The man goggled at him.

"I will not hurt you," Angel said. "Unless you make me. Lie down in the back seat."

The man looked up and down the road, decided that there was no help immediately forthcoming, and lay down on the seat. Angel was becoming quite an expert, now. Belt and tie went into action and a moment later the driver was incapacitated. Angel rolled him off the seat and on to the floor, borrowed his peaked cap; it was far too small, and sat on the back of his head in a rather mischievous fashion. It would still be necessary to avoid any road blocks.

He ran his fingers through the driver's pockets, found his wallet, flicked it open to discover his name and number, and then replaced it and got behind the wheel, immediately swung back towards the main road; this would have to be crossed before he could get anywhere near Antibes, and it was essential to do so before the police could really begin operating. Now he switched on the radio.

Route 97 was busy. Cars streamed along in both directions, in and out of Toulon and heading east for the motorway into Cannes. There would be road blocks, soon enough. But for the moment the radio was telling him what he wanted to know.

"All cars," came the girl's voice. "I have a police message for all cars. A dangerous criminal has escaped from the office of Maître Audier, in the Rue Anatole France. This man is English, he is armed, and is very large, perhaps two metres tall, with brown hair and blue eyes. He is wearing a blue open-necked shirt, blue trousers, and blue canvas shoes. He is pale skinned. He is wanted for murder, and is known to be violent. The police have established that he has managed to leave the vicinity of the Rue Anatole France, and it is thought that he will attempt to get to Antibes, by either car or train. It is requested that a lookout is kept for this man. I would like all cars to report in, as quickly as possible."

Angel took a deep breath, flicked the switch, spoke in a hoarse whisper. "Control," he said. "Number seven five. It is Pierre. Can you hear me? Speak low."

"I can hear you, Pierre," the girl said. "What is the matter with your voice?"

"Listen," Angel said. "I can speak no louder, eh? My fare to Hyères. It is the man."

"Eh?" Her voice squeaked.

"Be quiet," Angel begged. "He is a big man, English. But he speaks very good French. He wishes to go to Hyères."

"Hyères. Yes, yes. Where are you now, Pierre?"

"I am just approaching the town on Route 98," Angel whispered. "What shall I do?"

"Do not risk anything," the girl said. "I will call the police. Just remember where you drop this man. Call me as soon as you do this, with the address."

"Yes," Angel said. "I must stop now. I think he is trying to listen. Pierre out."

He left the key open, though. From the back seat there was a bumping as Pierre moved. But now he was approaching Carnoules, where he remembered there was a good road leading up into the mountains. He had bought himself about two hours of time, he figured.

CHAPTER 9

"Perhaps you would like something to drink," Inspector Levasseur suggested.

Lampagie Jarne focussed on his face with difficulty. It was odd how irrelevant things kept crowding into her mind. Such as how hard this chair was. Were all chairs in police stations this hard? It was three years since she had been inside a police station, and then she had been arrested for speeding, but released as soon as they had discovered who she was.

And such as how much she wanted to take off her hat and rumple her hair.

But Lampagie Jarne did not do things like that.

"I would like a glass of water," she said.

Levasseur nodded, got up, and opened his door. "Will you fetch some drinking water, please?" he said. "This news has frightened you, madame?"

"That the man Angel has escaped?" She shook her head. "I am still reeling under what you have told me about Justin. I cannot believe it."

Levasseur took the cup of water from the gendarme, closed the door, and returned to his desk. He held out the cup, and watched the woman drink. Her hand trembled.

"About the diamonds." Levasseur's hands came up, made to join each other, and instead fell to flicking, finger against thumb. "Of course he had retired from an active part in the business before you met him. You understand . . ." Again the shrug. "I hate to interfere with your grief, madame, but one reason that we were holding off arresting your husband was because we knew he had retired. But it is unlikely that his associates have also retired. Now he is dead . . . madame, if you can think of anything, any scrap of information . . .

where your husband kept his files, his papers . . . there must have been papers. He must have kept some sort of accounts. Madame?"

He is dead, dead, dead, Lampagie thought. It was impossible really to grasp what that meant. Justin was dead, dead, dead. She did not know whether she wanted to cry or laugh, now.

"I know nothing of my husband's affairs, Inspector. Neither his legitimate business affairs nor his criminal activities. As you must know, he spent very little time at home. Perhaps on the yacht . . ."

"We have almost taken that boat apart, madame. It is a boat. A very beautiful floating home. Nothing else."

"Well, then, my husband's private secretary, the man Harrington . . . ?"

"Mr. Harrington," Levasseur said. "He is very helpful, Mr. Harrington."

Lampagie frowned. "What do you mean?"

"What I said, madame. He is in Antibes now. Did you know that?"

She shook her head. But of course he would have come.

"He landed at Nice Airport some time ago. He was met by Mr. Colne, and driven off in Colne's car. But we do not know where he went."

Lampagie stood up. "I can tell you that, Inspector. He has gone to my house. He will wish to discuss my husband's affairs. His legitimate affairs, I mean. He is like that. Business comes before everything. I think I should get back and see him."

"You trust him?"

"As you say, Inspector, he is very helpful."

"And suppose I tell you that this story of Angel making for Hyères is a hoax?"

"So?"

"Angel is undoubtedly guilty of your husband's murder, madame. There can no longer be any doubt about that. Our trouble is that we are not certain of his motive. Was it a private revenge, because of his years in prison? Is three years long enough to create such a mood? Is Angel such a man?"

"What is the alternative?"

"That he is a hired killer, sent by some old associates of your husband's to murder him. And perhaps to obtain the very information we seek. In which case he may come looking for it at your villa. Would you not prefer to sleep tonight in an hotel?"

"I will sleep tonight in my own bed, Inspector. Have you no policemen to spare?"

"Oh, your house will be watched, at all times. But an armed and dangerous man . . . who knows what he may accomplish?"

Lampagie walked to the door, waited while he hurried forward to open it for her. "I have no doubt that your policemen will stop Angel long before he can reach Antibes, Inspector. And even if he does elude capture, you forget that apart from your men outside, not to mention my dog, I will have Mr. Harrington, inside. I do assure you, I shall be in no danger."

*

Angel discovered a road map in the glove compartment of the taxi, and this enabled him to reach the outskirts of Antibes by the quickest and least frequented routes. Once he knew where he was again, he located a minor road and turned down it, soon enough found a field into which he pulled. Once completely off the road he stopped the car, switched off the ignition, and wiped sweat from his forehead.

He was tired. It had been a long day, and no doubt the drug was still circulating in his system. But a lot of the sweat was tension. He had listened to a steadily building crescendo of excitement on the radio, first of all as the police had converged on Hyères, and then when they had not immediately been able to find the taxi. The girl at the control office had nearly gone wild trying to contact Pierre, and before very long she had been joined by a police sergeant. By then they had feared the worst for poor Pierre. Well, he supposed they were not so very far wrong.

And now they had also abandoned Hyères, and were throwing the net wide again, with particular attention to Antibes, so far as he could make out. But in any event, that figured.

It also figured for them to stake out the Jarne villa. But if he let that stop him, then he might as well find the nearest police station and turn himself in.

As if to add to his troubles, there were rain clouds building over the mountains, promising a return of the mistral, and before that, a wet night. But rolled up under the dashboard he found Pierre's raincoat; it would not fit him, but it could act as a cape, and as a useful cover for his much-publicised yachting gear.

He opened the door and got out, swinging his carrier bag. "I really am sorry about all this, old man," he told Pierre. "Here's your fare and a bit extra for the trouble. I should think someone will be along before long. In any event, I'll probably be back in custody by tomorrow morning, and I'll tell them where you are."

Pierre stared at him. He had not exactly made a friend, there. But then, did he have a friend anywhere? Was he accomplishing anything? He had a creeping feeling that his life was an exercise in futility. He was going through the motions, much as he had gone through the motions after leaving prison, in his search for Francine. Once again he was angry, and with a woman. But what would he do when he got to her?

If he got to her.

He studied the map again, then pocketed it and walked down the road with all the confidence he could manage. He was taking a chance, but it was a small one when compared with the over-all picture, and he did not think he was likely to encounter anyone who had been either listening to the radio or watching television in the middle of the day. Soon enough he was passed by a family of four, mother, father, and two teen-age daughters, panting along the road on bicycles, dreaming no doubt of their iced wine and *moules marinière*, casting only a glance at the tall man striding along the road. An envious glance, because he was so obviously fit, and so obviously had a good idea where he was going, and how far it was. They'd remember him tonight, at their hotel. By then it wouldn't matter.

And while he walked, he thought. Because just reaching Lampagie would hardly be sufficient. To think in terms of some homicidal drug was going a little beyond the bounds of credibility. But if she had drugged him, and Alison, it had to be for a reason.

And slowly the reason, or at any rate, a possible reason, began to take shape.

Lampagie Jarne.

The wood behind the house came upon him almost before he knew it. He left the road and walked under the trees. Dry bracken crackled beneath his feet, and it occurred to him that he was making a noise like a tank. And it still wanted at least two hours to darkness. There was nothing to be done until then.

Especially now that he had reached the fringe of the trees, on the crest of the slight hill, and could look down at the back of the villa. A track ran behind the wall, skirting the wood. A police car was parked there, and two gendarmes stood beside it, smoking cigarettes. There would certainly be another one out front, and possibly even a policeman in the house itself. They would not actually come looking in the wood until they knew he was in the neighbourhood; from the point of view of the French police he could be anywhere in the South of France, and all they could do was wait until he showed himself. Once.

He folded the raincoat to act as a pillow, and in doing so found a box of matches in the right-hand pocket. He took it out and looked at it for several seconds, then broke off some of the bread, ate it and the cheese, washed it down with a bottle of beer. Quite apart from the police, there were the chauffeur and the butler, and he did not know how many other servants. And there was the dog. But the police would prove sufficient. So, how badly did he want to get in?

He lay on his back, his hands beneath his head, and gazed up at the trees, at the clouds slowly moving across the sky. There was already a bit of wind, northerly, about force two, he thought. Nothing very much, but it was just flicking the leaves as it passed. The very dry leaves.

He had always had a horror of fire, like most sailors; at sea it is the greatest of all dangers.

But did he have an alternative? The French police had an open and shut case. There was nobody else could possibly have murdered Justin Jarne. Nobody with the opportunity, and nobody with quite his motive. On the face of it. So now he knew how it had been done, if not why. It was not something he could prove. His only out was to provide the law with a confession.

So how would he go about getting that, he wondered, from a woman like Lampagie Jarne? He wondered if she was quite as formidable as she seemed. He was surprised, and disturbed, at the way the memory of her aroused him, where her presence had not aroused him yesterday. But yesterday he had supposed nothing more into their relationship than acquaintance. Today they were intimates, in the act of murder. More intimate than he knew, perhaps. If Rehabilitation Incorporated really was an underground organisation, then this thing had been set up a long time ago. As Hibbert had warned him. And he had laughed.

The more he thought about it, the more it all seemed to fit, and only Lampagie Jarne could give him the out he needed, no matter what it took to get it out of her.

No matter what. He watched the leaves rustling in the wind, tried to remember what lay on the other side of the wood. Other villas, to be sure. And fairly close. But it was his only way in.

He looked at his watch. Seven o'clock. Still an hour to darkness. But it would take an hour for the flames properly to catch, even in this breeze. He went a little farther into the wood, began accumulating leaves. His hunt even produced some stray pieces of paper. An arsonist's dream. He was staking his real innocence against another crime, to avoid the consequences of a yet more serious crime. Thomas Percival Angel was so firmly behind the eight ball that there was really no prospect of his ever coming out into the open air again.

That was better. Now the anger was back, replacing the bewilderment and the sense of despair. Only anger would get him out of this mess. Because once he struck this match there would be no stopping or turning back. Once the first flame licked upwards into these unlucky trees he would be on a narrow one-way track, which he could only possibly justify by bringing in the actual murderer of Justin Jarne.

And perhaps not even then.

Angel struck the match.

*

As he had calculated, it took some time for the flames to catch hold. In the beginning there was hardly more than a little smoke, and for some time he was afraid that his bonfire would just die. But slowly the tongues of flame licked up through the piled paper and into the dry bracken all around. Then one of the trees standing close by caught, and within a few seconds the whole wood seemed to be ablaze as the freshening wind sent the fire racing from branch to branch.

It was time to hurry. Angel left the trees, and ran down the sloping bank. It was quite dark now, and the only light, apart from the sudden glow above him, was from the villa. And the gleam of the gendarmes' cigarettes by the side of the track. But now the cigarettes were extinguished; they had seen the fire.

He reached the ditch by the road, fifty feet away from the car, and crouched there, panting to regain his breath. The villa wall was another hundred feet or so beyond. Simple enough, really, except that the moment he scaled the wall, and the dog began to bark, the police outside, and the police inside, if there were any, would converge on him like the claws of a gigantic crab. Unless they were sufficiently distracted.

He waited, for what seemed an eternity, and then watched the two gendarmes, hardly more than shadows in the gloom, climb the slopes towards the wood. They carried blankets from inside the car. There was a futile piece of optimism. But they would have called for assistance.

Angel crawled across the road, and ran towards the wall. He had not reached it when he heard the wail of a siren. Another police car, more men jumping out and running towards the burning trees. The men from the front of the villa?

Angel lay in the hollow against the wall, and waited. There were shouts from inside the villa now as well. Something for Lampagie Jarne to look at, while she ate. And now he heard the clanging of a fire bell.

And now, too, Jupiter began to bark, endlessly and noisily.

His cue. He stood up, found that he could just reach the top of the wall with his fingers, dug them in and with a tremendous effort got his elbows up. Now it really was dark, and now too the noise was deafening; men shouting, engines racing, and someone had left his siren on to add its wail to the cacophony, while from in front of him Jupiter matched anything the humans could manage.

Angel sat astride the wall, looked at the side of the villa. There were people standing outside the back door, gazing up the hill. At this distance he could not identify any of them. Someone shouted out to Jupiter to be quiet, but Jupiter ignored the command. His bark was very close. Angel released the wall and dropped down. The bushes rustled and Jupiter bounded forward, baying rather than barking, now.

"Hi, there," Angel said softly. "Remember me? I'm one of the staff. Your mistress told you so, remember? Angel belongs?"

Jupiter sniffed his pants.

"There's a good lad," Angel said, patting his head. "I think you want to have a go at those firemen on the other side of the wall. Nuisances, they are, disturbing the whole neighbourhood. Go get them, boy."

Jupiter threw back his head and barked again.

"Off you go," Angel suggested.

Jupiter trotted into the darkness, barking.

Angel moved through the trees, stopped where they ended, surveyed the house. From where he stood he could see the water shimmering in the swimming pool, the lights in the downstairs rooms. There were none upstairs. Neither the Mercedes nor the Alfa was to be seen, and the garage was closed, but there was a Peugeot parked outside the front door. So she was, after all, entertaining. Or being visited by sympathetic friends.

Still the fire blazed in the wood, still people shouted. And still the siren wailed. And still Jupiter barked. And much as he strained his eyes, he could see no movement inside the house itself. It was certainly a chance worth taking. After all he had followed his nose all afternoon, with a certain amount of success.

He left the tree screen, ran across the gravel path, checked on the patio to tap his deck shoes and get rid of any earth which might have clung to his non-skid soles. The front door stood invitingly open, and the lights within glowed softly. Angel moved to the door, checked again. To his left the table in the dining room was set for dinner, and they had in fact actually started to eat, as there were half-empty soup bowls on three of the place settings. But they had abandoned that course to go outside and see what was happening.

He ran for the staircase, made it in three long strides, mounted beneath the archway. The bedroom doors stood open. The first had no scent, and there was a suitcase in the middle of the floor, as yet unpacked, and a man's raincoat thrown across one of the beds. That wasn't so good. It hadn't occurred to him that she might have a house guest.

The second room was also scentless, and apparently unoccupied. But the third, at the end of the hallway, was the largest, and decorated in a very soft blue which included walls, drapes, and bedspreads, exuded Adoration.

As he entered the room, he heard the first drops of rain on the roof.

CHAPTER 10

The police sergeant's uniform was wet; apart from the rain he might have strayed under one of the fire hoses. But he looked cheerful enough as he touched his kepi.

"It is under control, Madame Jarne," he said. "Just a small blaze, and the rain came to our assistance. Perhaps some careless picnickers. Perhaps . . . who knows? I have telephoned Inspector Levasseur."

Lampagie had changed into a white silk evening gown, high necked but without arms or a back. She wore white pearl earrings, but no other jewellery. The removal of her rings was the only evidence of recent tragedy. "You still think Angel may be coming here? I still fail to see why."

"I think the sergeant is probably right," Harrington said. "I'm afraid there must be some link between this man Angel and Mr. Jarne. Believe me, Mrs. Jarne, it really is on my mind. I picked him from amongst at least six applicants."

"So he had the best qualifications." Lampagie led Harrington and Colne back through the house. "Presumably we can continue our dinner now, Henri. Anyway, Martin, if Angel knew Justin, I can assure you that Justin knew nothing of Angel. I was with them when they first met. Have you ever seen the man before, Harry?"

Colne shook his head. "He's not the sort of man one would forget."

Lampagie sat at the head of the table, surveyed the two men. Her composure, Harrington thought, was fantastic. She showed no sign of weariness from her very long day, her chat with the police. He must find out just what the police had said to her, and even more important, what she had said to the police. But then, she had shown not the slightest surprise on returning home to find the pair of them waiting. Perhaps she had expected him to come. Nor was there now the slightest evidence of the strain she must be under. There were so many questions he wanted to ask her; she had carefully avoided being alone with him, even for a moment.

"What I do not understand," she said, "is why, if Angel has so clearly demonstrated his guilt by running away, they are still keeping poor Alison down in Toulon. Surely her innocence is now beyond question?"

Harrington leaned back to allow Henri to place roast pork in front of him, sipped Pouilly-Fuissé. "I would have said the police are working on the theory that they must have been in it together. Which seems pretty obvious to me. I mean, this story of hers that she must have been drugged, well . . . it's not very likely, is it?"

"They'll be carrying out tests," Colne said knowledgeably. "On what's in her blood, and on her real strength. Although I don't suppose there can be much doubt that Angel did the actual throttling. Oh, I really am sorry, Mrs. Jarne."

Lampagie was staring at her plate; she had not touched her food. Now she raised her head. "Why, Harry? Do you think I am going to break down and weep like a child? Do you know, I almost did that, when I saw Justin's body. When I saw his face. It was so completely relaxed. He had no idea that someone was standing behind him about to kill him."

"In front of him," Harrington murmured. "He trusted his crew."

"He had no reason to distrust them. But I did not cry then, and I am not going to cry now." She pushed back her chair and stood up. "But I do not really feel like any dinner. I think I shall go to bed."

"What about this inspector fellow?" Harrington asked. "The sergeant suggested he might be on his way here."

"We have already said all there is to say," Lampagie said. "But if he insists on seeing me again, you may call me. Are you staying the night, Harry?"

"Eh? Oh no, I'd better be getting back to the wife," Colne said.

"If you change your mind, tell Henri." She walked across the room, her gown faintly rustling. In the archway she paused, and turned, and smiled at them. "I really am more than glad you came down, Martin. We'll have a long chat about everything, in the morning."

The two men watched her climb the stairs.

Then Colne said, "What *do* you think about Angel breaking out? Think he may be coming here?"

Harrington sat down and began to eat his dinner. "I have no idea. If I were him I'd try to get out of the country."

"Hm." Colne chewed slowly and thoughtfully. "Do you think he really knew Jarne before? It's odd, you know, when you come down to it, how very little anyone really knows about Jarne. What do you know about him, Harrington?"

Harrington shrugged. "He owns ninety per cent of the J and J. And he likes birds. And boats. Nothing more than that, I'm afraid."

"I imagine Lampagie knows more than she's letting on. I wonder if Angel could be tied in with her? It was odd, you know, her going out to the airport to meet him. I think he is coming here, all right. And he is armed, the police say. He could turn out very bad. I think it was he who set that fire."

"And you think he's out there now, looking at us, and gnashing his teeth, an impotent monster? Then if I were you I'd drive straight home, and very fast. But if you'll take my advice, I would stop worrying about Mr. Thomas Angel, as of now."

Colne hesitated, and then shrugged and put down his knife and fork. "I'm sure you know best, Martin. But if you have a fault, it's a tendency to underestimate people." He went to the door, did Lampagie's trick of looking over his shoulder. "Have fun with the little lady."

*

Angel stood just inside the bathroom, watched the door swing wide. There had been no other sound apart from the steady drumming of the rain on the roof; the corridor was tiled, but she had stepped out of her shoes, as usual, and moved noiselessly. Now she dropped her shoes on the floor, and kicked the door shut behind her. It closed with a slight click.

Lampagie Jarne walked slowly across the room, stood at the french door to the balcony, gazing out at the night. Then she drew the curtains, holding the cord tightly but pulling slowly. She turned, her right hand reaching over her shoulder for the catch of her halter neck. If it was going to be done at all, it might as well be done now, while the men were still downstairs and the rain pounded on the roof.

He took a long breath, stepped out of the bathroom, the sergeant's revolver in his hand. He felt inexpressibly foolish, and for a moment could not think of anything to say which would not sound banal.

Lampagie gazed at him for a moment. Her expression never changed, although her eyebrows rose a little.

"If you scream," Angel said, "I shall have to kill you, and then perhaps somebody else."

"As you have already killed my husband?" she asked.

"I didn't do that, Mrs. Jarne."

Lampagie released the clasp, and the gown came loose. "As you didn't commit the crime for which you were sent to prison."

Angel crossed the room, held her shoulder, and threw her away from him. Her knees hit the bed and she fell across it, as he had calculated she would. Now, why had he done that? Because all his pent-up irritation and anger and fear demanded that he should? Because she was a murderess, and a most cold-blooded one?

Or because he just wanted to touch her?

She rolled on to her back, her gown crumpled on her stomach. Still her expression had not changed.

Angel stood above her. "I'm getting very tired of people pulling that one, Mrs. Jarne."

At last a reaction; she rubbed her shoulder, where his fingers had left a red mark. "The police suggested you might come here. How did you manage to escape?"

"I decided to act like a violent criminal," Angel said. "That's what I'm supposed to be, isn't it? You'd be surprised how simple it can be."

"And was it you who set that fire?"

"Yes."

"That was not a very good thing to do. Fires, on the Riviera, can cause a lot of damage. The wood is so dry, you see."

"So can the guillotine. Damage people, I mean." He sat beside her, wrapped the fingers of his left hand round her throat. This had worked with Doreen.

Trouble was, this wasn't Doreen.

But at least her eyes had widened.

"Holding you like this," Angel said, "I can break every bone in your body, and you wouldn't be able to make a sound."

His fingers were only an inch away from her breasts. They were larger than he had expected, low slung rather than drooping. Christ, how he wanted.

Lampagie Jarne stared at him, and he allowed his hand to relax.

"If I pretend you didn't say that, Angel, and you forget that you did, we may even stay friends. May I get up, now?"

His hand fell to the coverlet. And a lead weight crashed into his belly. "What do you propose to do?"

She smiled, with her mouth. "I propose to clean my teeth and wash my face, have a cold shower, and then come to bed. Unless you propose to stop me."

"It doesn't bother you to have a murderer in your bedroom?"

"The police think you are a murderer, Angel, and I must say I find it difficult to understand how you can be anything else. I must also assume that, having murdered my husband and then come here, you also intend to murder me. Which is all the more reason for being clean when my body is found, don't you agree?"

If she was afraid, she didn't intend to show it. No doubt she had handled enough men in her time to know that her greatest asset was her arrogant awareness of her beauty and her personality. She was a lion tamer, and he was an unintelligent beast.

On the other hand, he knew that she wasn't as arrogant as she pretended.

He also knew of her guilt.

"So go ahead," he said.

"Thank you." She sat up, and then stood up, slowly sidling away from him. The gown dropped about her ankles, and she stepped out of it, left it lying on the floor. She wore nothing underneath, but that figured. She walked slowly across the bedroom floor, removing her earrings as she did so, laid them on her dressing table. Angel found himself sucking air through his nostrils, loudly. There was too much brown-skinned, hard-muscled perfection for a man who had been locked away for three years; even the little roll beneath her navel suggested firmness rather than softness.

"I gather you're not exactly overcome with grief about poor Justin." He also got up, leaned against the bathroom door.

Lampagie was peering at herself in the mirror. She wore no make-up, and there were no creams in evidence; this was more in the nature of an inspection than an adjustment. "As I told you yesterday morning, Angel, I do not, I beg your pardon, I did not love Justin. In fact, in many ways I hated him. My God, *was* it only yesterday morning?"

"Is that why you arranged his murder?"

Her head turned.

"I've had time to do a little thinking," Angel explained. "And a little reasoning. And even a little calculating. You see, Mrs. Jarne, unlike the police, I have one tremendous advantage in thinking about Mr. Jarne's murder; I *know* I didn't do it. Once that fact is accepted, a lot of other facts fall into place."

Lampagie nodded. She left the dressing table, walked past him, so close that her arm brushed his shoulder. She leaned over the washbasin, picked up her toothbrush. "And of course you have decided that it was me. You are a genius, Angel. The police would never have thought of me. When I have had my shower I will show you the wax doll, and the pins. I believe they have no range."

"Shall *I* tell *you* how it was done?"

Lampagie cleaned her teeth, slowly and thoughtfully.

"In the first place," Angel said, "I was drugged. Both Alison and I were drugged. By your champagne. That's why you insisted on taking the opened bottle down to the boat, but your ploy about forgetting it in your car wears a bit thin, when you think about it. And you were so careful to remind us to drink the stuff that same night."

Lampagie rinsed her mouth thoughtfully.

"Once I realised all of that," Angel said, "I had to start thinking of why. Do you know, for a while I even toyed with the idea that you might have managed to get hold of some drug to turn me into a homicidal maniac?"

Lampagie put away the brush and stepped into the shower stall. "According to the police in Toulon, you also accused Alison of doing all of this."

"Well, I did, because frankly, I was panicking a bit at the time. I knew I was in a very hot seat, having just come out of prison. As you also knew, Mrs. Jarne. But I think my instincts were warning me all the time that Alison couldn't have been involved."

Lampagie pulled a rubber cap over her hair, switched on the water. Angel waited until the noise subsided. She was certainly thinking very hard. Well, that figured too. But she still did not look particularly apprehensive, either of him or of his theories.

"So how was it done?" she asked, taking off the cap and starting to towel. "I beg your pardon; how did *I* accomplish Justin's death, by strangulation, at a distance of . . . what was it, eighty miles?"

"You arranged his death, Mrs. Jarne," Angel said. "Because you knew your husband so very well. Do you know what he said to me, yesterday afternoon, after you had left? 'I regard navigation as an exact science.' And so it is, to a professional. And Justin Jarne was just about a professional when it came to the sea. As you pointed out, it was his only real love. He then went on to insist that we cruise at seven knots, regardless of the weather. He was rather proud of having had *Twin Tempest* built to do just that. I imagine he has said those very words to you, time and again."

Lampagie Jarne draped her towel on the hot rail, returned to the bedroom. "He did," she agreed. "But I do not see how that could have caused his death."

"Well, you see," Angel explained, "there are no tides in the Mediterranean, and a ship like *Twin Tempest*, with a nice deep keel and lots of ballast weight, will carry very little leeway in light airs. Now, normally when making a passage in a small boat, one has to work out the leeway and the tidal conditions from hour to hour as one goes along, and make the necessary adjustments to course and speed. But in this case that wasn't necessary. So therefore, once the time that *Twin Tempest* left port was established, and her speed and destination were known, her track and thus her exact position could be plotted for every hour, every minute, almost every second of the journey she was making, whether you were on board or not. Thus, once it was certain that she was making for Ibiza, it would have been the simplest matter in the world for anyone with but the slightest knowledge of navigation to work out exactly where she would be, say, at midnight last night, and arrange for another ship to be there too."

Lampagie sat at her dressing table, and resumed staring at herself in the mirror. "Would it interest you to know that I have no knowledge of navigation at all?"

"Doesn't matter," Angel said. "Obviously you have an accomplice, or perhaps two, who are seamen; the men who met *Twin Tempest* in another boat. But of course that wouldn't work if any of the crew of the ketch had been awake and on deck, on watch. So that was where you came into it. You drugged the champagne, and made sure that we drank it. And it affected me rather quicker than Alison, because for three years I had had no alcohol at all."

Lampagie got up from the dressing table, crossed the room, and lay down on the bed. Angel followed, sat beside her.

"And Justin?" she asked.

"Justin wasn't drugged, because of course you knew that the police would hold a post mortem."

"I do not see how I made sure that he would not drink the same wine as you and Alison."

"Because you knew he did not like Clicquot. He said so, yesterday afternoon. But you also knew he was going to drink a fair amount of the Krug, as he wasn't due on watch until two in the morning. And all this while the other ship, the murder ship, was tracking us, and gradually closing on us. As a matter of fact, Jarne and I spotted a blip on the radar screen, fifteen miles astern of us, about nine o'clock last night. So if she was making ten knots, she would have come alongside just before two o'clock this morning. That ties in with the time of death suggested by the police; with fenders out all along her side there would have been only the slightest jar, and not the slightest mark upon *Twin Tempest*'s topsides."

"And what was Justin doing all this time?"

"In bed, as I told you," Angel said. "But the jar, however slight, of the other ship coming alongside would have awakened him, as it would certainly have awakened Alison and me if we had not been out cold. So he came running on deck, and was met by his murderer."

"How incredibly simple," she murmured, "it is to commit murder. At least, according to you. But you must admit that your theory is remarkably far-fetched."

"Try it on a sailor," he suggested.

"Oh, I am sure it is practical, Angel. But how do you go about proving it? Or how would the police set about it, supposing they were disposed to believe you?"

"They might try finding your accomplice's boat." But the lead weights were back; she was just too confident.

"Hundreds, perhaps thousands, of boats, yachts, fishing vessels, anything you can think of, are coming and going out of the Riviera ports all day long, and all night long too, as a rule. Besides, you have just proved that it would have been possible for this other ship to have been at sea for several days, and still know exactly where *Twin Tempest* was going to be at a certain hour."

"Providing its crew knew our destination, Mrs. Jarne. But your husband never decided that until just before leaving. And he told us we would be going to Ibiza after five o'clock yesterday afternoon. Which is the point of my argument. As Alison and I were going to sea with him, and not even you will try to tell me that Mr. Jarne would arrange his own murder, only you could possibly have given anyone else our first port of call."

"Now, I hadn't thought of that," she said. "But I'm afraid the police will still be interested in *why* I should murder my husband, Angel. The problem is, you see, that as Mrs. Justin Jarne I am one of the most pampered women in the world. I have unlimited credit in every major city in Europe, the use of this house and two others, and of my two cars. So would it interest you to know that I lose all of that now Justin is dead?"

"Oh, come now," Angel said. "He was a millionaire."

"He was a compulsive gambler, Angel. Oh, a successful one. But apparently insatiable. I spent part of this morning with his lawyer. I won't bore you with the sordid details of my financial affairs, but they seem to be in a mess. Justin did all his wheeling and dealing on margin, and living the way he did, the margin itself was all overdraft. With the stock market the way it is now, he is in a considerable minus balance. He owns a lot of real estate, but most of it was very speculative buying, which may be worth an enormous amount in a year or two, but right now is of no value at all, and even less once it becomes known that I *have* to sell. It seems that by liquidating the houses I may possibly rescue a few thousand francs. Yet according to you I am proposing to share that pittance with at least two other persons. For I will have to share, won't I?"

Angel got up. He had been looking forward to this moment. But somehow it no longer seemed important. "That's your story, for the world, Mrs. Jarne. Total innocence. But the police know all about Mr. Jarne's smuggling activities."

She gazed at him, frowning.

He stood above her. "You're not going to pretend you didn't know about that?"

"As a matter of fact, I do know about that, now," she said. "The police told me this afternoon."

"You expect me to believe that?"

She shrugged.

Angel gazed at her in utter frustration. For, as with Alison this morning, deep in his gut he knew she had neither done it nor engineered it. Everything was wrong. He had figured out the true relationship between the Jarnes yesterday afternoon on board the boat.

But his *theory* had to be right. It was the only way the murder could have been committed.

Unless he *was* a homicidal maniac.

"I think you are beginning to have doubts, Angel," Lampagie remarked. "Fortunately, I am beginning to have doubts about your guilt, also."

"Why?"

"You are not acting like a guilty person. When I saw you standing there I thought I was about to be killed."

"It didn't seem to bother you very much."

She smiled. "Death is one of those inevitable things. Mind you, I am rather glad that you did not kill me. It would have been a frightful waste. And then, this theory of yours is very interesting. Yesterday, this morning, even, I would not have given it a second thought. But I did not know then that Justin was a criminal. Now, I can at least understand that there may have been quite a few people in the world who might want to get rid of him, and before the police could actually arrest him. And as you say, you would certainly be a perfect foil for them." She half turned her head, to listen to a car crunching on the gravel of the drive. "I have an idea that that is your friend, Inspector Levasseur."

*

Angel moved to the window, parted the blinds just enough to look down on the car below. "With Alison Somers," he said.

Lampagie got up, put on her dressing gown.

"Where do you think you are going?" Angel demanded.

"He has come out here to see me, Angel," she pointed out. "And before I came up, I told Martin Harrington that he was to call me when the police arrived. I think it would be best to meet them halfway."

"Who is Martin Harrington?"

"My husband's accountant and private secretary. He is also the secretary of my husband's holding company, the J and J. The legal side of my husband's life. He has come down here to help me, and I have no doubt at all he will prove to be very useful. He is a very efficient, very clear-headed man."

"And what do you propose to tell him? And the inspector?"

"I think that should depend upon what the inspector has to tell me," she said. "Isn't that fair?"

"You wouldn't feel that you were pushing your luck, as regards me?"

"Not if you are innocent, Angel."

"Levasseur won't buy that."

"There I agree with you," Lampagie said. "So, unless he manages to prove to me, very rapidly, that you are a murderer, I shall not tell him you are here." She opened the bedroom door. "Is that good enough for you? I will not be long. But you are looking very tired. You may lie on my bed, if you wish. Oh, Angel, by the way, if I am going to help you, I would like you to co-operate with me. I would appreciate it if you would not mention the fact that Justin was a smuggler to Mr. Harrington."

The door closed, and Angel continued to stare at it. He was slowly realising that he had been completely outmanoeuvred, as usual. His feeling for her innocence was no more than a feeling. In fact, she had agreed that in many ways he had solved the way the murder had been carried out. And then she had just walked away from him.

He sat on the bed and scratched his head. She could return at any moment with half a dozen policemen. In which case, his best bet was to get out as rapidly as possible.

He stood at the window, looked through the curtains. Two policemen leaned against Levasseur's car, wearing capes and smoking cigarettes, despite the drizzle. Jupiter wandered around them, slowly and suspiciously.

Besides, more than ever, Lampagie Jarne was his only hope.

He sat on the bed, and then lay down. By God, he was tired. Almost the moment his head touched the pillow the room began to whirl around his head, and the general headiness was compounded by the scent of Adoration which rose from the pillow and seemed to surround him like a mist. Lampagie Jarne. Lampagie Jarne. The most desirable woman in the world.

Or the most dangerous.

He awoke when the engine started. He looked at his watch, discovered that it was nearly ten. He had slept for over an hour.

He looked through the drapes, watched the police car driving away, water spurting from its tyres. An hour. So she hadn't betrayed him, at least.

Then why hadn't she returned to tell him that everything was all right?

He paced the room, twice, pausing each time he turned to stare at the door. Perhaps Levasseur had laid an elaborate trap. Perhaps he had merely sent for reinforcements. Lampagie would have reminded him that Angel was armed.

He stood against the door, listening, and heard nothing. He watched the second hand of his watch, sweeping endlessly round and round, listened to the minutes ticking away.

Cautiously he grasped the handle, tightening his fingers and depressing the catch. Gently he eased the door open, stepped outside on to the corridor, turned, and saw Lampagie walking towards him. She was accompanied by Alison Somers and by a man he did not know. Alison carried a tray on which were four cups and a percolator.

"Now that was silly of you," Lampagie said. "I might have had a policeman with me."

Angel's right hand had already settled on the gun in his pocket. "Am I any further ahead?"

"Considerably. I have persuaded Martin and Alison to listen to what you have to say. Martin Harrington, Tom Angel."

They came up to him, and Angel offered his hand, empty, to meet Harrington's.

"Mr. Angel, this is quite a pleasure," Harrington said. "In view of everything I've heard about you."

He didn't make the obvious and inane comment about his size. Angel thought they might just get on.

"And Alison you have met, of course."

Like Angel, Alison still wore her sailing clothes. And, like Angel, she looked very tired. But her eyes had lost some of their hostility.

"If you are innocent," she remarked, "you have behaved in a most guilty fashion."

He took the tray. "Did they give you a hard time?"

"Not particularly. They knew I couldn't have done it. They were only interested in proving that you and I were in this thing together, and as they couldn't manage that at the moment, they decided not to hold me. But I'm restricted to this area."

"While you are very much the wanted man, Mr. Angel," Harrington pointed out, "I must say my first reaction to this situation is to advise you to give yourself up. Even if you do have a theory as to how the crime was committed which will clear yourself. In fact, that seems to me to be all the more reason for giving yourself up."

"But first you are going to listen to what Angel has to say, Martin," Lampagie insisted. "We'll go up to the studio." She led the way, up a short flight of stairs, to another floor, and another doorway, this time a large arch which seemed to reach up to the flat roof. Beyond was a large, empty room, at least, empty by the standards of the other rooms in this house, although there were two divans along the walls and two low tables, as well as a huge cupboard against the right-hand wall. The entire wall facing the door was a single enormous sheet of glass, looking out over the hillside as it drifted down to the sea. Lampagie closed the door, and drew the drapes. "Put the tray down, Angel, and take the floor. But as Martin suggested, do make it good."

He wondered why they were not afraid of him. Or had Lampagie's overwhelming confidence reached them all?

Yet they were not as calm as they appeared. They exchanged glances as they sat together on one of the divans.

Angel repeated what he had told Lampagie, while she poured the coffee and gave them each a cup.

And then he waited.

"That is about the most far-fetched thing I have ever heard," Alison said at last. "You don't really mean to try that on Levasseur? He'd laugh at you."

"On the contrary," Harrington said, "I think Mr. Angel may have put his finger exactly on it. Presuming we accept his plea of innocence. I take it that you do, Lampagie?"

Lampagie was sitting by herself on the other divan. "Yes," she said. "That great big sad character is starting to grow on me."

Alison sighed, and raised her eyes to heaven.

"And that means," Lampagie said, speaking a trifle more loudly, "that I am prepared not only to go along with his theory, but to finance his defence, if it comes to that. Not, believe it or not, Alison, so much for his sake, but because I believe that is the best way to discover who really is responsible for Justin's death. And believe me, I do mean to find that out. I expect you both to help me."

"Well, of course you can count on me, Mrs. Jarne," Harrington said. "But at first hearing, as Miss Somers says, Mr. Angel's tale is just a little far-fetched. And again as she says, it may not sound very convincing to a bunch of policemen who are starting from the premise that he is guilty. I wonder if you'd be prepared to stake all on a demonstration, Mr. Angel?"

"I'd be prepared to give a demonstration, certainly."

"Just what do you mean?" Lampagie asked.

"Well . . ." Harrington got up, paced the floor. "It will be extremely risky, of course, but I think I can swing it. If you will trust me, Mrs. Jarne."

"Of course I trust you, Martin," she said. "Justin always did. And Angel is prepared to trust you as well, I have no doubt of that."

"Do I have a choice?" Angel asked.

"Well, what I propose is, that you let me have a chat with Levasseur. I dare not tell him that I have spoken with you, of course, Mr. Angel. I'm afraid he is unlikely to play ball on that one. But I can say I have been discussing the crime with Mrs. Jarne and Alison, and that we are not at all convinced that you are guilty, and that, in fact, we have come up with a way in which the murder could have been committed. An almost perfect crime, in fact. He will most certainly not accept the theory, as a theory, and so I will offer to prove it to him. I think I will be able to persuade him. Then he and I will put to sea in *Twin Tempest*. Oh, don't worry, Mrs. Jarne, we will take a couple of the coast guard along to navigate and actually crew the ship. We will leave Toulon and make for Ibiza, and I will guarantee that at an appointed time, another boat, named by me, will come alongside. In the meantime, if we can procure another boat, Angel can take her to sea, having been provided, just before he leaves, with the time of our departure and the course we shall be following. If you do bring your ship alongside *Twin Tempest*, Mr. Angel, at the hour stated, and in person, why, then, I think even someone like Levasseur will have to think again about your guilt. Certainly any jury would."

"Whereas, if you are guilty, Angel, you will just sail away into the sunset," Lampagie said. "And really give the police something to chase. You are quite a smart fellow, Martin. I can see why Justin had such faith in you." She glanced at Angel. "Will you go along with that?"

"If Mr. Harrington thinks he can get Levasseur to sea in *Twin Tempest*, and if he can find me a sea-going ship as well, capable of making more speed than the ketch, I'll come alongside whenever he wants me to."

"But you'll need a crew," Lampagie said.

"That depends on the ship I'm given."

"I'll crew you," Alison Somers said.

They all turned to look at her.

She flushed. "Well, it rather seems to involve my neck as well, doesn't it? The police can't *prove* anything about me. But I wouldn't like to swear they've given up trying."

"So then," Lampagie said, "all you have to do is talk with Levasseur, Martin. You may leave the obtaining of the other boat to me. I know the Riviera ports very well. Now I propose to go to bed. I have had a rather tiring day. Angel, I think you had better sleep on one of these divans up here. Then Alison can have the other spare room." She walked to the door, waited for Harrington and Alison to pass her on to the steps. "But I intend to make an alteration in the general scheme. As it was my husband who was murdered, and as you still seem to have some doubts about my innocence in the matter, I intend to accompany you and Alison on board your ship, and watch you put your theory into practice."

CHAPTER 11

Harrington knew she would come, and so stayed awake. He switched off the lights in his bedroom, undressed, lay on top of the coverlet, and watched the door. There was no moon, and the rain clouds shrouded the stars; the bedroom was utterly dark.

Incredible that he should be sleeping in the same house as Angel. Incredible that he should have met the man in these circumstances. But that figured, now he had met the man. They had made a mistake there. Angel might not be very bright, but he was far too determined to be the perfect patsy.

On the other hand, he was not quite determined enough to match Martin Harrington. There was a comforting thought. Harrington's insurance, against any awkwardness on Angel's part, had been the women. He had reasoned that a man like Angel, after three years in prison, would be walking around with a permanent erection. And he had been right.

And as long as Angel was in that condition, all his acuteness, all his sound reasoning, was not going to get him anywhere. Except into the morgue.

Or in this instance, to the bottom of the very deep, very blue Mediterranean Sea.

His door handle turned, and then the door itself opened inwards. For just a moment she was silhouetted against the faint light which still glowed in the hall, then the door closed again.

"Martin?" Her voice was only a whisper across the darkness.

"Waiting for you, my darling."

His eyes were by now accustomed to the gloom. He watched her cross the floor, slowly, inhaled her scent as she came closer. She wore no nightdress. But he had not expected her to.

She stood above him, next to the bed. "I suppose you know what you're doing?"

"I could ask the same thing of you, volunteering for a trip like that."

"I thought you wanted me to, having gone along with him that far."

For how much had his desire to do this been responsible for his anxiety over Shelley? In looks, Shelley could not compare with this woman. In sheer animal sexuality, Shelley could not compare with this woman. So Shelley had the manners and the background and the general charisma he wanted. This woman had the body.

And tonight she could no longer put him off with a cold smile. Tonight she was all his because she had to be, all his.

She sat down beside him.

"Don't you think, after all, it would be simpler to get Levasseur back? Angel is a dangerous man, but even dangerous men sleep."

"And have him tell the police what he told us just now?" He lay back, but she was still close enough to touch. For how long. Christ, he was going to burst in a moment.

"No one would believe him," she said. "By running away, by coming here above everything, he has proved his guilt to their satisfaction."

"I doubt that. He knows the truth of the business, up to a point. He has worked it out. He will even be able to prove his theory, I have no doubt. But Levasseur is not a fool, either. Running away from the magistrate's office is really the only guilty thing Angel has done on this whole trip. I'm afraid his reactions on the boat were rather disappointing, so far as I can gather."

"I don't see what else you expected him to do, as he *was* innocent," she pointed out.

If only her voice would change timbre, or her body would start to sweat. This was his curse, his total inability to arouse women, to obtain any reaction from them at all, except by hurting them.

But he had finally made the grade with Shelley. He must always remember that.

"I want you," he said.

"And Peter?"

"We share and share alike on this one. Remember?"

She hesitated, and then lay down.

"And is Angel not now going to prove his theory to the world?" she asked. "Anyway," she said, "Levasseur will not allow *Twin Tempest* to be taken to sea without him on board. And a few gendarmes."

He found her mouth, made his kiss as brutal as he could. Suddenly he was happy. What a magnificent way to plan a murder, a double murder.

Or a triple murder?

"So it won't be *Twin Tempest*, my darling," he whispered. "Angel will home on the blip on his radar. On a moonless night, and there is no moon at the moment, he will not be able to identify another ship until he is very close. By then it will be too late. Peter and I will be waiting for him."

"And what about me, Martin?" Her voice was softer than ever.

"You have to go now, darling. Having said you would. But had I thought of it sooner I would have asked you to go. Your presence will make sure he does not get cold feet and run away. Take a weapon, and if necessary, use it. And actually it will fit rather well. Listen. Tommy Angel escaped from the magistrate's office and disappeared. But he will have made a previous rendezvous with his woman, his accomplice, and he has managed to keep that rendezvous, despite the police. The two of them mean to make their way down to the coast and procure a boat. But of course they will be forced to take you with them, because you were here when he came. Right? So maybe they have a choice, to kill you here or take you with them. So maybe Angel is soft hearted, not as bad as he is painted. Or maybe he thought of you as a hostage. You aren't sure why. So you are forced on board the boat they have arranged, and they put to sea, making for North Africa, you understand, although they will have to stop at one of the small ports in the Balearics to refuel. This will account for their making for Ibiza. But somewhere on the way there will be an explosion; again you cannot be sure what happened, but you think there may have been a gas leak. Anyway, after this tremendous explosion, you find yourself in the water. The boat has disappeared, and so have Angel and the Doll. And you suppose you are also certain to die. But fortune favours the innocent. You are picked up by two yachtsmen, and brought back to France. I can see you now, a heroine to the newspapers."

"And suppose these fortunate yachtsmen do not come along?"

"There won't be any yachtsmen, my darling. They will be Peter and me. Sometimes I think you are not very quick on the uptake.

Who do you think is going to cause the explosion on board Angel's boat? He'll come alongside, as I said, and we'll be waiting for him. And her. And you. You won't even get your feet wet." He kissed her on the nose. "Although perhaps we will have to pour some water over you, just to make it real. Believe me, I have worked it all out. That's my business, my darling, working it all out. The French police will be happy to close such an awkward case, and you will have nothing to worry about."

"As long as I trust you," she said.

Harrington smiled at her. "As long as you trust Peter Smith," he said. "And you do that, don't you, my darling?"

*

Angel awoke as Lampagie entered. For a moment he did not know where he was. He only knew that for the first time in a very long time he had awakened in a totally relaxed frame of mind. He had slept heavily, the residue of the drugged champagne combining with his own exhaustion to lay him out.

The drugged champagne. Somehow, last night, the question of the drugged champagne had been gently pushed to one side.

She drew the curtains from over the big window, smiled at him. She wore a yellow sun dress, but her feet were as usual bare.

"Good afternoon," she said. "I'm sure you feel like a good breakfast."

The smell reached him first, and he watched in amazement as she now brought in a laden tray, which she placed on the table.

"I have given Henri the day off, in the circumstances," she said. "And I cooked all this myself. Bacon, eggs, tomatoes, and mushrooms; toast and marmalade; fruit juice and coffee. Is that English enough for you?" She sat beside him, handed him a glass of chilled orange juice, and took one herself.

"I shall start again," she decided. "Good afternoon, Angel."

"That's what I was afraid you'd said. Afternoon?"

"You have slept for sixteen hours. I felt you needed the rest."

"And made sure of it?"

She laughed. "But of course. Just a sedative in your coffee."

"You don't think that might prove something?"

Still she smiled. "I don't see why it should, Angel; as a matter of fact you gave me the idea with your theory. Anyway, I am admitting this one. I had nothing to do with what happened on board the yacht."

Angel drank orange juice. As always, when she sat as close as this there was not a hell of a lot of use in thinking about drugged wine. Or about anything else that she might be planning.

"So how is the merry widow?"

She put down her glass and got up, for a moment disturbed. "I do not know." She walked to the window. "Please eat your breakfast, Angel. I do not know, about the widow. I am distressed, about Lampagie. Lampagie is suddenly becoming aware that she is free."

"Even if destitute. Stuck with two cars, a house, and a yacht. I presume they will return *Twin Tempest* to you, when they are finished with it? Oh, I forgot, and a dog. My heart bleeds for you."

"And various employees," she said. "Like the dog, they will expect to be fed. And even paid, from time to time."

Angel ate bacon and eggs.

"But they are a detail. Lampagie is the problem. Was Lampagie acting, these four years, trying to compete in outrageous behaviour with her husband? Is Lampagie really like that? Or is she just a simple girl who wants someone to love her?" She came back across the room and poured coffee. "You have not forgotten that, after we have proved your innocence, you will still be skipper of *Twin Tempest?*"

"Is that why you are coming along on this trip your friend Harrington mapped out? To see if I'm good at my job?"

"As a matter of fact, that is one of the reasons, yes. It has occurred to me that *Twin Tempest* could prove to be a small source of income, at any rate. And you have experience in the chartering business. But I would also hope to try to make sure that you do nothing foolish. I think you are inclined to do foolish things, Angel."

Angel drank coffee. "You're wrong, you know. Were I really inclined to do foolish things I would drop this cup and grab hold of you."

"I assume your intention would be to murder me?"

"No," Angel said. "I do not think I wish to murder you, at the moment."

"Then why would it be such a foolish thing?"

"Ah," Angel said. "There you have it. Because you wish me to grab you, certainly, but not, I think, out of any desire to have Thomas Percival Angel hold you in his arms. Out of sheer curiosity."

"And that is insulting to you."

"And because you are not yet a widow of forty-eight hours."

"And that offends your sense of gallantry. I really had not suspected that on top of everything else you would turn out to be a gentleman."

"Also because you are my employer, as you have just reminded me."

"And the whole thing smacks too much of some *droit du seigneur*."

"Also because, having been a little out of touch with all women, but especially women like you, over the past three years, I wonder if I would be able to measure up to what you would require."

"And failure there would humiliate you."

"And also because," Angel said, "there is the little matter that if I am to prove my innocence, it may still be necessary to prove you guilty, of Justin Jarne's murder."

"Of course," she said. "And once you had made love to me you would be unable to send me to the guillotine." She poured herself a second cup of coffee. "Tell me something about Thomas Percival Angel. I mean, before things started to go wrong."

"Thomas Percival Angel was one of those men who had it too good," Angel said. "He was blessed from a very early age with health and strength and size and a gift of the gab with women, and with a complete self-confidence. He worked in an office in the city and had done extremely well, and he spent his holidays and the weekends sailing his sloop *Marianne*. And when *Marianne* was finally paid for, he sat back and thought to himself, Why spend the rest of your life inhaling the smog and the exhaust fumes. All you want to do is sail your boat, and it really doesn't matter who you do it with. So he quit his job and took his boat down to Sète and chartered her. She slept five, two pairs in separate cabins. She went with skipper, and unlimited cruising. As you probably know, a lot of chartering is a bit of a swindle. The skippers limit themselves to twenty miles a day and they refuse to leave port in anything over force three. This saves fuel and wear on the boat. Thomas Percival Angel advertised *unlimited* cruising in any weather the charterers could stand. He earned himself a bit of a reputation and did very well. He slept around and he enjoyed himself. Life was a four-year-long holiday. He did so well that one autumn he felt homesick and decided to come back to England, just for the winter. After all, when you travel with your bed and board it is just as cheap to travel as it is to stay in one place. But being lazy he thought he'd come back up the Canal du Midi to Bordeaux, and this meant he needed a bit of help with the locks. So he picked up a bird in Sète. He didn't realise that the bird had actually picked him up by showing the right amount of thigh at the right moment."

"For an intelligent man you often act very unintelligently," Lampagie observed.

"Occasionally I act very lazily," Angel corrected. "Because I am, by nature, lazy. I wanted someone to sleep with, and there was someone very attractive to sleep with. I'd done it before, often, and got into no trouble."

"But this one really became interested in you only after you had told her you were coming back to England."

"Why, yes," he said. "That didn't strike me as odd, at the time."

"And so, having been sent to prison for three years, you come out and land foursquare in the middle of an even bigger mess. You need looking after, Angel."

"I won't quarrel with that," Angel said. "But of course it is all the same mess, isn't it? It began with your husband, although I didn't know it at the time, and it looks as if it is going to end with him."

"Or with you." She shrugged. "So sometimes I hated Justin. I think most of the time I hated him. So I knew him well enough to feel that perhaps he could have been a criminal, once. So perhaps I even knew him well enough to feel that he might have committed murder. But he was as capable of inspiring love as he was capable of inspiring hate or loathing. When I sounded off to you about him I think it was probably just because of the resentment I felt at his going off with that lovely child and leaving me here. But I did not hate him enough to wish him dead. Do you believe that, Angel?"

Angel hesitated. "I don't have much choice, Mrs. Jarne."

"Then it is time we left. The boat is waiting. So I would like you to get dressed. We have a fair distance to travel." Her smile suddenly debouched into that fascinating laugh, but as his hands came up she stepped away. "I will expect you downstairs in five minutes."

CHAPTER 12

Harrington stood at the huge window in the reception lounge of Marseilles Airport, and gazed at the runway and beyond, at the Étang de Berre. He wore a raincoat, although it was a cloudless day at the moment and he was indoors. But there was a fresh north-westerly wind raising ripples on the lake. It was going to be a bumpy night at sea.

A young man with a little black moustache walked past, and checked, close to him.

"I say, you look English. Would you by any chance have a light?"

Harrington offered him a gold lighter.

"All set?"

Smith flicked the lighter, failed to ignite his cigarette, and tried again. "All set. Sure you won't come along?"

"I hate boats," Harrington said. "Here, let me do that for you." He took the lighter, flicked it, held the flame close to Smith's face. "Anyway, my business is to be snugly back in England long before anything devolves."

"We take the risks, you collect the profit."

"I also do the organising," Harrington pointed out. "And from this one, Peter lad, there is going to be enough profit for all. Besides, what risk is there for you? Only that our friend Angel is not as good a navigator as he thinks he is. In which case it might be a good idea for *you* to find *him*. I am assuming he can at least get his ship within radar range."

"I am quite sure he will bring her alongside, if he wants to. I was thinking more of the weather. That mistral is on its way back."

"And that is dangerous?"

"It may complicate matters."

"Rubbish," Harrington said. "It will make it all the more likely that Angel's little boat will sink. There's my flight."

"What about our girl?" Smith asked.

"She is going to be holding the fort at the villa," Harrington said. "Don't worry, Peter lad. She'll sit it out, and be as clear as day this time tomorrow."

"Yeah," Smith said thoughtfully. "This time tomorrow, we'll all be clear as day."

"So contact me when you get home. And good luck." Harrington hurried towards the exit. He had a plane to catch.

And Shelley would be waiting at the other end.

*

"I told Juan to take the day off as well." Lampagie led Angel and Alison down the stairs, carrying an overnight bag; Alison carried a portable icebox—apparently Lampagie Jarne did not mean to be uncomfortable if she could help it. "We shall take the Mercedes, which will give you plenty of room to stretch out on the back seat floor, Angel. I'm afraid that will be necessary, as the police are still looking for you."

She opened the door from the pantry into the garage, where the two cars waited side by side.

"May I ask where we are going?"

"St. Tropez, Angel. There is always so much going on in St. Tropez, such a crowd, you know, that they will not even notice us."

"And what about the boat?"

Lampagie spread a rug for him. "I do not think we will be stopped, but if we are, there is another rug you can pull over yourself. You will sit in the front beside me, Alison." She waited for them to get in, started the engine, and drove out of the garage. Jupiter sat on the front porch and gazed after them, somewhat sadly. "Ah yes, the boat," Lampagie said. "It is a motor cruiser. Quite fast, I do promise you. Very comfortable, too. But her speed will allow you ample margin for error in your efforts to overtake *Twin Tempest*."

"And is that also arranged?"

"Oh yes, indeed. Martin really is very efficient, although he told me on the telephone that Levasseur took a little bit of persuading." She skidded round a corner, narrowly missing a truck.

"So all we have to do is reach our boat."

"I have never had an accident yet."

"I wish I could feel happier about the weather," Alison remarked. "Doesn't it strike you that there's a lot of wind, Tom?"

"So we're back to first names, are we?" Lampagie said nastily.

"Well, it seems we're all in this together, now."

"It could be building up," Angel agreed. "How big did you say this motor boat is, Mrs. Jarne?"

"Twelve metres long. Isn't that good?"

"That depends on how much the wind blows up."

But Alison was right; he would have said this was the beginning of a mistral. First thing to do when he got on board was pick up a forecast.

But would that do any good? He had no choice but to go to sea, and prove his point. Regardless of the weather.

He wondered if Lampagie had ever been at sea in a storm. He wondered what she would be like on a boat, a help or a hindrance. He really wondered why she was coming along at all. So she had given him some reasons. But to suppose that a woman like Lampagie Jarne could really be interested in a man like Thomas Percival Angel was ridiculous.

So wasn't he being an utter fool in trusting her? Because was it at all possible that a woman could not be aware of her husband's true identity? And if Jarne's legitimate finances were in a precarious state, her motive had to be to take over his criminal finances. Thus she had to have contacts in London. Because there would have been some anxiety in the underworld as well, if they had somehow learned what was going on. The police were slowly accumulating evidence against Jarne. And when they got around to arresting him, there was a chance he might talk too much. So Jarne had to die. But in such a way that it could not be linked back to his accomplices. Therefore, there had to be a fall guy. And it hadn't been difficult to find one.

But that didn't ring altogether true, either. If a whole criminal organisation was at work, it would have been too simple to hire a professional killer, and let him take his chances. To use Angel smacked more of a private operation, a core within the core, who could afford no publicity of any sort, either inside the organisation or outside it, and who therefore had to pin the killing quite definitely on an irrelevant source.

Which brought him back to Lampagie all over again, in a different context.

The next time his brain went in one of its complete circles.

But before that could happen again they were in St. Tropez. Ibiza with class. Or, more properly, Ibiza was St. Tropez without class. But it was the lack of class that made Ibiza so attractive. In St. Tropez one could not escape the feeling that the hippies, and the millionaire yachtsmen, were there because it was St. Tropez, and not because they liked the place.

But, like Ibiza, it was always crowded, and, unlike Ibiza, always bustling, always too busy to notice itself. And anyone in it. A good place to leave from unobtrusively, as Lampagie had said.

The car stopped in the park by the harbour office. "I think it would be best if you did not come on board until we are sure it is safe," Lampagie said. "I presume Alison is capable of making a ship ready for sea? There are no sails to be set, or anything like that."

"I am quite capable," Alison said.

"Then we will call you when all is ready, Angel," Lampagie said, and closed the door.

"Sit tight," Alison recommended, and then she too disappeared.

Angel tried to make himself comfortable on the floor, beneath the rug. It was at once hot and cramped, and grew harder with every second. And his mind was feeling equally hot, and uncomfortable. Because Lampagie was being distinctly cold, all of a sudden.

Very likely she was a little tense merely because she was going to sea, and she did not really care for the sea.

So then, *why* was she coming along? If she still felt that Angel was guilty, and perhaps in partnership with Alison, after all, then she was putting herself into terrible danger. And quite unnecessary danger.

And not only from human beings. He listened to the rattling of rigging from all around him. St. Tropez was a large harbour, containing an enormous number of yachts, of which at least half were sailing boats. So it would not take much above force four to set all the loose halliards swinging. But he had an idea it was going to be a lot more than that by midnight.

On the other hand, by midnight they should have made contact with *Twin Tempest*. And would *that* really prove anything?

The car door opened, and he sat up. "You can come now," Lampagie said. "There does not seem to be anyone about."

She had changed into white nylon trousers and a blue sweater. Her hair was once again tied up in a head scarf, white silk this time, and she wore flipflops. She looked good enough to eat.

But no better tempered. Angel got out of the car and followed her across the park to the dock. The harbour office was closed and, although to their right the town of St. Tropez itself babbled with sound and noise, there were few people around the dock.

The motor cruiser lay stern on, looking extremely small between two large Bagliettos. Her name was *Douce* and she was of a typical Mediterranean variety, with a semi-displacement hull—which meant that she was both capable of a fair turn of speed and, theoretically, able to take a fair amount of sea as well, although of course she would be neither so fast as a pure planing hull nor as good a sea boat as a pure displacement hull. She had a large cockpit aft for fishing or sunbathing, a flying bridge with a second steering position, and her console was a mass of dials recording everything from engine oil pressure to whether the stereo cassette recorder was switched on. The wheelhouse doubled as a dinette which could be converted into a twin berth, and down a short companion ladder there was another saloon containing the galley and also meant for use as an occasional sleeping cabin before the forecabin was reached. Her furnishings were opulent, and she was in superb condition, at least at first glance.

"Not your type of boat?" Lampagie asked.

"She'll do for what we have in mind," Angel said. "You'd better hope along with me that the weather stays kind, though, or she may prove very uncomfortable. Would you like to move?"

She was standing in the middle of the cockpit. "Why?"

"So I can have a look at the engines."

"They're all right. I was guaranteed that."

"I propose to take this thing to sea, Mrs. Jarne. And I'd like to see what is going to get us there, and back."

She sat on the transom. Alison was still up on the foredeck, sorting out warps. Now she came aft to join them. "Well?"

Angel lifted the board, was suitably impressed. The twin Mercedes were indeed in good shape. He found the dipstick and tested the fuel level. There was enough for about twenty hours' cruising, he figured, and they would certainly not need all of that.

"Well?" Lampagie asked in turn.

"So why are we waiting here?"

"I'm to give you the facts and figures," she said.

"On the chart table would be best." He closed the engine hatch and went inside.

"The time is now sixteen minutes to six," Lampagie said. "Oh, I am sorry. I should have said seventeen forty-four, shouldn't I?"

"I'm glad you find all this amusing, Mrs. Jarne," Alison said.

"Oh, I am a positive bundle of nerves, Alison. Really. *Twin Tempest* is going to leave Toulon at six o'clock, Angel, and steer due south for six hours. That will put her roughly where she was when you called Grasse. At midnight she will alter course for Ibiza. You will have to work out what course she will be steering. The arrangement is that you go alongside her at two o'clock tomorrow morning. Not a moment later, and not a moment before."

Angel got to work with his dividers and parallel rule. "At two o'clock tomorrow morning she will be here." He made a cross on the chart. "That is seventy-seven nautical miles south west by south of Cape Camarat, which gives us five and a half hours at a cruising speed of fourteen knots to catch up with them. Say half an hour from the pier heads to the cape, and we want to leave here at eight o'clock this evening. Twenty hundred hours to you, Mrs. Jarne. We have a lot of time in hand."

"Well, then," she said, "I suggest we have an early dinner. Alison, will you look after it?" She opened her icebox. "There is cold meat and salad, and some apples. Oh, and I have brought along two bottles of Clicquot." She smiled at Angel. "This time they are nice and cold."

*

Lampagie leaned back and sipped her drink. She seemed amused. "Neither of you seem worried that this may be drugged."

"If it is, as you drank it as well, we'll probably spend the night going round and round in circles." Angel checked the chronometer on the console. It was half-past seven. "I think we could make tracks."

"You've just time to do the dishes, Alison." Lampagie left the wheelhouse, went into the cockpit, and climbed the ladder to the flying bridge. "I'll let go, shall I?"

"I thought you didn't know anything about boats?"

She shook her head. "I said I didn't like sailing, Angel. Although as a dutiful wife, I tried to like it, once. When Justin and I were first married, I crewed him for a full year. Motor boating, now, I have always enjoyed. As a matter of fact, this is my boat."

Angel gaped at her. "Say again?"

She smiled at him. "Where do you imagine we managed to find a boat waiting, so conveniently to be used, Angel? With no questions asked?" Her smile became a laugh. "Oh, you do look bothered. Don't tell me you're starting your sums all over again." She climbed down the ladder.

Angel scratched the back of his head, then turned the starboard ignition key, and listened to the engine growling into life. It sounded good. So did the port. And all the gauges and dials were taking up their correct positions. There was going to be no trouble below decks.

And that was about the sum of it. Because the wind had freshened quite a lot during dinner and was now a north westerly four, here in St. Tropez, which promised quite a bit more when they left the shelter of the land, and with probably a further actual increase to come during the night. And now Lampagie was stirring the pot. Why? Why *should* she risk her neck by coming at all? But the stern of the motor cruiser was already free, and Alison had joined Lampagie on the foredeck, one pressing the switch on the electric winch, and the other standing by with a boat hook just in case the anchor came up crooked. A good crew.

Why, indeed? Because she was Justin Jarne's wife, and wished only to discover the identity of her husband's murderer? Or because she wanted to keep an eye on her boat? Or just because she was hoping to rendezvous with some friends?

And what was Tommy Angel going to do now? What *could* he do now, except keep right on going. It was really quite amusing, now he came to think about it. He had been following a carefully laid path since walking through the door at Parkhurst. Everything had been decided for him. So perhaps once or twice there had been a choice of two ways to go, two paths to follow; but each had been just as carefully charted. He might not have gone to Doreen's flat. That had not mattered. He had had to go to his own flat, the one the man called Smith had rented for him. Perhaps they had even known that Hibbert, or someone like Hibbert, would pay him a visit or counted on it, just to get his wind up, to drive him the more quickly out of England. They could not have known he would visit Dave Bracken, but the word had gone out, Angel is poison, and Dave had not been quite as good a friend as he had hoped.

After that it had been too easy. Lampagie had met him at the airport. Had that been suggested by someone else, or had she chosen to go on her own? Just to create a little more motive, just to unsettle a little more an already unsettled mind.

If Lampagie were guilty, they could not have been sure he would not also murder Alison Somers. Oh yes, they would have been sure. Because they would have known that Tommy Angel was no murderer. Once that fact was established, Alison's reactions were perfectly easy to establish, and so would be the decision, whether ultimate or immediate, to call Grasse. Because it was what an innocent person would do.

They could not have guessed he would snap the traces at Maître Audier's office. He wondered if there, for the first and only time, he had for a moment held a trump by the very unexpectedness of his action.

But of course he had never held a trump. Not by escaping. Escaping had merely proved his guilt. Perhaps he had for a moment held a trump by turning up at the Jarne villa. Had he thrown his weight around he might have upset one or two people. But instead he had allowed himself to be overwhelmed by Lampagie all over again. She had extracted his theory from him, the right theory, of course, and she had laid her plans. She had even conned Harrington and Alison into going along with him. Lampagie Jarne could con anyone into anything.

The bow of the yacht was free. Lampagie turned towards the bridge and gave the thumbs-up sign. Angel eased the engines into slow ahead, and the motor cruiser slipped out from between her companions and turned slowly and quietly towards the harbour mouth. The women returned to the wheelhouse.

After which she had suddenly decided to come along. Now why? Because when he made his rendezvous, he would have proved his point.

So obviously he was not going to make his rendezvous. Perhaps she had slipped up by admitting just how much she knew about ships and the sea.

The pier head dropped astern, and Angel gave full throttle to bring the ship on to a course wide of the Rabiou Shoal. He watched the light beacon on La Mouette come into view on the starboard bow, and then the tower on Cape Camarat. A few minutes later he altered course to the south west. Where was *Twin Tempest* now? He could only hope. But it was going to be a long six hours. Which he meant to spend right here. It was safer.

The lights dwindled and the night darkened. They were travelling faster than the wind, and only occasionally found a deep trough. Maybe the mistral would hold off until morning. Maybe.

It was midnight when he heard feet on the ladder behind him. Which one?

"Christ, this feels good," Alison said, and dropped into the co-driver's seat.

"What's up with the boss?"

"She's turned in." Alison watched the white water spurting away from the flared bows below them. "I've been thinking. If this theory of yours is right, and you are innocent, then I owe you quite a large apology."

"Faults on both sides."

"And if you are guilty," she said, "presumably I'm asking for trouble."

"Terrible fate, when you come down to it, Alison, to be stuck on board a small boat with Lampagie and me."

"I couldn't agree with you more. She terrifies me. She always has done."

"And I don't?"

Her head turned. Her face was just outlined in the phosphorescent darkness.

"No," she said. "You don't. You never did. Somehow . . . I never really supposed you had killed Jarne. Oh, I reacted. For a few moments I just panicked, you know. But after you had called Grasse, and we were on course for Toulon, I suddenly had the wildest desire to say let's toss his body overboard and just sail and sail and sail."

"Only you didn't."

"It wouldn't have worked, would it?"

"It might have, for a while. If we'd got our story straight. On the other hand, I suppose it wouldn't have worked in the long run, for us. But if it's any consolation, I had exactly the same urge, almost immediately after finding his body. And at that time I supposed you had done it, because I knew I hadn't."

She smiled; her teeth flashed in the gloom. "I'm glad you wanted to do that."

"So maybe there'll be a next time, for you and me, on a boat."

"Maybe," she said.

"When this is sorted out. Did you know this was Lampagie's yacht?"

"No. But I imagine Lampagie likes her secrets."

"I'm inclined to agree with you," Angel said.

"Have you any idea why she chose to come along on this ride?"

"Only that she had an interest in the outcome."

Alison stared at the darkening sea. "So here we go on the merry-go-round all over again. How do you feel about it?"

"I'm beginning to wish I was still in Parkhurst."

"But you aren't, Tom," she pointed out. "So you had better come down heavily on one side or the other."

"Did you have any idea that Jarne had a shady past? I mean, criminally shady?"

Now she turned her head. "What on earth are you talking about?"

"My mistake, and it doesn't matter. Actually, it does matter. Your not knowing about Jarne, I mean."

"You are going to have to explain all of that," she said.

"I'd say the less you know about this entire business the better off you will be," Angel decided. "But I agree it leaves me with a problem. She has me across a barrel, you see. If I default on this one, then I'm proving my own guilt more conclusively than ever. And perhaps yours, by implication. If I go through with it, I can't escape the feeling that I'm falling in with some plan of hers."

"It's a bigger barrel than you think," Alison said. "She has a gun."

"By God." Angel slapped his pocket, discovered for the first time how empty it was.

"It's a fact," Alison said. "I picked up her overnight bag by mistake, and there is a revolver in it. I felt the shape through the canvas."

Angel stared into the darkness. "Do you think you could take her for a while? You're steering just south of south west. Try to hold two three five."

"Will do." She moved over; he had to retain his grip on the helm until her hand closed on the spoke, and their shoulders brushed. "What are you going to do?"

"First thing, regain control of the situation. Then perhaps the lady and I will have a chat."

"But you'll go through with the rendezvous?"

"As I said, I don't think either of us has too much choice."

She settled into the seat, and after a preliminary tremble the motor cruiser settled back on to course; but the seas were now starting to heave.

"Do be careful, Tom. She is probably the most dangerous woman you'll ever meet."

"I think I'm just generally unlucky when it comes to women," Angel said. "Although . . . you never know."

He climbed down the ladder. It was time to take a firm grip on himself. His trouble was that he was a very ordinary human being, not in the least cut out for the principal role in a murder case. He could still remember the feeling of total inadequacy he had known in her bedroom, and then *he* had held the gun.

This time he could not afford to make a mistake. Or be overwhelmed. But this time he had Alison to help him.

He opened the sliding door into the wheelhouse. It was empty, but Lampagie's overnight bag lay on the starboard settee berth, behind the dinette table. A break at last. Angel crossed the swaying deck, leaned over the table, and picked up the bag.

"I imagine this is what you are looking for," Lampagie said from the steps down to the saloon. She held the police revolver in her right hand.

CHAPTER 13

The airport bus deposited Harrington and sixty-odd others, sun-browned and happy at the end of their Riviera holiday, at the foot to the terminal building. Harrington lacked the tan, but he was as happy as anyone; he had drunk champagne from take off to touch down. And, having only an overnight bag, he was first through the barrier. It was just half-past nine.

Well, he thought, he had every reason to be happy. Angel's escaping, which might have turned out to be a disaster had he not been on the spot, had been neatly channelled into a tremendous success. Because it would get rid of both the bitches in one sweep, and leave him with only Smith and the crew on his plate. But Smith and the crew he could trust. They would ask nothing but their share of the money, and then quickly disappear. If they made trouble, they would be sending themselves to gaol.

Everything had really turned out very well.

And to top it all, he had got that marvellous hunk of woman into bed. For how long had he wanted to do that? Now he could let her go to her death without the slightest regret. For now there would be only Shelley, and total respectability.

As if, so far as any human being knew, there had ever been any-thing else but total respectability.

"Hi." Shelley wore a pink minidress.

He kissed her on the mouth, stood back to look at her. "You almost look as if you've been missing me. I've only been gone thirty-six hours."

"It was a long night," she said. "The car's outside."

He followed her down the stairs. She looked so neat, so proper, and so ladylike. A lot of leg, but everyone showed a lot of leg nowadays, providing they had legs worth showing. For the rest, her hair was neatly combed, and she wore a little summer hat, in straw with a flower on the brim. Her shoes were white high-heeled sandals, and she carried a white handbag. In leather, of course. Shelley Beattie would never settle for anything artificial.

So, starting at this moment, he must put artificiality behind himself. He sat beside her and she started the engine. "How were things?"

"Chaotic. They always are on occasions like this."

"And how was Mrs. Jarne?"

"Upset. More about her finances than about his death, though, I think."

"Are they bad, then?"

"They are nonexistent," Harrington said happily.

"What's she like?" Shelley drove into the tunnel. "I've seen photographs of her in the newspapers, of course."

"I think the best thing I can say is that she is exactly like her picture in the newspapers. Very composed, very calm, even in circumstances like these. I shouldn't think anyone but me would guess how much she has on her mind."

"And of course, she is very beautiful," Shelley said.

"Oh, very. But hers is the sort of beauty that frightens men."

Shelley concentrated while they negotiated the various roundabouts and got the car on to the motorway leading into London. Then she said, "Do you believe this rumour that has cropped up in one of the evening papers? That Mr. Jarne was mixed up in diamond smuggling?"

"Got here already, has it?" Harrington asked. "I'm afraid it's true."

"How can you know?" Shelley asked.

Harrington leaned back and smiled. "Because I'm the one who put the police on to it."

The car slowed as she turned her head. "You, Martin? I don't understand."

"You can't work as closely with someone as I have worked with Jarne over the past five years and not get to know all about him. You observe little things," Harrington said pompously. "And you start to think. And when you are trained as I am to check on every detail, you start to wonder. Take his finances, for instance. They were in a razor edge state all the while. He lived like a millionaire, and everyone thought he was a millionaire, including Lampagie, incidentally, but there was no cash around. And yet there always was, when it was needed. Things like that, and a whole lot more, which convinced me that he had some private means, or some private life, of which I knew nothing."

"So you decided to find out," Shelley said. The car engine missed. "Oh, bother," she said. "What shall I do?"

"You'll have to pull off the motorway," Harrington said. "At the next shoulder. I'll have a look under the hood. You *do* have petrol?"

Shelley peered at the dials. "Oh, bother. I don't think I remembered to fill her up."

Harrington raised his eyes to heaven. "Well, then, pull on to the shoulder just along there. The next service station is about half a mile down the road. We can walk along and get some petrol."

"Will do." Shelley eased the car into the inside lane, and then on to the shoulder. It was quite dark now, but the night was far from quiet as the endless row of cars hurtled past a few feet on their right.

*

Douce hit the first big wave, and gave a little skip across the crest. They were moving away from the shelter of the land. Angel sat down, and Lampagie leaned against the bulkhead.

"I suppose," he said regretfully, "that I am the biggest fool who ever lived. I mean, I knew you had to be involved, from the start. And yet I let you lead me around by the nose, all the time."

"That, I regard as a compliment." She came into the wheelhouse, holding on to the grabrail with her left hand. "I take it Alison is on the helm?"

"Not steady enough for you?"

"I imagine it will get more bumpy than this." She sat in the helmsman's seat, gazing at him from behind the revolver. "I just wanted to know where she was. But I'd like to talk with her as well. Before you get her down, though, will you tell me why you came looking for this gun?"

"It seemed rather a good idea, a few minutes ago. After all, I stole it in the first place. I have never owned a gun in my life, before. It really is remarkable, though, how quickly you can get used to the feel of having one in your pocket. Now I feel positively lonely without it."

"And how did you know where it was to be found, so exactly?"

"Alison spotted it."

"And it was her suggestion that you come down and regain possession of it, I imagine," Lampagie said. "I wouldn't be surprised if she is

up there waiting for the sound of the shot. So let's disappoint her."
She reversed the revolver and held it out, butt first. "Don't you want
it any more?"

Angel considered the weapon, and the woman. "Have you ever had
the feeling that life has got completely out of control?"

"No," Lampagie said. "I believe that life, or one's place in life, at
any rate, should always be very strictly controlled." She leaned forward, placed the gun on the table. "And I should think that I have
had even more shocks than you, these last few days. Just for the
record, and for the last time, I did not know that Justin was a
diamond smuggler, and I did not kill him. Or arrange to have him
killed. As regards the first, I suppose I have been somewhat
complacent and somewhat blind. He had a great deal of money; he
was an international figure here on the Riviera and in the Mediterranean generally, and he offered me a good home and unlimited security. Or so it seemed. Although I come from a very good family, the
trouble with the age in which we live, Angel, is that the very good
families no longer have any money, and so it is necessary for a young
woman to take care of herself, instead of merely waiting to inherit
when Daddy drops dead. So no doubt you will say I was utterly cold
blooded and deserved everything I got. But I did get it, Angel. My
four-year prison sentence was quite as rough as your three-year term, I
do assure you of that. As for Justin's death, as I now know that the
police were working themselves up to arrest him in the very near future in any event, presumably I would then have been destitute in any
event, and even more unfortunately, I would have been lumbered
with a husband who was in prison, whereas now I am at least free to
starve in my own fashion. But I do intend to clear myself of any possible implication in his murder."

"I think we've been through all this before." Angel picked up the
revolver, broke it, checked the chambers to make sure it was still
loaded, and replaced it in his pocket. "As there has to be a woman involved, you are not going to try to convince me that Alison is the
guilty party?"

"Of course."

"How do you propose to do that?"

"By using your own method. You explained to me that once you
started with the premise that you were not guilty, it was merely necessary to work out how the crime could have been committed by some-

one else, sticking you with the dead body. Well, if I start with the premise that I am not guilty, it seems to me that the whole question of my guilt hinges on the fact that I am the only person who could have given the murderers that vital piece of information, the time of your departure from Antibes and your destination, which would have enabled them to intercept *Twin Tempest*. Right?"

"You said it. Not me."

"But, if I start from the premise that I am not guilty, Angel, only one person could have done it. Don't you agree?"

"Except that no one went ashore but you, Mrs. Jarne."

"No one, Angel? Did no one even step off the ship between the time Justin told us of his plans and your departure?"

Angel frowned. "Alison got the champagne from the boot of your car."

"Which was parked next to a telephone booth, you may remember, and on the far side of the harbour office from *Twin Tempest*."

"Good God," Angel said.

"And then, of course, Alison also served the champagne later on. After you had put to sea, and after you had drunk quite a lot of Justin's. That is, she didn't wish you to fall asleep too soon. She had to make sure that you would stay asleep until at least dawn."

"But she also was drugged."

"Of course. More drugged than you were, according to what you have told me. She took hers four hours after you, at the end of her watch."

Angel scratched his head. "That kid?"

"That kid, I should imagine, is a very hardened criminal. Don't you think you should ask her about it?"

"Take the helm for a moment," he said, and went outside. "Alison," he called.

"Thank God you're back," she said. "She's getting a bit hard to hold."

The sea had suddenly become an endless mass of whitecaps.

"So come below," Angel said. "We'll steer her from inside."

She came down the ladder, went inside, stared at Lampagie. "Is she . . . ?"

"Oh, I am all right, darling," Lampagie said. "Angel and I have sorted out our little difference." She let him take the helm. "I'd like to talk to you, though, about Martin Harrington."

"Harrington?" Angel turned away from the wheel without meaning to. Now they were well south of the Hyères Islands and the waves were distinctly lumpy, throwing the motor boat from side to side and occasionally causing the engine to race as the ship galloped down a particularly steep trough.

But he couldn't afford to reduce speed, if he was to catch *Twin Tempest* within the next couple of hours.

"I'd say," Lampagie remarked, "that it has all been a little too pat. Sending us out here on a wild goose chase?"

"But he is out here as well," Alison said. "Waiting for us on *Twin Tempest.*"

"Is he?" Lampagie demanded. "Suppose *Twin Tempest* isn't out there? Won't Angel just have proved his guilt all over again by forcing me to take him down to my motor boat and attempting to leave France? Mightn't that even point me up as his accomplice?"

"And you seriously suppose that if I were involved in such a plan I would have come along on a trip like this?" Alison asked.

Lampagie smiled at her. "Why not? I have come along, and you seriously supposed that I was involved. But there will have to be a reason, Alison my dear, and I should like you to tell us what it is."

Douce was fighting back now, twisting to and fro in the buffeting waves, kicking against the helm. The wind had started to howl, and Angel even had difficulty in hearing the two women. He wondered if they had any idea at all that, apart from the machinations of their various friends and accomplices, they might be in some danger from the sea itself, before the night was finished.

"I think you are talking nonsense, Mrs. Jarne," Alison said. "*Twin Tempest* will be waiting for us."

"What do you think, Angel?" Lampagie asked.

Angel had been looking into the radar screen. "I've stopped thinking, Mrs. Jarne. Because there *is* a ship ahead of us, right now."

Lampagie got to her feet, appeared to realise for the first time that the sea had got up, and staggered across the wheelhouse. She grasped the grabrail, brought herself back to the console, peered into the screen. "Twelve miles," she said, and looked at the chronometer. "It's only seven minutes to one, Angel."

"So the stern seas have been pushing us a bit faster than they ought. But now I have her in my sights I can either slow down a little, or I can catch her up even quicker."

"I wouldn't dally," Alison said. "It's rough out there."

Lampagie looked through the window; the crests were now starting to break, and spray was flying, still mostly from astern.

"Will this boat take a gale, Angel?"

"Up to a point, Mrs. Jarne."

"Life jackets," Alison said. "I suppose you do have life jackets, Mrs. Jarne?"

"In the cockpit locker."

"Well, I think we had better put them on." She pulled open the sliding glass door to the cockpit, and shuddered as a big sea broke against the transom and cascaded white water around her feet. A good deal of it got in the door to soak the carpet.

"Shut it, for God's sake," Lampagie shouted.

Alison slammed the door behind her as she went outside.

"Are we in danger, Angel?"

"Not so long as everything works. Sorry you came?"

Lampagie stared into the night. But the glow of the cabin lights shut out the night; all they could see was the breaking of the waves close at hand, and the swell of foam racing away from the bows.

"No," she said. "I had forgotten what it was like, to be at sea in a storm. Is there anything more exhilarating?"

"It's nicer looking back on," he said. "I think you'd better kill those lights. I'll be able to see more of what is happening, and they won't be able to see us so well, except on the box." He shut down the navigation lights as well; according to the radar there was only the other ship in the vicinity, and she was still ten miles away, although closing rapidly. He listened to the throb of the engines; they sounded all right, as they had looked all right earlier. But he did not know them. And on them everything depended; engine failure in these conditions would result in *Douce* turning beam on to the seas, and if she did not roll over it would not take that much to swamp her.

But at least half the responsibility of avoiding that catastrophe had to be his, and already rivers of pain were running up and down his shoulders from the strain of holding the ship in front of the waves.

The noise of the wind and the sea boomed again as the sliding door opened to readmit Alison. She was soaking wet, but carried three life jackets. "I really would feel happier if we put these on."

She was a very efficient crew.

"I'll do his." Lampagie dropped the jacket over Angel's head, pulled the cords tight around his waist, tied a bow. "You look splendid."

"I wish I could say the same for you," he said, when she had tied her own. "Somehow there seems just too much of everything. Now, I'd like you to take over the radar watch."

Lampagie buried her face in the eye shade, twiddled the brightness control. "Range eight miles," she said. "I suppose he can see us just as well as we can see him."

"Every time we come out of a wave," Angel said. "But he's fairly constant, is he?"

"Yes," she said.

"Then I imagine he's a pretty big boat."

Her head came up, and he glanced at her. They could both pray, he supposed.

"Can't I be of any help?" Alison asked.

"Just hold tight."

A larger than usual wave slammed against *Douce*'s quarter, and tried to spin her round. Angel cursed under his breath and gave hard left rudder; he didn't fancy taking any seas on the beam in these conditions, certainly in this make of boat. *Douce* straightened and mounted the next wave at an exact right angle. For a moment they climbed, and then hung on the crest, slowly gathering speed as the wave surged forward.

"Christ almighty," Angel said. He watched the engine revolution counter, which had been hovering just under the twenty-five hundred mark, moving past the three thousand, and closed the throttle. But the needle refused to come back, and now they were over the crest of the wave and aiming downwards. In front of him there was nothing but blackness.

"She won't do it," Alison gasped.

"I've lost my friend," Lampagie remarked, still deep in the neon world of the radar screen.

Angel closed his fingers on the wheel tightly; he dared not let her deviate an inch. *Douce* raced down the trough, propelled by the breaking crest which was now under her stern, lifting and pushing. Her bows went into the back of the next wave, in and in and in. Green water rose up over her pulpit, drowned her anchor, came smashing aft. From below there was the crash of shattering glass.

"Oh, God," Alison shouted.

Angel could see nothing but green over the windshield. But it was whitening as it broke, and now he could feel the bows lifting. She was a better boat than he could have hoped, had cut her way through several tons of water. Alison had fallen over on to the seat, and Lampagie was holding on with all her strength.

"Up she comes," Angel said.

"Let's hope there aren't too many like that wandering around," Lampagie said. "It even showed on the screen."

"Um," Angel agreed. He could see the bow again now, clear of water, tossing spray backwards, preparing to hit the next wave, coming to life as the sea issued its challenge. He gave the helm half a turn to starboard to straighten the yacht up for the next crest, and the wheel spun free in his hand.

"Angel," Alison screamed.

"God damn and blast," he shouted. "Grab something."

He held on to the spinning wheel, Lampagie threw both arms around the display unit. *Douce*, having started her turn, kept on going, and was struck on the beam by the next wave, fortunately a moderate one. Yet she went right down on her port hull, engines screaming as the starboard propeller came free, and sagged there for a moment before turning back. Angel closed the throttles.

And that had been a small one.

"What happened?" Lampagie asked, her voice remarkably calm.

"The steering has gone. Maybe there was just a shade too much strain last time round. Or maybe there was a fault in the wire from the beginning. When last did you have it checked?"

"The steering? I don't think I have ever had it serviced. I mean, I really never expected to take her out in something like this."

"God save me from women owners," Angel grumbled. He had one hand on each throttle control, and now he gave her a burst ahead on the starboard engine to bring the bows straight for the next wave. But to steer her on throttles alone meant he had to reduce speed to only a crawl, and now the waves were catching up with them. *Douce* settled into the trough of the next big swell comfortably enough, but water slapped over her stern. There was actually less violent movement now she was no longer hurrying, but she rolled viciously. And what would happen when the next really big one came along didn't bear thinking about.

Every rule of survival at sea demanded that he turn her to take the waves bow on; that way he would keep her going in some safety for as long as his fuel supply lasted.

But to do that meant abandoning his last hope of keeping the rendezvous.

He switched on the electric bilge pump, gave a burst on the port engine. "Have you got our friend back yet?" he asked.

Lampagie was tenderly feeling her left eyebrow. "I think I am going to have a black eye."

"Tell me where that ship is."

"You are a harsh and brutal skipper, Captain Bligh," she remarked, but she turned back to the set. "About four miles. I think he must be coming this way."

"Well, he'd better hurry. Take the ship, Alison. Can you steer on the throttles?"

"I'll try." She grasped the levers.

Angel switched on the transmitter. "Pan, pan, pan," he said into the microphone. "Pan, pan, pan. *Douce, Douce, Douce,* calling. I am thirty-six miles south south east of Cape Sicie, in heavy seas, with my steering broken. I say again, I am thirty-six miles south south east of Cape Sicie, in heavy seas, with my steering broken. I have a vessel four miles south west of me on my radar screen. Would she reply, please? Over."

He flicked the switch, and Lampagie raised her head to look at him.

But the reply came back both quickly and loudly. "*Douce, Douce, Douce,*" said the strangely familiar voice. "*Soft Lady, Soft Lady, Soft Lady* calling *Douce.* We have you on our screen, man. I say again, we have you on our screen. Are you in immediate danger of sinking? Over."

"By Christ," Angel said.

"Friend of yours?" Lampagie asked.

"At least they sound English," Alison remarked.

"*Douce, Douce, Douce,*" the voice said. "*Douce, Douce, Douce, Soft Lady, Soft Lady, Soft Lady* calling *Douce.* I can still see you on my screen, but I cannot hear you, man. Are you all right, *Douce?* Over."

"You have to answer," Alison shouted. "Or we *will* sink. There may not be any other ship for miles."

"There isn't," Lampagie agreed from the radar screen. "And he will have to come if you do call, Angel, no matter who he is. There could just be another ship listening."

"He'll have thought of that one too," Angel muttered. But there was his proof. He would never find any more. Whatever risks were involved.

Besides, he *had* recognised the voice, and the anger was back, bubbling in his belly.

"*Soft Lady, Soft Lady, Soft Lady,*" he said. "*Douce, Douce, Douce* calling *Soft Lady*. I would be grateful for a tow into Toulon or any French port. Over."

"*Douce, Douce*. Of course, man," came the voice. "We shall be with you in half an hour. You send up a flare in twenty-five minutes so we don't make any mistakes. Got to go now. *Soft Lady* over and out."

Angel replaced the microphone on its bracket slowly. As he did so a wave struck *Douce* again, and over she went once more; he lost his footing and his handhold and fell across the table. Lampagie still grimly clung to the radar set. But now there came an ominous slurping sound from beneath them. Fortunately, he reflected, it would take more than a little water to kill a pair of diesels.

"Well?" Lampagie demanded.

Angel pulled himself up, looked at Alison. "You wouldn't like to choose this moment to declare once and for all how you fit into this?"

"I told you . . ."

"Because it's shortly going to be a case of we all pull together or we'll all sink separately."

That voice. That ship. *Soft Lady,* not *Twin Tempest.* Roaring towards them through the storm. With who on board? With how many on board?

And coming to their rescue?

"*Did* you know that voice?" Lampagie asked.

"I think so. How far now?"

She thrust her face against the eyepiece. "Just over two miles. We should be able to see her. But Angel . . ." For the first time in their brief acquaintance it occurred to him that she sounded a little afraid.

"She's the one we came looking for," he said. "Whoever she is."

He hunted through the lockers, found a Very pistol and a handful of cartridges. He jammed a red one into the breech, closed the pistol, waited his moment, and pulled open the sliding door. The wind howled at him like an animal, and struck at him, too. It was still getting up. A wave slapped *Douce*'s stern, and spray splattered in his face like a handful of gravel. But she was still afloat and taking the seas well. Alison was a very capable young woman. On the other hand, the seas hadn't reached their peak yet by a long way. He pointed the pistol into the air and fired.

The glowing orange ball arced over his head, and then hung, perhaps a hundred feet above the yacht. If *Soft Lady* was within two miles her crew would see that without difficulty. But just to be sure, he fitted another cartridge into the chamber and sent that after the first.

"Aren't they beautiful?" Lampagie shouted.

Angel closed the door behind him, pushed wet hair from his forehead. Time to plan. If this was to be a proper rescue, the larger boat would come close on the leeward side of the stricken motor cruiser, and they would heave her a line. And that would have to be made fast forward, which involved someone going up on the foredeck. Which meant he had better start finding and rigging a life line.

But this might not be a proper rescue. What would they intend?

He glanced at the two women. Lampagie still watched the screen, face lost in the eye shade, legs spread wide, feet anchored on the deck, brown hands tensed as they gripped the handholds on either side of the display unit. She seemed to have quite recovered her courage. Or her confidence? In what? Or whom?

Alison worked the throttles with equal efficiency. She also did not seem afraid.

But then, she had not been afraid when she had thought herself alone on board a boat with a murderer.

Because she had known from the start that he was not, could not be, a murderer?

It occurred to him that if he ever did get out of this mess he was going to be the greatest misogynist the world had ever known.

But the boat out there would know that their woman was on board, and would have to act accordingly. In fact, they would be expecting her to assist them, at the vital moment. By doing what? The only idea they could have in mind would be that Angel and whichever of the women was innocent should not get back again. But how could their woman help them in that? Was she supposed to be armed?

But even if she was armed, if they were intending to fake a shipwreck, they wouldn't want to risk a body being picked up by another ship, with a hole in it.

So, why have her along at all?

"By Christ," he said.

"What's the matter now?" Lampagie asked, without raising her head. "They're only a mile away."

"They mean to do us all."

"Eh?" Now her head did come up.

"You didn't suppose they intended to rescue us, did you?"

"Well, I . . ." She frowned. "I suppose I didn't."

"They just mean to be sure that we go down, and can be considered lost at sea. For them, this is the best weather they could possibly have. And just supposing anyone else was listening to our conversation just now, they are doing all the right things, rushing to our assistance. But they won't get here in time."

"Oh, they must," Lampagie said. "They're less than a mile off, and we're not going to sink that quickly. If we sink at all. I mean, Angel, why start coming in this direction if they just wanted us to sink?"

"Because, Mrs. Jarne, as you have just pointed out, the odds are that we shall *not* sink, unless they are here to help us."

"That ridiculous," Alison said, giving the port engine a burst. "I mean . . ."

"That there should be someone on board they will want to pick up?" Angel asked. "I wouldn't count on that. They mightn't want her around any more, either, now she's done her bit."

They both stared at him for a moment, and then Alison turned back to the helm, and in the same instant screamed, "Look."

Angel swung round as *Douce* rolled down the side of a trough. Seeming to hang immediately above them, although she was at least two crests away, was a large motor fishing vessel, a sea-going juggernaut of heavy wooden timbers and an iron-bound stem, with a forward wheelhouse and an enormous diesel sending her ploughing through the waves at an unchanging ten knots, while aft a steadying sail reduced her big, slow roll. She was all in darkness, and looked the more sinister for that.

"She hasn't seen us," Alison shouted. "Send up another flare."

"She's seen us, all right," Angel muttered. But *Soft Lady* was disappearing again, sinking into the following trough, although she was now so close that her radio aerial and the radar scanner on her wheelhouse roof remained visible.

But the next time she appeared . . .

"She's going to run us down," Lampagie breathed, at last raising her eyes from the radar screen. "What must we do, Angel?"

Angel pushed Alison out of the way, grasped the throttles, put the port engine astern and the starboard ahead, and watched *Douce's* bows come round. But only slowly. The next wave picked them up and carried them sideways far more quickly than his engine manoeuvring could adjust their speed. *Soft Lady* appeared, right alongside, still shrouded in utter darkness. She looked distressingly dangerous, a ghost ship determined on destruction. Then she was swept astern.

"Oh, well done," Lampagie said.

Alison moaned.

Angel put both engines full ahead and skated down the next wave, looked over his shoulder, and watched the big ship turning in their wake, rolling scuppers under in the heavy seas. He tried to think, with desperate haste. He had really only delayed the inevitable. Without steering he could neither keep *Douce* on a straight course away from the danger, nor manoeuvre fast enough to avoid a collision indefinitely. And to abandon ship would be worse than useless; in the life raft they'd be absolutely helpless.

"Our only chance is to get on board her," he said. "Outside."

For those huge bows were back, hardly more than a ship's length astern. Angel opened the sliding door, dragged Lampagie into the cockpit. A wave struck the motor cruiser and the woman fell across the transom. Angel had to grab her legs to stop her being swept overboard.

She sat up, stared at the thirty tons of wood and metal riding down on them. "I couldn't get up there," she shouted. Water had extinguished the effervescence of that shining hair, as it had swept her scarf away. "*You* get them, Angel."

Alison had also come into the cockpit; one arm was wrapped around the ladder leading to the flying bridge while the other waved frantically. "No," she screamed, into the wind. "Peter. Martin. No, it's me."

The women didn't have a hope in hell, unless . . . Angel snapped his fingers with inspiration, dropped to his knees, tore open the aft locker. There, as he had hoped, was the kedge anchor, a light grapple with four flukes curving backwards; and already attached to the shackle was a length of nylon line. He freed the end, tied a bowline round Lampagie's waist, saw it settle under her shoulders.

"Climb if you can," he shouted. "If not, just hang on."

She nodded, still staring past him at the looming M.F.V.

"What about me?" Alison shrieked.

"Swim," Angel suggested, and left the cockpit, on the side away from the charging ship, the anchor and the coil of rope in his right hand while he clutched the grabrail with his left. On the heaving foredeck he dropped to his knees, shook his head to clear his eyes as a shower of spray rattled across him, and drew back his right arm. The M.F.V. was not twenty feet away; impact was going to be within two seconds. Angel hurled the grapple. It whipped up into the wind, and then descended on the deck of the M.F.V. with a crunch which was immediately lost in the roar as *Soft Lady* seemed to rise up in anger to crush the little yacht. Angel threw himself forward, wrapped both his arms around the huge anchor protruding from the hawsepipe in the bows of the fishing boat, and was struck a paralysing blow in the stomach and groin. An explosion of pain boomed away from his belly into his arms and legs, sent his head swinging. Yet through it all he heard the crunch from beneath him as wood bit into fibre glass. Then the pain reached his eyes and he had to shut them, while his arms and fingers seemed to lose their connection with his body as they clawed into the anchor.

A wave broke over him, and then another, and he realised to his amazement that he was still there, pinned to the bows of the M.F.V. as she came round and stuck her nose into two successive big ones. For a moment he couldn't breathe as salt water clogged his mouth and nose, but now at last the pain was beginning to recede. He shook his head to clear his eyes again, and looked astern. But astern there was nothing. The motor cruiser had gone down like a stone.

But the warp trailed away from the anchor he had thrown; the grapple had lodged itself on the iron horse surrounding the base of the fishing boat's mast.

There was shouting from above him. They had seen the trailing rope as well. He could wait no longer. He sucked air into his lungs and strength into his muscles, threw up his left hand to lodge his fingers on the rail, released the anchor, and followed with his right hand, giving himself a jerk upwards and at last finding a lodgement for his feet on the anchor itself as he half vaulted and half fell over the rail. He landed on his hands and knees on the foredeck, and slid across to the other side. Coming towards him from the wheelhouse was a big, heavy man clad in oilskins but capless, who now stopped in surprise at the sight of Angel getting up out of the scuppers.

"Well, for crying out loud," he said, his hand brushing the crisp black hair back from his forehead in a mixture of surprise and embarrassment.

"Hello, Dave," Angel said. "How's the wife?"

CHAPTER 14

"I'm sorry, Angel, man." Dave Bracken held on to the shrouds as he slowly came forward. "That's the way it goes."

"From the beginning?" Angel remained crouching against the rail, bracing himself to the roll of the ship, shoulders hunched under the spray which came flying over the bows with every wave.

"I liked you, man." Dave sounded positively distressed, although it was too dark to see his face properly. "But business is business. You know that, man."

"I'm beginning to find out," Angel agreed. His fingers closed on the revolver in his pocket. No doubt it would still fire, despite its soaking. He could use it now and drop Dave without ever letting him close. He could do that.

Trouble was, he had never shot anyone in his life.

"So what now, Dave?" he asked.

Dave stopped; he was only six feet away. His shoulders seemed to slump. "Man, you have to go. You must know that. There's too much at stake. You just have to go."

"And the women?"

"The women?" Dave asked. "You mean there was more than one?"

"Alison Somers was with us," Angel said. "I'd have thought someone would have told you that."

"Oh, Christ," Bracken said. And then shrugged. "But they've gone already. I don't think you have more than lumps of meat at the end of this rope."

And then he moved forward, with a surprising speed. Angel released the revolver and brought up his hands, and was amazed at the savage numbness which seemed to follow each blow. Bracken threw them from all angles. Angel caught the first three on his arms, and lost all feeling. His hands dropped and the next two thudded into his belly, and as his head came down, Bracken struck him on the chin.

It was difficult to tell which was deck and which was sky and which was breaking wave. He found himself in the starboard scuppers.

Bracken was breathing hard. "Man," he said. "You never learned nothing? You have to roll with the punches, Angel, man. You don't just stand there and take them, no matter how big you are."

Angel got back to his knees, his back once again braced against the rail of the rolling ship. He saw two prize fighters in front of him, but he supposed he would eventually discover which was which.

Bracken came in again. Now he had discarded the punching idea, had locked his two hands together, and reared above his victim. Angel threw both arms around the boxer's waist, and clutched. He could do nothing else.

A tremendous force descended on the back of his neck, seeming to dislodge his vertebrae and send them tumbling down to the base of his spine. For a moment he lost consciousness, but only for a moment, and his arms never slackened their grip around Bracken's waist. The M.F.V. slid down a trough and up another wave, and they lost their balance and rolled together, across the deck, to come to rest against the wheelhouse, while water scattered over them. Bracken moaned with pain, and struck again. But there was no strength left now. Only fear. And still Angel squeezed, expiating all the anger which had been bubbling inside his soul for three years. Another wave broke over them, and Bracken went limp. And still Angel squeezed, locking their bodies together, exerting all his tremendous strength.

It was not until he felt something give beneath him that he relaxed, and looked down. Bracken was unconscious. He might even be dead, Angel realised with horror. But the horror was at his own feeling of satisfaction.

And the night wasn't finished yet. The lights had come on in the wheelhouse, and the revolver still stuck in Angel's pocket. He rose to his knees, dragged out the gun, and was struck on the back by another wave; through the roaring of the water he heard the bang of the wheelhouse door. Smith had put her on auto and was coming out to see what had happened. Angel saw the man and the gun in the same instant, and fired. But the ship was rolling and the bullet went wide. And Smith also had a gun.

Fortunately he had stepped back as Angel fired, and so his own reply was wide. Angel slid down the deck as it fell away from him, gaining the far side of the wheelhouse, and looking aft, towards the saloon and the engine room, where the deckhouses were lower.

"Angel," Smith called, his voice high and drifting in the wind. "Throw out your gun and come forward. Or I'll cut Mrs. Jarne loose."

He was on the side where the warp trailed.

"I wouldn't," Angel shouted. "There are two women out there. One of them is Alison Somers."

There was no reply. Angel crawled aft, and watched Smith moving along the other side of the ship, pulling on the warp. Honour amongst thieves.

He took a long breath and stood up, holding on to the grabrail with his left hand, his right hand thrusting the revolver over the saloon roof.

"Drop it," he said.

Smith turned, and brought up his pistol. Angel found himself firing before he really intended to. The first bullet whined into the night, the second struck the cabin roof and ricochetted, the third hit Smith in the shoulder and half turned him round, the fourth exploded against his left side ribs and knocked him against the rail, and the fifth hit him on the head as he went down. Then there were several clicks as Angel found himself still pulling the trigger. And while he did that he slumped to his knees, and vomited.

There had been, after all, too much hate in his system. Too much anger. But now it was gone. His arm hung limp, and the next wave broke over him as it shifted Smith, and the spreading blood, farther down the deck.

All Angel wanted to do was sleep. And sleep and sleep and sleep.

And forget, perhaps.

Until he remembered. He scrambled to his feet, and ran round the deckhouse, and made his way aft, clutching the trailing rope. Beneath his feet the big Kelvin diesel chugged away happily; of all engines it was least likely to be disturbed by rough seas, and the autopilot was whirring with its usual reassurance. The ship was all right, making north, slowly and steadily, for France. With at least one dead man on board.

And how many dead women trailing astern?

He reached the rope, began pulling. He could see Lampagie now, supported by her bowline and her life jacket. But not using her arms. Because she was holding something. Something equally lifeless?

The rope burned his soaked fingers, but at least right aft he was less exposed to the waves breaking on the bow. And he panted, with fear as much as with exhaustion.

"Lampagie," he shouted. What a feeble croak. "Lampagie."

They were directly under the stern, and still Angel coiled in the warp, moving mechanically now, hand over hand.

"Lampagie," he mumbled.

"Well, take her," Lampagie shouted, from just beneath the rail.

Angel leaned over, grasped Alison's life jacket, pulled her across the rail and dumped her on the deck. Then he reached for Lampagie, grasped her hands, and dragged her up.

"I heard firing," she said.

"Mainly me."

She glanced at him, and then sank to her hands and knees on the deck. "God. Whoever said the Mediterranean was always warm?"

Alison had not moved.

"Is she all right?"

"I don't think so, Angel. We'd better get her inside."

Angel scooped her into his arms, made his way forward. The wheelhouse door still banged, and beyond was the lighted warmth of the saloon. How secure and dry it seemed, after the noise and the wet and the anger outside.

Angel laid Alison on the carpet, and Lampagie slammed the door.

"Who was that I fell over?" she asked.

"A man named Smith."

She hunted around, found the liquor locker, pulled out a bottle of brandy and drank, and then sat on the settee berth, shoulders drooping, water running out of her hair and down her face, gathering in a steady pool between her legs.

Angel knelt beside Alison, watched the foam bubbles gathering around her nostrils and at her mouth.

"Oh, Christ," he said.

"Give her the kiss of life," Lampagie suggested. "It cannot have happened more than a few seconds ago."

Angel held the girl's nose, placed his mouth on hers, pressed down on her belly with his other hand as he alternately blew and sucked.

"And if you have killed Smith you will need her as a witness." Lampagie drank some more brandy.

"I think the other one is alive. If he hasn't drowned as well."

"You mean there were two?" Lampagie flopped against the cushions. "You are quite a lad, Angel. When you get yourself worked up."

Angel released Alison, and she gasped for breath, and retched.

"Do you think you could keep her going?" he asked. "I have to see about Dave."

"Was that the voice on the radio telephone? Your friend?" She knelt beside the blond girl.

Angel paused to check the wheelhouse. But there was no need. This was an ocean-going ship, and although the seas were bigger than before, and the wind certainly stronger, *Soft Lady* ploughed her way steadily into them, tossing spray over her foredeck, slicing through each breaking crest as if it were a ripple, autopilot whirring and diesel throbbing relentlessly under the deck. Angel made sure they were on course for Toulon, and went on deck.

Both men lay where he had left them. Smith had drifted against the rail, Dave Bracken remained in a huddled mass against the wheelhouse bulkhead. Angel dragged Smith inside first. He was dead, with bullet wounds in his head and chest. Angel left him on the wheelhouse floor. Then he went out for Dave, was relieved to find that the ex-boxer still breathed. And was, indeed, trying to regain consciousness, face twisted with pain.

"You broke my ribs, man," he muttered at Angel.

"So now I'm taking you to a doctor," Angel said, and braced his back against the bulkhead to lift his friend up, and carry him also into the wheelhouse.

"I guess you're pretty sore," Bracken gasped.

"Pretty," Angel agreed. "Every time I turn around I seem to lose another friend."

"Man," Bracken began, and then his face twisted as he doubled up with pain.

"What's the matter with him?" Lampagie asked from the saloon doorway.

"A broken rib. Maybe more. Do you think you could spare him some of that brandy?"

"I imagine so." Lampagie tossed her head. "She's awake."

Angel returned to the saloon, where Alison was propped against the settee berth.

"Oh, Christ," she muttered. "Oh, Christ. They tried to kill me. Oh, Christ."

Angel sat above her. "That's right," he said. "But they didn't quite make it, thanks to Lampagie and me. So why don't you work out which side your bread is buttered on, and tell us about it?"

Her head came up, blond hair plastered to her cheeks and neck in wisps; her eyes gloomed at him.

"It might make it a lot easier on yourself," Angel said.

"Where's Peter?" she asked.

"Peter?"

"Peter Smith. Wasn't he on board?"

"He was," Angel said. "I'm afraid he's dead."

"Oh, Christ," she repeated, and her shoulders drooped.

"Friend of yours?" Angel asked.

Her eyes came up again. They were filled with tears. "Martin too?" she whispered.

"Harrington isn't on board," Angel said.

"But . . ." She bit her lip.

"I think you have been scuppered but good," Angel said. "I'm sorry about your friend Peter. Believe me. On a caper like this someone was certain to get killed. I think we're a trifle lucky to have got away with just one, even if from your point of view it was the wrong one. And if it's any consolation, he lost his life through trying to save you when he realised what had happened."

"Your friend Dave is moaning and groaning," Lampagie said. "But I think he'll survive." She sat beside Angel. "Well, Alison, darling, all the chickens have come home to roost."

"Not quite," Angel said. "But Alison is going to co-operate. Aren't you, sweetheart?"

She looked from one face to the other, and her shoulders sagged. "Does it matter?"

"To me," Angel said.

"And remarkably enough, to me also," Lampagie said. "I am wondering if you did not know more about my husband than I ever did."

"Oh, him," Alison said, in tones of the most utter contempt.

"Him," Angel said. "And me. And Francine Dow. And your friend Peter Smith. And even, perhaps, Martin Harrington. And Dave Bracken, of course. Rehearse what you are going to tell the police for me, Alison. Just so we know what to expect."

"Why should I?" Alison demanded. "Why should I put you in the clear?"

Lampagie knelt beside her. "Because, darling, he is in the clear in any event. Tonight has proved that. And because if you don't tell us exactly what was going on, and exactly who killed my husband, he is going to break every bone in your body. Aren't you, Angel?"

Alison gazed at Angel.

"And he's awfully good at it," Lampagie said. "He showed me, last night."

"Oh, what the hell," Alison said. "Jarne? Jarne was nothing but a pimp, really."

"On second thoughts, I might have a go at you myself," Lampagie said thoughtfully.

"I'm telling the truth," Alison insisted. "That's how he began. Five girls and five London apartments. Just after the war. Oh, he always thought big. And while he had been in the Army he had made the acquaintance of this man who had a foolproof method of getting diamonds out of Kimberley. But at that time it was just a dream. An idea, between the pair of them. Then Jarne found he could market the stones in England, and he put his girls to work, travelling. And he built up the chain. The stones came up to Morocco or Tunis, Jarne picked them up in his boat, and sometime during the summer he contacted one of his girls, who'd be cruising with her special friend, and they'd take them back to England. It was really very simple."

"You worked for Jarne *then?*" Angel demanded.

"For God's sake, do I look that old? Of course not. But the time came, seven years ago, when Justin decided to retire. His original contact in South Africa had died, and he didn't altogether get on with the new lot. By then he was building up his legitimate business interests, and he wanted to get away from any association with the smuggling or the girls. But he still retained an over-all interest. After all, he had created the chain. His successor was to pay a royalty."

"And who was his successor?" Lampagie asked, her voice cold.

Alison sucked air through her nostrils, noisily. "Peter. Peter Smith. So each girl had her local pimp, you see. This was part of the system, not only for her protection, but to accompany her on her summer trips. Peter was one of them, and he was the one Jarne picked as the next leader. Then Justin just moved out, earned world-wide fame as the wizard financier in charge of the J and J Corporation, and spent most of his time cruising in the Med." She glanced at Lampagie. "And marrying. He'd already been married once, but she had left

him. Now he started going through them pretty rapidly. I think you
had just about completed the course, Mrs. Jarne."

"Stick to the facts, darling," Lampagie suggested.

Alison shrugged.

"And then Smith got the idea he could do away with Jarne's ten
per cent," Angel suggested.

"Thirty," Alison said. "Thirty per cent. But Peter had no idea of
ever taking over from Jarne. He was too frightened of him. Justin
could be a terrible man. And he was utterly ruthless. You knew that,
Mrs. Jarne."

"I knew that," Lampagie agreed.

"So he had laid it on the line for Peter. 'I have friends, Peter,' he'd
said. 'They worry about me. And if anything ever happens to me, I've
told them where to look.'"

"So what changed Smith's mind about the risk?" Angel asked.

"Martin," Alison explained. "It all happened because of you and
Francine Dow. She was the first one of Jarne's couriers ever to be
picked up. And Peter got scared. He tried to contact Justin, and Justin
wouldn't have anything to do with it. So Peter lost his head and went
to see him, openly, at the J and J building. You can imagine, Justin
was furious. He virtually had him thrown out; the responsibility for
anything going wrong was Peter's, not his. But Martin overheard
some of the conversation, and it made him think. A lot about Justin
had apparently made him think, already. At this time, you see, he was
a legitimate accountant, handling Justin's affairs. I suppose he must
always have had a bent streak, though. He went after Peter and
conned him into spilling the situation, and then thought some more.
Because what interested Martin, you see, was not the actual
smuggling; he agreed with Peter that the whole thing was far too dangerous, and it was his idea in fact that they shut down the chain, although Peter told Justin that it was only a temporary stoppage, until
they could be sure that Francine hadn't actually spilled anything to
the police.

"But Martin wanted to know what had happened to Justin's share
of the profits. Over fifteen years he had taken a minimum of thirty per
cent out of the gross, in cash, and Martin, who handled all of Justin's
business, knew that very little of that money had ever come back into
circulation. Only now and then, when Justin really seemed to be stuck
for cash, there was suddenly a large amount available. But when Mar-

tin sat down to calculate just what was outstanding, he got to a figure of something like four million quid, just put aside, somewhere, and apparently in notes."

"Four million pounds?" Lampagie whispered.

"And Martin figured he knew where it was," Alison said. "In the course of his duties as Justin's private secretary he had come across the rental for several large safe deposit boxes in a West End bank, but so far as he could see they were used neither for the business nor Justin's private papers. He mentioned it to Justin, and was told to mind his own business. Justin could be very brusque. That settled it for Martin. He began to watch, and plan, and at last, by the old subterfuge of the two papers, you know, got Justin to sign an authority for him to have access to the boxes. But of course he had already begun to plan the murder as well, because he did not dare use the authority while Justin was alive, as the bank keeps a record of everyone who uses their boxes, and Justin would have been sure to find out. Martin was every bit as afraid of Justin as Peter was."

"But they couldn't just have him killed," Lampagie said thoughtfully, "because when the police started to investigate they might find out about the smuggling." She frowned. "But the police were on to him anyway."

Alison almost smiled. "Martin wasn't afraid of the police, Mrs. Jarne. It was he who had given the information which first led them to investigate Justin at all. He was the honest secretary and accountant who had inadvertently stumbled upon his employer's guilty secret and couldn't keep quiet about it, because of his conscience. It was a part of the murder plan, and was done a month before Angel came out of prison, so that they would just have started their investigation when the murder was committed. No, like Peter, Martin had to be clear with Justin's friends."

"The Big People," Angel murmured.

"That's right. The Big People. They had to be satisfied. But by now Martin had discovered the perfect murderer."

"Thomas Percival Angel," Angel said. "And he was willing to wait three years, for me?"

"What are three years, with a certain four million on the end of it? But in any event, it took very nearly three years to set everything up. First of all we had to find someone in prison who could get close to you, and find out what you were like, how you might react to various situations, and who could take care of you, too, and keep you out of trouble, so that you'd be sure to get maximum remission. Fortunately, Peter knew Dave already, and Dave was a natural for joining us, because he had been in the Navy and knew ships and the sea. Then we had to buy this boat, and Peter had to come down here every summer to establish that he was the owner and that he spent his summers in the Med. Martin thought of everything, to make quite sure no one could ever come back to any of the four of us. It was a million each, with not a single tie."

"And he even had Francine murdered too," Angel said.

"Just before you got out. Dave rang her up and asked to meet her on a lonely street, and when she went down there, Peter knocked her over with a stolen truck. Martin wanted the news of her death to knock *you* over with surprise and shock and maybe anger, to unsettle you and make you more certain to take the job. But he always figured you would go along to see Dave, and he knew that once Dave told you the deal sounded all right that would satisfy you."

"And where did you fit into the scheme?" Lampagie asked.

"I was Peter's girl." Alison looked at the dead body in the wheelhouse. "Up to tonight I thought I was still Peter's girl. But they wanted someone close to Justin. Believe it or not, I was his body-guard. Because had anything happened to him before we were ready, or perhaps even before we knew about it, the police might have got on to the safe deposit boxes and we'd have been left with nothing. There was also the possibility that Justin might remove the cash himself. That was my responsibility. I just had to keep him real happy, happier than ever before in his life. So he liked a lot of women," Alison said, with some satisfaction. "But he always came back to me in the end. Whatever he did or said, I just smiled and took it and got on with being good to him. I think I could have had him divorce you to marry me, Lampagie, if I'd really wanted to."

"Only you didn't really want to," Lampagie said. "You hated him."

"Oh, sometimes. Always, I think, when we were apart. When we were together, I often loved him. There was something about him . . ."

"And you also had to drug the champagne, and make sure *Soft Lady* was overhauling you on schedule," Lampagie said. "But weren't you taking the biggest risk? Actually being on board the ship at the time of the murder? You could easily have been arrested."

Alison shook her head. "They couldn't hold me. It was a physical impossibility for me to strangle Justin like that."

"You could have been accused of working with Angel."

"We had never seen each other before, or even heard of each other. The police had to fall down on any attempt to link us together. Besides, I acted the complete innocent, forced him to telephone Grasse. I told you, Dave had studied Angel's character pretty closely, in gaol. We had a good idea how he would react."

"And Dave had also assured you that I wouldn't cut loose and go for you when I found Jarne dead," Angel said thoughtfully. "But you still held on to your little gun, just in case."

"Well, there was no point in taking an unnecessary risk. None of us was to do that. It was the perfect crime. It just couldn't go wrong."

"Except that you had, after all, picked the wrong man," Lampagie said. "Angel had far more intelligence and far more guts than you had reckoned."

Alison shook her head. "It should still have been the perfect crime. Maybe we hadn't really expected him to work out how it was done. But even after Angel had done that, all Martin had to do last night was call the police and have him arrested. Even if they had believed his story, I don't see how they could ever have traced it back to any of us. I had washed the glasses and got rid of any trace of the drugged champagne. The whole situation would have been so confused that I think they would have got nowhere. And Angel's theory would have remained only a theory, whereas he *did* have the motive, the opportunity, and the strength for committing the murder. I tried to tell Martin this, last night, after you had gone to bed, but he wouldn't listen. He must have lost his nerve. That was certainly something we had not anticipated. His whole idea was to get you out here where Peter and Dave could sink you, apparently while you were trying to get away."

"With you on board as well?" Angel asked.

"I was his insurance that you would keep the rendezvous. Martin was very good at closing every possible loophole. You all would have kidnapped me, you see. Then when *Douce* blew up and sank, I was to be the only survivor, picked up by the cruising English yacht *Soft Lady*." Her breathing was now back to normal, and with an almost casual air she reached into the hip pocket of her jeans and pulled out a small automatic pistol. "And it seems that, after all, he was right to send me along."

They stared at her. Angel was suddenly aware of how exhausted he was.

Then Lampagie smiled. "You poor little girl. Do you really believe that is how Martin planned it? His real idea was that all three of us would disappear without trace."

Alison stared at her, her mouth making that disturbing O.

"Think about it," Lampagie suggested.

But the gun muzzle was already drooping.

Very gently Lampagie leaned forward and removed it from Alison's hand.

Angel wiped his brow. "And who did actually kill Justin Jarne, then? Or need I ask?"

Because only one man possessed the strength and the determination and the viciousness.

Alison looked at Dave as the ex-boxer rolled and groaned in the wheelhouse.

"I'd better get on the phone and have a doctor standing by," Angel said. "They'll be used to that, from me."

"And I would like a word with Levasseur," Lampagie said. "I want Martin Harrington in custody by the time we get back to Toulon. You will hurry, Angel? They are burying Justin today."

*

There were few people at the funeral. Colne and one or two other obvious business employees and acquaintances, the butler Henri and the chauffeur Juan, Lampagie Jarne, Angel, and several policemen. And Detective Inspector Hibbert standing beside Inspector Levasseur. The directors of the J and J Corporation were not represented at the last rites of their chairman.

At a discreet distance from the actual mourners there was a group of onlookers, mainly women.

The service was suitably brief. Everyone, even the priest, seemed anxious to get Justin Jarne six feet under and forgotten as rapidly as possible. Lampagie was first to turn away, to lead the group down the gravel path towards the gate to the cemetery. She wore a black pants suit and a black toreador hat; huge dark glasses hid any sign of grief, and also the slight swelling where she had hit her eye on the radar screen.

Inspector Levasseur walked at her side. "Inspector Hibbert will explain," he said.

Hibbert walked on her other side. "We found Harrington at last, Mrs. Jarne," he said. "He was sitting in his car, on the shoulder of the motorway from Heathrow Airport into London. The car was about five miles from the airport. He had been shot twice through the heart with a small-calibre revolver."

Lampagie stopped, and turned to stare at him. "But . . . when did this happen, Inspector?"

"Time of death has been placed at about ten-thirty last night. His flight landed at nine-thirty. So that seems to fit."

"But who in England would want to murder Harrington?" Angel walked behind them, flanked by two gendarmes.

"Now there's the point," Hibbert said. "We are forced to the conclusion that the four conspirators you have unearthed must actually have been five."

"I'll swear Alison didn't know that."

"Neither did the man Bracken," Hibbert agreed. "I spoke to them both in hospital this morning. On the other hand, Martin Harrington is most definitely dead, and the safe deposit boxes you mentioned are most definitely empty. And the murder was most carefully planned. The driver would have stopped on the pretence of having run out of petrol, and by heaven the car would have run out of petrol, just in case Harrington looked at the gauge. So it must have been worked out to the last inch. We are looking for a woman, we think."

"You *think?*" Lampagie asked.

"Well, frankly, Mrs. Jarne, we have almost nothing to go on. It seems likely that Harrington was met by his murderer at Heathrow, but who that was we cannot say, exactly. The arrival lounge was crowded, and once he got outside it was almost dark. His car had been picked up from the park a few minutes before the plane landed, but no one remembers by whom. He just walked off the aircraft, and disappeared, until his body was found this morning."

"But he was killed on a very busy main road, you say."

"Which made it easier for the killer. The car windows were shut, and it was dark. No one would have heard two shots above the roar of all that traffic, and if the killer had then just got out of the car and walked down the verge to the nearest service station, which was only half a mile away, and picked up her car—there are always at least thirty parked outside the restaurant—and driven away, who'd be any the wiser? But as I said, we do have one lead. Harrington's secretary has disappeared."

"His secretary?"

"A girl called Shelley Beattie, who had worked for him for the past year. She is our only suspect, but a good one; everything about her seems to have been false. She gave an address in Wiltshire on her card, but no one of that name either lives there now or has ever lived there. Her references, which were very good, were forged, but of course no one bothered to check them when she was employed. She kept to herself in the office, and none of the other girls got to know her at all well. But her typing speeds and general ability as a secretary were excellent, and her London address was legitimate enough, although unlike most girls in her position she lived alone, in a rather expensive flat, incidentally. But she never did more than camp there. The flat is empty of her, and of anything which could be connected with her."

"All of which isn't very conclusive," Angel said.

"It's sufficiently circumstantial to get us interested, Angel," the policeman said. "There are other things, which might be coincidences but don't seem so now that Harrington is dead. She began to work for him just over a year ago, as I said. Her predecessor, a girl called Elizabeth Hartnell, was, remarkably enough, fired by Jarne himself; he seems to have lost his temper just because he telephoned the office very early one morning and she wasn't there. I gather he was rather like that."

"He was," Lampagie said.

"Anyway, the girl Beattie applied for the vacant job the same day it was advertised, and as she had those splendid qualifications, she was taken on. I think Harrington probably engineered the whole thing."

"And she killed him," Lampagie said. "And has disappeared with the money. She must have been more than his secretary. Have you any idea where she might have gone?"

"None. But we do have a description. She's short, good figure, blond hair, fairly long, pretty features."

"Oh, brilliant," Angel said.

"Yes," Levasseur agreed. "It will be difficult. Everything about this case is difficult. Do you realise that the only three men who could have told us how the actual smuggling was done are now dead? Presumably the African half of the partnership will now merely locate a fresh European outlet."

"Oh dear, that *is* bad luck," Angel said. "Believe me, I didn't plan it that way."

Levasseur smiled. "But at least we have Miss Somers and the man Bracken. And we also have you, Mr. Angel."

"But he has cleared himself," Lampagie protested.

"Of murder, Mrs. Jarne. Mr. Angel is going to be charged with assault on Maître Audier, assault on my detective sergeant—his jaw is broken, you know—assault on a taxi driver, resisting arrest, stealing a revolver, stealing a taxi, stealing a raincoat, arson . . . I am speaking from memory, you understand. There are one or two more, I am certain."

"Very well," Lampagie said. "You may issue a summons, Inspector. I promise you that Angel will answer it."

"You wish me to let him go free, for the time being? But, madame . . ."

"I will be his surety. I will also stand his bail. And I will also pay his fine. Because I am sure there will only be a fine, Inspector." She smiled at Levasseur.

"Now that I cannot say, madame. A fine, for so many grave offences . . ."

"First offences, Inspector. Is that not so, Mr. Hibbert?"

Hibbert sighed. "I suppose they are, technically, first offences, Mrs. Jarne. But arson is a serious crime at any time."

"In this case it was not, Inspector. Because the rain extinguished the fire before it properly started. And Angel knew it was going to rain. Didn't you, Angel?"

"Well, I . . ."

"Of course. He's a sailor, you know, Inspector. He understands the weather. The rest of your charges are hardly more serious than a teenage boy out larking on a Saturday night. They were serious in the context of an escaping murderer, but we now know that Angel was not that, don't we?"

"Do you mean to defend him yourself?" Hibbert asked sarcastically.

Lampagie continued to smile. "He will be defended by the best lawyer in France, Mr. Hibbert. He will be in touch. And incidentally, unless you and he manage to come to some agreed formula for the charges, Mr. Angel will be filing an action against the Toulon police for false arrest. But as I say, I am sure that something, a fine, can be worked out. Now we will wish you gentlemen good day. We have business to discuss."

She turned away from the policeman and walked towards the gate of the cemetery.

Hibbert sighed. "You'd better go with her, Angel. I wouldn't have thought she was the sort of person you'd want to lose sight of."

Angel caught her up. "I don't think you realise what you've got yourself into, Mrs. Jarne," he said. "For one thing, it is likely to be a very stiff fine. And the lawyer is going to cost a lot of money, which you haven't got any more. Better let them get on with it."

"I have arranged to place the villa on the market," she said, without looking at him. "This will cover my personal debts, and leave a little over. Enough to pay for the lawyer. And of course, selling the house, and the cars, for I mean to do this as well, will relieve me of Henri's and Juan's salaries. Your salary will remain a problem. I will have to ask you to take a share of the profits."

"What profits?"

"From the charter business. We are going to use *Twin Tempest* for charter, remember?"

"I'll need a crew."

She paused at the gate, and turned to smile at him. "You don't suppose I could go on living in Antibes, or anywhere around here, with every neighbour knowing that my husband was a diamond smuggler?" Her smile changed into a frown, as she looked past his left shoulder. "Why, for heaven's sake. Shirley?" She raised her voice. "Why didn't you tell me you were coming over?"

The girl was short and solidly built, neat rather than pretty; her black hair was bobbed. She wore a black dress and a large black hat, and had previously been lost in the onlookers.

"I didn't wish to embarrass anyone, Lampagie." Her voice was low.

Lampagie took both her hands. "How can you say that, at a time like this? Angel I want you to meet Shirley Jarne, Justin's daughter."

"My pleasure, Miss Jarne."

But she spared him only a glance. "I must go, really, Lampagie."

"But, darling, I haven't seen you in ages. Oh, over a year. And you've cut your hair."

"Well, it's much easier to manage, when travelling."

"Is that what you're doing? Travelling? And now you are going back to England?"

Shirley Jarne glanced at Angel once again. "No. No, I don't like England. I mean to go on travelling. I've a plane to catch now, for Rome. I'm sorry about Daddy, Lampagie. I mean, about his being a smuggler. It must have been a terrible shock."

"Not to you?"

"Oh, Mother knew he was bent, years ago. That's why she left him. But after she died, I suppose I looked on things a little differently. He was always very kind to me. I really must go."

"But, darling," Lampagie said. "All this travel . . . these clothes . . . we just have to have a talk. I mean, there can be no more allowances. Really. I'm just about destitute."

Shirley Jarne almost smiled, and then controlled her face. "Oh, poor darling Lampagie," she said. "I *am* sorry."

"It is you I am thinking about," Lampagie said.

"Well, please don't. I'm all right, truly. I . . . I have a little put by. Now I just have to go. It has been a pleasure, Mr. Angel. I only wish it could have been in happier circumstances. Oh, and Lampagie, I'd be so grateful if you wouldn't mention to anyone that I'd been to the funeral. I really don't want to be followed all over the place by reporters. Justin Jarne's daughter, and all of that."

She left them and went through the gate, hurrying for a waiting taxi. The spectators were starting to disperse.

"Now, isn't that strange," Lampagie said.

"That she should attend her father's funeral?"

Lampagie glanced at him, frowning. "I suppose not. But . . . what did Alison tell us? Jarne had warned Smith that there would be someone watching him all the time? Do you think he also had his doubts about Harrington?"

"By God," Angel said. "You don't suppose . . ."

"She used to wear her hair shoulder length," Lampagie said. "Dye it yellow, and you'd have Shelley Beattie, according to Inspector Hibbert. I imagine it was Justin arranged her employment, and not Harrington, as your policeman supposes."

"And she doesn't want to return to England," Angel said. "But you mean you think that kid met Harrington at the airport, drove a little way into London with him, then shot him in cold blood, got out of the car, and walked away?"

"If perhaps he had told her something of what he'd been doing? She was Justin's daughter. And there was a great deal at stake. Not just revenge, I mean."

"My God," Angel said.

"Yes," Lampagie agreed. "What with Alison and now Shirley, you must have lost all faith in modern womanhood."

"I was thinking that she's scooped the lot," Angel said.

"I would say she has. What did Alison estimate? About four million pounds?"

Angel turned. Levasseur and Hibbert were still a good distance behind, walking slowly, talking. "Shall I . . . ?"

"Let her go," Lampagie said. "I imagine, as she was Justin's daughter and mixed up in the business, she has earned herself a bit of a holiday. And no matter how hard she runs, with how much money, the police will catch up with her eventually. They always do." She led him to the Mercedes, where Juan held the door. Henri already waited in the front seat. "I intend to concentrate entirely upon my own affairs from now on, Angel. And that means *Twin Tempest*. Where was I?"

"Disposing of your staff. You forgot Jupiter."

"Oh, Jupiter will come with us on board. He will be an added attraction, and a very good watchman." She sat down and patted the seat beside her. "I'll have vodka and tonic. We may as well enjoy the car for the last time."

Angel poured two.

"That leaves me needing only a skipper, Angel. Will you accept the job?"

Her fingers brushed his as he gave her the glass. "Why *did* you come along, last night?"

"I wanted to be able to prove Harrington's guilt. He gave himself away, you see, at dinner, the night before last. He knew nothing of the crime at all, apparently, yet he said that Justin had faced his murderer. As indeed he had. Because when he rushed on deck, as the two ships touched, there would have been Peter Smith. And while Justin was staring at him, and no doubt demanding to know what was happening, Bracken stepped forward and gripped his throat. But how could Martin Harrington have known that was how it happened, unless he had planned it that way? At the time, not one word of how Justin had died had been released to the press."

"But . . . wouldn't it have been a whole lot safer merely to have called Levasseur?"

"Martin would then have said I was mistaken in what he had said, and probably contacted Smith and abandoned the whole idea of last night. I told you, I wanted my husband's murderers. All of them. I wasn't even sure then that it didn't include you, you know."

"And that it might have cost you your life as well didn't bother you? Has anyone ever told you that you are a remarkable woman, Mrs. Jarne?"

She smiled at him. "I don't think anyone knows me well enough to decide that, Angel. Yet. And now I really think you should start calling me Lampagie. I am only the crew, remember?"